"WE HAVE TO DO WHATEVER WE CAN TO KEEP THE CARS FROM ROLLING."

"Including violence?"

"What violence?"

"There were some officers who had rocks, sticks, and snowballs thrown at them. I heard one in Flatbush was knocked out from a rock."

"We're not looking to attack the police. Most of them are in solidarity with us. And considering how little they did to help the trolley companies yesterday, I see no reason why any of our members would want to harm them." Coppinger shrugged. "Of course, we can't control everyone. If somebody gets excited and wants to throw a rock, is there any way we can stop him?"

"What about the militia?" Webb asked. "Do you think *they'll* be in solidarity with you, too?"

Coppinger looked grim. "No, I don't. But I think it's an idle threat on Mayor Schieren's part. Do you really believe a mayor will call in troops against citizens of his own city?"

"He also owns shares in the railroads. He wants this strike over and the trolley companies making money again."

"That may be, but—"

The office door was flung open and Scott Berner pushed through. "Mike," he said breathlessly. "Just got a phone call. A cop's been shot on Atlantic Avenue—he's dead."

"Damn it, *no*." Coppinger looked as if he'd just been shot himself.

STREETS OF FIRE

TROY SOOS

KENSINGTON BOOKS
Kensington Publishing Corp.
http://www.kensingtonbooks.com

KENSINGTON BOOKS are published by

Kensington Publishing Corp.
850 Third Avenue
New York, NY 10022

All Kensington Titles, Imprints, and Distributed Lines are available at special quantity discounts for bulk purchases for sales promotions, premiums, fund-raising, and educational or institutional use. Special book excerpts or customized printings can also be created to fit specific needs. For details, write or phone the office of the Kensington special sales manager: Kensington Publishing Corp., 850 Third Avenue, New York, NY 10022, attn: Special Sales Department, Phone: 1-800-221-2647.

Kensington and the K logo Reg. U.S. Pat. & TM Off.

ISBN-13: 978-0-7582-0625-1
ISBN-10: 0-7582-0625-9

First Kensington mass market printing: May 2008

10 9 8 7 6 5 4 3 2 1

Printed in the United States of America

CHAPTER 1

Marshall Webb wasn't even aware of how far he'd rolled his oak swivel chair back away from his desk. By now, he'd become almost transfixed by the winter street scene outside the window and was oblivious of the dreary routine unfolding within the office.

Harper and Brothers was the largest publishing house in America, producing an extensive list of book titles every year. The company also published some of the most popular periodicals, including *Harper's New Monthly Magazine*, devoted to arts and literature; *Harper's Bazaar*, a ladies' fashion publication; *Harper's Young People*, a children's magazine; and *Harper's Weekly*, an illustrated newspaper that arrogantly billed itself as "A Journal of Civilization." Webb was employed to write for the latter publication.

The Harper's offices and presses were all housed in a single building in Manhattan, half a dozen short blocks east of City Hall, at the junction of Pearl and Cherry streets in busy Franklin Square. The five-story structure towered above the bustling square, and its elaborate facade looked like something that might have been carved by the same medieval stonemasons who'd constructed the great European cathedrals. Overall, it presented an image entirely in keeping with the publisher's inflated opinion of the firm's importance.

As imposing as the exterior of the building was, the office shared by four of the *Harper's Weekly* staff writers was of modest size and bleak decor. A calendar that displayed nothing but days and dates in plain block letters, a telephone with a broken magneto, and some framed brittle covers of earlier issues of the publication were all that adorned the beige-painted walls. Every bit of boxy oak furniture—desks, file cabinets, and bookcases—was stained exactly the same shade and faded to exactly the same degree. A braided throw rug near the office door was so well used that it was almost impossible to tell if there had ever been a color underneath the embedded dust and dirt.

Two of the writers, both rather humorless young men, were as nondescript as the office. Dressed in standard-issue black business suits, they hunched over their desks producing tedious articles on society events and athletic competitions. Webb suspected that their information had to be either secondhand or entirely fabricated since, as far as he knew, neither of the young men actually went anywhere or saw anything himself. But then the publication's editor preferred that his writers remain at their desks so that he could monitor their production, as if journalists were the equivalent of factory workers whose output was judged more by the quantity of goods they produced rather than the quality.

The third writer covered business matters for the publication. Keith Hopkins, a man of about forty with a straggly mustache the same shade of red as the wisps of hair combed over his balding scalp, was at the desk nearest Webb's. Being only a little older than Webb, Hopkins was also the closest thing to a friend he had in the office. But the nation was mired in the worst financial depression in the country's history, and after three years of reporting business failures and stock market losses, Hopkins had largely surrendered to the national sense of despair himself and was a gloomy companion. He had once found amusement in composing mock obituaries for failed companies, but lately had gone back to an unfortunate habit of reciting execrable limericks. Webb usually tried to feign polite interest in Hopkins's attempts at humorous verse, but he had come to wish fervently that there had never been a place named "Nantucket."

So when Hopkins noisily cleared his throat, and began, "There was a young man from—" Webb had begun edging away, slowly rolling his chair back toward the window behind him.

In truth, it wasn't only a desire to distance himself from Hopkins that caused Webb to move. His attentions had been wandering away from his *Harper's* duties for weeks now, and he often found himself idly gazing out the window. Webb was aware that if he had been a factory worker, he'd have long since been fired for inattentiveness and lack of production.

The view of Pearl Street below was not a spectacular one. The street scene was almost as lacking in color as the office interior, but instead of the brown monotones within, Franklin Square was cast in shades of gray.

Even in summer, sunlight barely penetrated to ground level. The Manhattan approach to the Brooklyn Bridge was overhead, almost at roof level; its roadway and network of supporting iron trusses ran east–west, casting shadows in that direction. Beneath the bridge ran the tracks of the elevated train that traversed most of the island from south to north. This intersection of the bridge and the el left Franklin Square in perpetual shadow.

Nature further contributed to the gloomy atmosphere. New York had been in the harsh grip of a bitter winter chill for weeks. What little sky was visible through the manmade obstructions was a dull, solid gray. Drifting down around the tracks and trusses was a flurry of soft snow that swirled outside the window and left a small drift on the ledge.

Webb looked down at the street. This was a business area, and most of the pedestrians were men, heavily bundled in dark wool overcoats and treading carefully over the treacherous sidewalks. Some found warmth and refreshment in the hot cider or burnt sausages hawked by pushcart vendors. Traffic in the street was snarled, as usual during a Manhattan workday. An electric streetcar with icicles dripping like frosting from its roof ground slowly northward, not stopping or slowing for other vehicles, as if it had an inherent right of way. Delivery wagons were parked haphazardly, often blocking other traffic, while their drivers casually lugged their parcels and packages into the office buildings that lined the square. Meanwhile, carriages and trucks vied for any opening to move forward. Horses were brutally whipped to make them pull ahead, then abruptly reined in to prevent collisions with other vehicles pushing into the same spot.

There was nothing in particular to capture Webb's attention, except for the fact that there was *life* going on in the streets outside. As he stared out the window, Webb had the sense that he was suffocating in the confines of the *Harper's* office. The hissing of the building's cantankerous steam heating system seemed to grow louder, and the clanging of the pipes was jarring.

The scratching of pen on paper by the other writers began to grate on Webb's nerves. And the incessant sniffling of Keith Hopkins, who suffered from hay fever in the summer and chronic colds in the winter, was a sound of utter misery.

Webb wanted to open the window, to let in some fresh air and allow the sounds of street life to come into the stifling office. With the outside temperature barely over ten degrees, though, his coworkers would probably have thought he was trying to murder them if he had done so.

Suddenly, two wagons directly below Webb's vantage point attempted at the same time to plow into a small opening in the traffic jam. One was a colorful red-and-blue panel truck emblazoned with garish advertising for the *New York World* newspaper; the other was piled high with kegs of beer on its open platform and had J. RUPPERT'S LAGER BIER stenciled along its body.

They collided with a grinding thud that sent a shudder through Webb. Neither was going fast enough to cause injury; on the contrary, both teamsters seemed spurred on by the impact and they whipped their straining horses to forge ahead and gain the advantage over the other vehicle. Their efforts were in vain, as their wheels appeared to lock together.

The burly driver of the brewery wagon then shifted his attention from his horse to his rival in the newspaper truck. As he hopped off his running board, with a wrench clenched in his hammy right fist, Webb's view of the scene fogged over. He suddenly realized that he was so close to the window that his breath was steaming up the pane, and he felt the cool glass on his forehead as he pressed against it.

Webb then noticed that Keith Hopkins was honking his nose like a frantic goose. It sounded like something far more severe than a mere head cold, and Webb glanced back at his coworker who was clutching a wrinkled handkerchief the size of a pillowcase. Although Hopkins's inflamed nose nearly matched the color of his brick-red hair, and his droopy mustache glistened from a substance other than mustache wax, Webb could tell that his noises had been intended as a kind of warning signal. With watery eyes, Hopkins caught Webb's look and then flicked his gaze toward the door as if relaying a throw.

Just inside the office door stood Harry M. Hargis. The *Harper's* senior editor puffed on a long black cigar and stared at Webb with disapproval. Hargis's elegant attire—smartly tailored alpaca suit, silk cravat with an ostentatious diamond stickpin, and high white wing collar—would have made an impression in the most stylish Fifth Avenue drawing room, but his appearance was especially striking amid the drabness of this office. The waxed tips of his dainty mustache were curled up to the exact same height, and his manicured hair was plastered down with pomade. A fresh red carnation bloomed cheerfully from the buttonhole of his lapel—in stark contrast to the scowl that creased his face.

Webb rolled himself back to his desk, trying to remember what he was supposed to be working on. Was it a piece on Tammany Hall's latest political machinations? Another article on the Lexow Committee's hearings into city corruption? Or more speculation about the impending consolidation of Brooklyn, Manhattan, and other nearby municipalities into a single city? It seemed that he'd been working on nothing but these issues for the past several years, and they were so intertwined that none of them seemed clear anymore. He glanced over the papers on his desk, struggling in vain to recall his current assignment. He looked back up at Hargis.

The editor's gaze lingered on him for a long moment, long enough to make clear his displeasure. Then he turned his attention to the young writer at the desk nearest the door.

Webb accepted the silent reprimand as a deserved one. Since he had written a series of articles for *Harper's Weekly* that exposed the Tammany political machine with enough detail to trigger a state investigation into its control of New York City politics, both he and the publication had received wide acclaim for his efforts. In almost every issue thereafter, *Harper's* included at least a brief follow-up to the stories along with a reminder that its own Marshall Webb had helped bring about these historic efforts to reform city government. That made Webb a valuable commodity for the publisher, and Hargis had given him a lot of freedom. But there was a limit to the editor's forbearance, as Webb could see.

Webb tried to force himself back to work, to no avail. He stared without recognition at a sheet of notes he'd written about the new mayor. Then he eavesdropped on Hargis, who was instructing the young writer to make prominent mention of one of Hargis's friends in a report about Mrs. Astor's latest ball, and glanced at Hopkins, who was scribbling what was probably just another limerick but at least gave the appearance of productivity.

The radiator hissed like a whistling teapot, and shuddered with a metallic rattle. Webb looked back to the window, yearning to get out of the office. As the room seemed to close in on him, Webb looped a finger behind the knot of his carefully tied four-in-hand to make it easier to breathe. The effort failed.

On impulse, Webb stood, pulling himself to his full six-foot height, and almost sprinted toward the door. Hargis turned to him, a stunned expression on his imperious face.

"I'm going to lunch," Webb blurted in an effort at explanation. He reached for the coat rack.

Hargis made a show of pulling an ornate gold watch from his vest pocket, and stared incredulously at its hands.

As Webb slipped into his caped overcoat, he realized that it probably wasn't even ten o'clock yet. But he attempted no further explanation, quickly grabbing his derby and stepping out of the office.

Webb didn't recall giving a thought to what Harry Hargis or the other writers must be thinking of him. Nor could he remember making his way out of the stifling office building. Not until he felt the sting of winter on his cheek and cold air filling his lungs, did Webb feel his senses revive. Even then he walked as quickly as his long legs would take him, as if making an escape but not wanting to attract the attention that a full run would garner.

He was vaguely aware that even his walking pace was hazardous. Earlier snows and inadequate shoveling had left the sidewalks hard-packed and icy. With flurries still coming down from the low sky, loose fresh snow settled softly onto patches of ice, and at times Webb's boots slipped as if he were trying to walk across a floor covered with marbles.

Although he had no destination in mind, Webb headed north from Franklin Square, up the Bowery. His eyes were kept lowered to monitor his footing, but he did notice the people around him. Whereas he had run eagerly into winter's cold grasp, most of them were struggling to fend it off. In alleys and park areas, shabbily dressed men, women, and children huddled around feeble fires to avoid frostbite. Scruffy boys, probably with no other shelter, trotted beside slow-moving streetcars, jumping on whenever the conductors weren't looking so they could stand for a while in the relative warmth of the trolleys. As he walked, Webb turned down numerous offers from peddlers of hot pies, roasted corn, and similar foodstuffs—even if he had been hungry, Webb knew well that nothing sold by a New York street vendor was ever actually hot all the way through.

Webb finally slowed to a stop. He was breathing heavily and felt a slight strain in his calves. Looking to the street sign, he saw that he'd come all the way to Houston Street, about a mile north of the *Harper's* office. He paused to catch his breath and took out a pocket handkerchief; brushing it over the thick mustache that obscured his upper lip, he found that his breath had frozen on it, leaving the hairs stuck together in clumps of ice.

"Paper, mister?"

"Wha—?" Webb looked down to see a grimy, bare-headed boy of about ten holding up a copy of the morning *Herald*. He wore several layers of garments, but each was so tattered and threadbare that put together they would barely make a set of summer underwear.

The headlines of the newspaper held little interest for Webb: MAYOR STRONG SLOW TO ORGANIZE NEW ADMINISTRATION . . . BROOKLYN STREETCAR WORKERS THREATEN STRIKE . . . LEXOW REPORT DUE NEXT WEEK . . . POLICE SERGEANT PLEADS GUILTY. So far, the new year of 1895 appeared to be no different from the previous one. Financial hardship, labor unrest, political corruption, and police malfeasance seemed to have become entrenched in the life of New York.

"*Mister?*" The small boy's voice was insistent. He held the paper higher and stretched upward on his spindly legs trying to position it directly in front of Webb's face.

"No, thank you," answered Webb. "But since I *did* read the headlines—" He put a hand inside his coat and dug a shiny twenty-five-cent piece from his vest pocket. "Here you go."

The boy's smile nearly matched the gleam of the silver. "Thanks, mister!" That single coin, now clutched tightly in his ink-stained palm, probably equaled two days' wages for him. It would at least allow him to buy a decent hat. He hurried away, still smiling joyously at his sudden prosperity.

Having caught his breath, Webb briefly considered where to go. He aimlessly began walking west on Houston.

He'd barely gone two blocks when he noticed half a dozen boys about the same age as the news urchin. They were involved in a different sort of enterprise, and judging by their furtive glances and low voices Webb guessed it was not a legitimate one. Curious, he watched them to see if they were preparing to mug an unsuspecting passerby. He felt little fear himself; any experienced street thug would pick an easier target than Webb.

He finally realized that the object of their attention was a rickety coal wagon parked at the corner of Mott Street. The single driver was a squat man with the general appearance of an unhappy bullfrog. He was perched on the open seat of the dirty vehicle, swathed in a plaid blanket. Apparently taking a break from his deliveries, he sipped from a pint bottle of whisky while his ancient nag stretched its neck to the side to lick at a dirty snowbank.

The boys then prepared for their attack. They quickly packed a number of snowballs, favoring snow that had been doused with horse urine. The projectiles were no doubt heavy, icy, and vile. Two of the boys lifted the fronts of their ragged shirts and held them out while the others stacked the ammunition on the shelves created by the stretched garments.

The two armed boys crept along either side of the wagon, quietly working their way from the back to the front. The others huddled down behind the wagon to remain out of the driver's view should he happen to turn around—an unlikely event since he seemed totally absorbed in his drinking.

"Get 'im, Scotty!" The boy who barked the order followed up by hurling a snowball at the driver's head. It was a perfect strike.

"Goddamn it!" The driver's anger at the impact was increased by the fact that he'd dropped his bottle and it had broken on the footboard. His head was still tilted from the first projectile when he was hit again from the other side. Spotting his assailant, he yelled, "Yuh little bastard! If I get my hands on yuh, I'll wring yer goddamn neck!"

The rest of the boys scampered over the back of the wagon. They scooped lumps of coal into makeshift sacks while their two accomplices kept the driver pinned under a hail of snowballs.

As quickly as it began, the assault ended. The two boys in front had depleted their supply of ammunition and the ones in back had filled their sacks with precious heating fuel. The driver was still reeling and cursing by the time the boys vanished into a nearby alley.

Webb was so surprised at the suddenness and strangeness of the assault, that it took him a moment to realize what had happened. Then he walked up to the driver. "Are you injured?"

He received a bleary look in reply. The driver

didn't have any visible wounds. "Yuh got a flask?" he finally asked.

"No. Sorry."

"Then go to hell." The driver looked down forlornly at the broken glass and amber liquid on the floorboard.

Webb suddenly found himself feeling no guilt at not having tried to stop the boys. Not that he felt too badly, anyway. There were a million people living in Manhattan—*trying* to live, anyway. And in these hard times, surviving was as much as many of them could hope to do. If they had to steal some coal to keep from freezing to death during the night . . . well, it was nothing compared to the thievery that took place under the auspices of city government.

Webb continued walking, more slowly now. He looked at everyone he passed—a shivering peddler hawking pencils with not a customer in sight, an underdressed teenaged girl huddled in a doorway loudly whispering offers of a "hot time," children scavenging through the enormous heaps of garbage that sanitation workers would leave uncollected until the weather improved. And there were the more fortunate ones—businessmen walking full of purpose, women on shopping jaunts, and merchants manning their dry goods stores, butcher stalls, and bakeries.

The life of the city was in these people, Webb thought, not in the power brokers and henchmen who infested the corridors of City Hall and the back rooms of the political clubhouses.

Webb stopped to get his bearings, and quickly decided on a direction. With a deep breath, he headed south again. But he wouldn't be returning to the *Harper's Weekly* office.

CHAPTER 2

Three letters. Rebecca Davies ran her thumb over the edges of the thin envelopes. The morning mail had brought only three letters. She knew, without opening them, that there would be no good news within. But as long as they remained sealed, she could permit herself to fancy that one of them at least might contain a pleasant surprise.

Rebecca found herself in a peculiar situation. Although Colden House had never before been as well funded or staffed as it was now, Rebecca had a sense of hopelessness.

The shelter, on State Street overlooking the Battery at the southernmost point of Manhattan, provided a safe place to stay for desperate young women from all parts of the island. It had been a Davies family charity since before Rebecca was born, and she had been personally running the shelter for more than a decade. During most of her years managing the house, it had been an ongoing struggle to obtain enough food and coal to keep the residents fed and warm—often, the pantry and the coal bin were both literally bare and most of Rebecca's efforts were directed toward scrimping on expenditures and pleading for enough donations to keep the home going for just one more day. For the past year, however, her sister Alice, who'd married into an even more affluent family than the Davies, had ensured ample funding for the operations at Colden House. And yet Rebecca had seldom felt more discouraged than she did in recent months.

"I thought you might like some tea, Miss Davies. It's gonna be an awful cold one again today. Don't want you catching sick."

Startled, Rebecca turned around from her corner desk in the small, simply furnished sitting room that served as an office. There stood young Stephanie Quilty holding a tray with a blue enamel teapot from which a ribbon of steam curled up enticingly. "How very thoughtful of you," she answered. "Thank you." She would have preferred that Stephanie didn't dote on her quite so much, but she knew the young woman was happy to have a permanent position working in the house and it was futile to ask her not to work as hard as she did.

As Stephanie placed a saucer and cup on Rebecca's desk, and poured the tea, Rebecca briefly studied her. Although seventeen years old, the wispy young woman looked far younger, with her figure cloaked in a faded gingham dress of a girlish style. When Stephanie, who'd escaped a brutal life on the streets and overcome an addiction to morphine, first came to Colden House she had the careworn face and sad hopeless eyes of a woman in the twilight of her life. Although some of her history was still etched on her features, she now bore an expression of general contentment and often flashed a shy but heartfelt smile.

Stephanie stepped back from the desk. "Would you like anything else, Miss Davies?"

"No, thank you." Rebecca took a sip of the tea. "This is excellent—just the thing for a winter day."

The young woman beamed. "I've already finished preparations for lunch, so if you need anything, just give me a call."

"Take a little time for yourself," Rebecca urged. "Read for a while—yesterday we received a donation of some new books that look interesting. Or go for a walk—see what's happening at Castle Garden." She knew the suggestions would fall on deaf ears.

"I'm going to start a couple of the girls baking bread for tonight." Then, as silently as she'd arrived, Stephanie backed out of the room.

Left alone again, Rebecca took another sip of tea and picked up the thin stack of envelopes. Working slowly, to delay having her last vestiges of hope squelched, she opened each one and read its contents. As she'd expected, the news was not encouraging.

Colden House was intended to provide temporary shelter for women needing sanctuary from harsh streets, abusive husbands, or cruel sweatshop bosses. To make more permanent change to their lives, Rebecca tried to find them regular employment with decent wages and conditions so that they could then take care of themselves. For years, she'd been corresponding with a growing network of contacts throughout the Northeast, finding jobs, and sometimes housing, for her girls. But with the country mired in the grip of a depression, there were simply no jobs to be had. Rebecca continued writing regularly, but most of her contacts no longer even answered her letters. Those who did provided the sort of polite but brief responses that she'd received this morning. The result was that Colden House remained full, housing thirty young women who had no prospect of moving on to a new life, and leaving other unfortunates out on the street because there was simply no more space available to shelter them.

At least when Rebecca had to concern herself with keeping the house operating on a day-to-day basis, there was little time for her to dwell on future plans. Now, with Stephanie Quilty assuming charge of the kitchen chores and longtime assistant Miss Hummel taking care of the bedrooms and checking that the girls were getting treatment for any health problems, Rebecca was able to expend most of her efforts in finding opportunities for the residents to make more lasting changes in their lives.

She had the time now, but had no fresh ideas. There must be *something* that could be done, despite the bleak economy.

With a sigh, she reached for a fresh sheet of writing paper and picked up her pen. Until she had a better idea, she would at least keep sending out inquiries and hope for a positive response.

Just before pressing the nib to paper, though, Rebecca glanced at a cream-colored envelope on the corner of the desk. It had arrived in yesterday's mail, and Rebecca had already read it three times.

Laying down her pen, Rebecca picked up the envelope. It was of expensive linen, and bore a handwritten return address of "The Fields Hotel, Fulton St., Brooklyn." She extracted the note inside, of matching paper with an ornate watermark. The handwriting was feminine, yet bold. In direct language, the author expressed admiration for Rebecca's work at Colden House and requested a meeting to seek her advice on starting a similar shelter in Brooklyn.

The letter was signed "Miss Vivian O'Connell." Although Rebecca had no idea who this Miss O'Connell

might be, and the note failed to give any clues, she
had immediately replied and agreed to help.

While waiting to meet her, Rebecca could only
speculate as to what kind of woman this Miss
O'Connell could be—and to hope that she might
have some ideas that Rebecca could use herself.

Marshall Webb was happy to see the warm smile of
welcome that greeted him when he walked into Lawrence Pritchard's cramped office. It gave a lifelike appearance to a visage that could almost be mistaken for that
of a corpse.

"Well, well. It's been a long time," said Pritchard,
rising from his desk and offering a skeletal hand. The
middle-aged man's bony face, with sunken eyes and
clean-shaven pale skin, had a spectral quality that gave
the impression of a nervous ghost.

"Too long." Webb returned his clammy grip. "I
apologize for dropping in like this—I hope it's not a
bad time."

"Never. Come, sit down."

The single room that housed the business operations of Pritchard's Dime Library made Webb's office
at *Harper's* appear opulent in comparison. Several mis-
matched bookcases overflowed with books and manuscripts, the battered file cabinet was missing a drawer,
a small throw rug in front of Pritchard's chipped pine
desk was moth-eaten, and the two chairs squeezed
close to the desk were orphaned from a kitchen set.
Webb warily lowered himself onto one of the chairs,
hoping it was stronger than it looked.

Pritchard blinked rapidly behind his pince-nez and
ran a hand over the three strands of gray hair combed

carefully over his scalp. "How have you been? And how is your young lady—Miss Davies?"

"We're both well. And both busy." Too busy, thought Webb with some sadness. "How about you?"

"*I'm* fine. But to be honest, business hasn't been nearly as good as when you wrote for me." He reached to a shelf behind him and took down a thin paper-bound volume. "This is still the best seller I've ever had." He put the book on the desk in front of Webb, who read the cover:

Pritchard's Dime Library Presents
THE COURAGEOUS CAVALRYMAN
or
How Sergeant Frazier Saved The Day
by David A. Byrd

Webb chuckled at the artwork, a lurid, full-color illustration of a Union cavalryman about to slash a Confederate soldier with his saber. It had only been a couple of years since Webb wrote thirty-two-page dime novels for Pritchard under the Byrd nom de plume, but it seemed so long ago. Although it was considered such a disreputable occupation that, to save his family embarrassment, he used an assumed name and told no one of his work, he'd come to realize that it was some of the most satisfying writing he'd ever done. Justice was always meted out at the end; there was a happy ending for the good, and punishment for the evil. In real life, he knew from his recent political investigations, the powerful—whether good or evil—prospered while the poor suffered.

Webb ran a finger over the garish cover, tracing the figure of the rearing horse. In a soft voice, he asked, "Could you use me again?"

Pritchard started so suddenly that his spectacles slipped from his nose and he had to move fast to catch them. "Are you serious? Would you write for me again?" Then he hesitated, appearing to brace himself in case Webb was only kidding. "What about your work for *Harper's Weekly*?"

"That hasn't been turning out quite the way I'd hoped."

Pritchard nodded thoughtfully. He pulled a linen handkerchief from the breast pocket of his tweed jacket and meticulously polished the lenses of his pince-nez before positioning them back on the bridge of his nose.

Webb tried to discern what his former publisher might be thinking—a difficult task, since Pritchard's emotional range was limited to the narrow spectrum of "worried" to "nervous."

With a sigh, Pritchard leaned back and folded his bony fingers together over his vest. "I have to be a fool for saying this, but you're doing important work at *Harper's*—I've read your stories and you're bringing serious issues to public attention. If you started writing for me again . . . Well, to be honest, I only want to sell books and provide some entertainment, not change the world."

Webb smiled. Pritchard's statement was a refreshing one. Unlike with Harry M. Hargis and the other *Harper's* editors, there was no pretension, no arrogance about the importance of the publication. Lawrence Pritchard simply provided the public with an inexpensive way of escaping their own lives for a little while. Webb replied, "I've come to the conclusion that the world *doesn't* change. And I'm tired of deluding myself into thinking that I *can* change it."

"How can you say that?" Pritchard squinted, causing

his spectacles to tilt precariously. "It was your work that helped lead to the Lexow investigation. Isn't their report due out soon? You'll see: New York City is never going to be the same—it will be a better place in no small part due to your efforts."

"You're more optimistic than I am." It was true that Webb's reports of election fraud and police corruption, all orchestrated by the Tammany Hall political machine, had helped lead the state legislature to launch an investigation. And it was true that a number of police officials had been convicted of bribery and other charges. But Webb was skeptical that there would be a real change in the way government worked. "Do you know what caused the most outrage?" he asked.

"What?"

"The fact that police were taking payoffs from brothels and saloons. And that wasn't even news—anyone who's lived in New York for any length of time already knew the cops were on the take. But the newspaper editors found they could sell a lot of papers by including salacious details in their editorials against the corruption. *Vice* is what got most of the attention. Not the fact that politicians sold themselves to an evil political machine. Not that Tammany was rigging elections and disenfranchising voters. No, what people were angry about was the fact that police were providing protection for the sex and liquor businesses. And do you really believe any of those will be going *out* of business?"

Pritchard shook his head. "No, of course not."

"Despite what they might say in the newspapers or the pulpits, there are too many powerful men who want those businesses available to them—and who want a share of the profits from them." Webb had already learned that some of the fired police officers' replacements were taking the same payoffs as their predecessors. They were simply more discreet about the graft.

"Still . . ."

Webb was finding some relief in giving voice to his frustrations. "And *Harper's* isn't even really pursuing the story anymore. After my first series of articles, things began to develop so fast that the daily papers were beating us to every new aspect of the investigations." That was understandable, Webb realized; a weekly newspaper simply couldn't keep up with rapidly changing news stories. "So all *Harper's* did was keep publishing reminders that it had been the first publication to expose the corruption schemes."

With a smile that made him look like a grinning skull, Pritchard said, "With the 'Rogues Gallery.'"

Webb nodded. Every time a police officer or municipal official was exposed as a crook at the Lexow Committee hearings, *Harper's* ran a front-page portrait of the offender under the heading ONE FOR THE ROGUES GALLERY. It was as if the paper were mounting their heads as trophies.

"But there *has* been a change," Pritchard went on. "Tammany lost the mayor's seat. That's something."

It was true. In the November election, the Tammany candidate had been soundly defeated by a Republican who promised reform. "Yes, they lost the mayor's seat. But they're gaining a city."

"Brooklyn."

Webb nodded. On the same election day that brought William L. Strong into City Hall, Brooklyn residents voted to give up their independence and merge into a single city of Greater New York. "Fewer than three hundred votes," he muttered. Despite news reports, many of them written by Webb, demonstrating that Tammany Hall was looking at Brooklyn as fresh territory for expanding its operations, Brooklynites had narrowly voted to relinquish their status as a separate city. And now, Webb had learned, Tammany was indeed making moves across the East River and taking over Brooklyn's local political machines.

No, nothing changed. Webb had written about the mistreatment of the immigrants who came in to Ellis Island every day, hoping to improve their lot; but with the depression, resentment of the newcomers had only gotten worse. He exposed corrupt city officials, hoping to change the system; instead, those who were ousted in disgrace were simply replaced by others eager to fill the vacancies and collect their share of the graft.

Pritchard leaned forward again and cleared his throat. "So you're serious about writing for me again?"

Webb recalled the satisfaction that he'd had writing dime novels, working at home and creating fictional yarns that he could spin however his fancy struck him. "Yes, I am."

"What kind? You know, detective stories are becoming popular."

No, Webb wanted something more removed from his daily reality. He thought of the boys he'd seen this morning, ambushing the coal wagon. In his imagination, the event transformed into an Indian attack on a lone stagecoach. "Westerns," he answered.

"There's always a market for westerns." Pritchard was beaming. "We should celebrate. Are you free for lunch?"

Webb laughed. Nothing was settled in the publishing business unless it involved a lunch. "I am indeed." After all, that's where he'd told Harry Hargis he was going.

CHAPTER 3

Precisely at the appointed time of two o'clock, Thursday afternoon, there was a forceful knock on the front door of Colden House. Rebecca Davies hurried to answer it herself, curious to meet Miss Vivian O'Connell, and opened the door with anticipation.

Standing at the threshold, apparently impervious to the bitter winter chill, was a rather stout woman of about forty draped in a lustrous sealskin cape. She had large, piercing blue eyes that she fixed on Rebecca. "I have an appointment with Miss Davies," she said in a brusque, smoky voice.

Rebecca introduced herself and welcomed the woman inside. Before closing the door, she hesitated a moment to look toward the curb. Parked there was an elegant one-horse brougham painted in dark green enamel. Its liveried driver was standing near the rear wheel, running a small whisk broom over the carriage body to dust off the snow and dirt that had been kicked up during the drive. Miss O'Connell was obviously able to afford first-class transportation.

She then shot a quick glance past the carriage. Across the street, the bare limbs of Battery Park's

American elms and London plane trees shivered in the frosty air. Beyond them, the choppy water of New York Harbor was barely visible, the flickering white-caps seeming to merge with the overcast, snow-laden sky. It would be another bitter cold night, and Colden House was sure to be full again—so full that Rebecca would no doubt be forced to do what she hated most: turn away girls who needed shelter. She closed the door firmly, as if trying to shut out the thought as well as the cold.

Rebecca took Miss O'Connell's cape and matching fur hat and led her through the foyer to the sitting room while exchanging polite comments of no consequence. Many of the young women who came to Colden House were shy about discussing their lives upon their initial arrivals, so Rebecca had developed a practiced eye, and was accustomed to doing quick evaluations of the girls in an effort to discern any injuries or diseases, as well as pick up any clues that she could as to their life circumstances. Partly out of habit, and impelled by curiosity, Rebecca made a similar study of her present visitor.

Vivian O'Connell wore a stylish mulberry silk walking suit trimmed in black velvet. Although what had probably once been an hourglass figure now had a capacity of more than ninety minutes, she carried herself gracefully, with a proud bearing and a haughty tilt to her fleshy chin. A fine strand of pearls was draped around her neck, gold earrings adorned her lobes, and an elegant hairpin kept her luxurious brown hair in a controlled bun.

By the time they'd reached the sitting room, Rebecca had made her assessment: Vivian O'Connell was a society matron who had decided to become active in charity work. The question was whether Miss

O'Connell would be truly committed to establishing a shelter or it would be the short-lived interest of a bored woman seeking a diversion.

Rebecca motioned for her visitor to take a seat at one end of the room's single settee; she then sat next to her and the two women twisted slightly so they could face each other. In the better light, Rebecca found that she had to reassess. Miss O'Connell's round face was lightly powdered, a touch of rouge gave color to her lips and cheeks—although tastefully applied, the makeup was more than a respectable society lady would wear. And her hair, a rich shade of brown with a coppery tint, was of an unnaturally uniform color—probably from a bottle. Rebecca also revised her estimate of the woman's age to late forties.

"They smell delicious," said Miss O'Connell.

It took a moment until Rebecca realized that her guest was referring to the cookies on the parlor table. While Rebecca had gone to answer the door, the refreshments had appeared as if by magic—the work of Stephanie Quilty, her quiet hardworking assistant, no doubt. A tray held a plate of ginger snaps, still warm and fragrant, along with a large pot of tea.

"I'm sure you can use something warm after being out in this weather," Rebecca said, reaching for the teapot.

"Yes, thank you so much." O'Connell smiled. "Uh, three lumps—and heavy on the cream."

A terrible thing to do to perfectly good Earl Gray tea, Rebecca thought, but she prepared the cup as requested.

After they'd each taken a sip, O'Connell said, "I want you to know how much I appreciate you seeing me—I'm sure you have many demands on your time operating a home like this." She then began nibbling on a cookie.

"I found your note intriguing," Rebecca answered. "You mentioned that you wish to start a new shelter in Brooklyn."

"Yes. And I'm hoping you can tell me how to do so." O'Connell followed the statement with a piercing look from her startling blue eyes.

Rebecca felt as if she were pinned in the beam of a police lantern. "I'll advise you as best I can," she replied. "But may I ask why you came all the way to Colden House? There are other homes nearer to you."

"Oh, you weren't my first choice," O'Connell answered. Both her eyes and her speech were disarmingly direct. "I've been to 'Saint this' and the 'Home for that' all over Brooklyn and Manhattan. No one was interested in helping me."

"They weren't?" Rebecca tried to imagine why O'Connell had been turned away from the other homes. With so many young women needing help, why not encourage someone who wanted to take a share of the burden?

"No." O'Connell shook her head. She took a dainty bite of another ginger snap. "These really are very good—although you might want to try adding a touch of cardamom."

Rebecca felt a flash of annoyance. "Thank you for the suggestion, but our food is simple here. We don't have a lot of spices." In fact, the cookies were something of an extravagance.

"Of course. Please excuse me." O'Connell smiled; her teeth gleamed as bright as her sapphire eyes. "I suppose I'll have to start getting used to simpler fare myself, if I'm going to get a shelter started."

"Where else did you visit?" Rebecca asked.

O'Connell washed down the cookie with a swallow of milky tea, and again fixed Rebecca in her stare. "Let me save us both some time by telling you up front . . ." She hesitated for effect. "I am a whore." The sentence was spoken like a dare, challenging Rebecca to respond.

The announcement was a surprise, but Rebecca didn't think she indicated any outward reaction. The young women who came to Colden House usually had to survive in any way that they could, so Rebecca had certainly met prostitutes before—but none of them had ever before arrived in a brougham, nor were they capable of passing for a society matron as Miss Vivian O'Connell had. "I see," Rebecca finally replied, although in fact she didn't.

"I am no longer active in my profession," O'Connell went on. "But I know how society views me: damaged goods. No matter how long I'm retired, people will believe that 'once a whore, always a whore.'"

Rebecca started to understand the reason O'Connell had made the announcement. "That's why the other places you went to wouldn't help you? Because you, uh, you're a . . . *were* a . . ."

"Whore." O'Connell reached for another cookie.

Rebecca would have preferred that she used a less blunt word, but Miss O'Connell seemed to delight in speaking bluntly. "Yes, a whore," she repeated softly, thinking that a quieter tone might take the edge off the word.

Miss O'Connell smiled slightly. "I've been to a dozen homes in the city, but it was made clear to me that such shelters are only reserved for 'virtuous' women." She leaned forward. "You see, I'm planning to establish a home for young women of my profession who no longer want to be . . . prostitutes."

It was Rebecca's turn to smile; O'Connell's choice of language was clearly a concession on her part. "I think that's a fine idea. I've had girls from all sorts of backgrounds here, but I don't believe there is any home dedicated to helping prostitutes make a new life."

"There aren't." Another ginger snap slid between O'Connell's rouged lips. "In fact, most homes won't take them in at all." Her forehead creased. "I've found that most shelters are connected with churches or missionary societies, and they're more interested in saving souls than people. Seemed to me that some of the nuns and preachers I met would be perfectly happy to let a girl starve to death as long as they'd gotten her to accept Jesus. 'Now you're saved, so hurry up and go to heaven' seemed to be the attitude."

Rebecca nodded in sympathy. She knew that Colden House was unusual in that no religion was preached, and it had brought on a fair amount of criticism. But Rebecca had never found much use for religion; there was too much work to do saving lives, and she gave little thought to the notion of an afterlife.

A small smile appeared on O'Connell's lips. "But they certainly wanted to know every detail of what prostitutes do for a living—before condemning them as degenerate 'sinners' of course. Do you know Saint Theresa's Foundling Asylum—on the Bowery, near Broome Street?"

"I've heard of it."

"Father Justin—a little gnome of a man—took me to his office and asked me no end of questions. Although he never lost his scowl, I realized that he was taking pleasure in what he was hearing." She chuckled. "So I really let him have it—every sordid detail and every embellishment I could think of. He offered me no assistance, of course, but by the time I left him he was unable to stand, if you know what I mean." She touched her hand lightly on Rebecca's forearm and laughed again.

Rebecca did indeed know what she meant and although she didn't consider herself prudish, she felt herself blushing.

O'Connell tapped Rebecca's arm again. "Come to think of it, I should have charged him for the experience!"

Rebecca laughed, too, then got to the point of the meeting. "As I said, I think establishing a home for former prostitutes is a fine idea. I'll be happy to help, but what exactly do you want from me?"

After fortifying herself with one of the few remaining ginger snaps, Vivian O'Connell answered, "I would like to know how a place like this operates—from top to bottom. I want to make my shelter work, and I want to be able to keep it open for some time to come." She again displayed a mischievous smile. "I *have* run a house, but not of this kind."

"There *is* a difference," Rebecca said. Not only in the activities, she thought, but in the funding. A charity was very different from a profit-making venture. "How do you plan to finance the home?"

"I've managed to save a fair amount of money, enough to purchase an adequate home, I'm sure."

"And to keep it going? The daily expenses are enormous—food, coal, medicine—you'd be surprised how much it can cost to shelter twenty or thirty girls." Rebecca didn't want to deter Miss O'Connell from her mission, but wanted to give her a realistic picture of what it would take.

"I'll have to give that some thought," O'Connell

replied after some hesitation. "But for now, may I see how you operate here?"

Rebecca hesitated now. She was protective of the young women residing in Colden House and wary of bringing strangers into their home. But Vivian O'Connell wasn't an angry father or a possessive husband, who often tried to get inside but rarely asked permission. "Yes, of course." She stood and smoothed her blue serge bell skirt. "Shall we begin upstairs?"

On the second floor, Rebecca introduced O'Connell to Miss Hummel, a short woman with iron-gray hair pulled tightly back in an impeccable bun. She was dressed, as usual, in a starched dress that matched her hair and a stiff white apron. Rebecca knew that she was much softer on the inside than her severe outward appearance would indicate. "Miss Hummel has been working at Colden House longer than I have," she said. She then explained the purpose of Miss O'Connell's visit, and Hummel took the information in stride—but then she rarely did reveal whatever she might be thinking or feeling.

Led by the longtime assistant, they toured the upstairs of the three-story Federal-style row house. A couple of girls were changing sheets in the bedrooms, while others were working on some schoolbooks. As they walked, Miss Hummel explained the sleeping arrangements, the girls' work responsibilities—all who were able had to contribute to the operation of the house—and some of the educational and vocational programs that were being implemented.

Back on the second floor, she led them into the infirmary, a converted bedroom that didn't contain any real medical equipment. A couple of cabinets were stocked with basic supplies—bandages, headache powders, and miscellaneous salves and ointments. There were two narrow beds, a ladder-back chair, and a washstand with a large enamel basin. The chair, cabinets, and the iron rails of the bed were painted the same antiseptic white as the walls.

"Yes, we'll need something like this," O'Connell said. "Perhaps even a doctor or nurse on hand, if possible. Disease and injury are sadly an occupational hazard in my profession."

"Doctors are expensive," Miss Hummel replied. "And most of them are quacks. You'd probably do just as well to learn how to use these medicines yourself. You'll soon find you can tell what's wrong with a girl readily enough and then begin the appropriate treatment."

Rebecca concurred, adding that they did bring in a physician for unusual or severe cases.

Leaving Miss Hummel, Rebecca led O'Connell back downstairs to see the kitchen.

"Oh my," was O'Connell's reaction when she got her first look at the brightly lit room.

The kitchen had ample space but few laborsaving devices, and some of the fixtures looked as if they'd been installed when the house was originally built more than a hundred years earlier. Despite the fact that the ancient wood-burning ranges had recently been replaced with coal stoves, there was no escaping the fact that food preparation was hard work.

Young Stephanie Quilty, wearing an apron over her faded gingham frock, was in command and had divvied up the tasks among six other girls: two were kneading dough for bread, two were chopping vegetables, one was monitoring the coal burning in the stoves, while the last was cleaning a couple of kettles that would be used for cooking soup. Quilty herself was cutting up several chickens that looked as if they might have died from starvation.

Rebecca made the introductions, adding, "Miss Quilty hasn't been with us very long, but she's already become invaluable—I don't know what I would do without her."

The slim young woman beamed at the praise and ducked her head shyly. "Thank you, ma'am," she murmured.

Rebecca tried to get Quilty to explain the kitchen's operation to Vivian O'Connell, but the girl's shyness made it a futile effort. So Rebecca took over, describing how much coal was used, how many loaves of bread were baked and consumed on a typical day, how many gallons of milk were needed, what foods were worth purchasing and what were more cost-effective to prepare from scratch, and what foods could be stretched out when times were lean.

Stephanie Quilty had quietly eased away from them and returned to preparing the chickens.

Before leaving the kitchen, Rebecca paused and quietly thanked her for her thoughtfulness in bringing the tea and cookies.

"You're welcome, ma'am."

Vivian O'Connell had overheard. "Oh, you made the ginger snaps! Very good, but next time—"

"Next time you might want to make more," Rebecca finished, shooting a sharp glance at O'Connell. She wasn't about to have Stephanie's recipe criticized. "They really were delicious."

"Exactly what I was going to say," added O'Connell, her teeth and eyes sparkling.

Back in the sitting room, Rebecca asked, "Is there anything else I can tell you about how we do things here?"

"Not that I can think of at the moment."

O'Connell gave a wistful look at the now-empty cookie plate. "But I know I'll have a lot of questions as I proceed with this."

"Anything I can do to help, I'd be glad to."

"There is *one* thing. But it might be quite an imposition."

Rebecca had a sudden sense of unease. "Yes?"

"I've been looking at several properties in Brooklyn, but I don't know what would be most suitable." O'Connell again pinned Rebecca with the glow of her startling blue eyes. "Would you be willing to visit them with me and give me your opinion?"

Rebecca hesitated. The request was a reasonable one, but she always hesitated at the thought of leaving Colden House for any amount of time.

"I must tell you up front that it could end up being a long day," O'Connell went on. "I've already been turned away from the nicer areas of the city—people seem to think a house full of former whores is still nothing but a whorehouse—so I've had to look on the outskirts of town, mostly in Flatbush but one place all the way out in Canarsie."

"I'd be happy to," Rebecca finally answered.

"Thank you so much." O'Connell smiled warmly. "Now, I won't take up any more of your time today." She gathered her skirts, about to rise from the sofa.

"I do have one question for *you*, though." Throughout the day, Rebecca had been giving answers and advice. But she had a question of her own that had been gnawing at her all along.

O'Connell eased back down. "Yes?"

"Why are you doing this? As you said, you've saved a fair amount of money, you're retired from your, uh, profession. What makes you want to take on the task of opening a shelter?" In her experience, she had encountered few altruistic people; most were motivated by hopes of personal gain.

"A fair question." The eyes dimmed a bit. "I never expected to take on a job like this. I've been fortunate in my career: I remained healthy, found some pleasures in my work, and earned enough money to keep me in creature comforts for the rest of my life." She hesitated. "But I came to realize that my experience is the exception. Not many girls—well, there was one—" Her voice caught.

Rebecca waited, then prodded her gently, "One girl?"

O'Connell nodded. "Frenchy Sayre. She worked for me for several years, and even though I was her boss we became very dear friends." She coughed. "A whore should know better than to get close to anyone, but I was very fond of Frenchy. And when she told me she wanted out of the business, I couldn't have been happier— even though it meant I would be losing one of my best girls. Everyone wanted Frenchy. She was a lovely young girl, and *so* . . ." O'Connell caught herself before describing any more of Miss Sayre's attributes. "But she didn't get a chance."

"What happened?"

"Somebody beat her to death."

"I'm so sorry."

"And to the police it was as if she never existed. There was no investigation, and when I tried to make a fuss about it, they made it clear they weren't going to waste their time on the death of a whore." She added grimly, "There was a sergeant who actually said to me, 'You go into that line of work, you got to take the risks that go with it.'" O'Connell sat a bit straighter. "Anyway, I've decided there are just too many risks. I know there are girls who want to get out of that life, but don't know how. They're threatened by their pimps, in debt to feed their children—another risk of the trade—or they just don't know how else to make a living. So I'm going to do something to help them. I don't want another girl to end up like Frenchy Sayre." She looked up at Rebecca, fire having returned to her eyes. "Shouldn't a girl have a chance to change her life and start over?"

Rebecca agreed emphatically, and began thinking to herself how she could help Vivian O'Connell's goal become reality.

CHAPTER 4

For the first time in many weeks, Buck Morehouse found himself grateful for the bitter cold weather that had gripped Brooklyn. There was nothing worse than a warm morgue.

Just before stepping into the morgue of King's County Hospital, he inhaled deeply, causing his potbelly to strain the buttons of his rumpled sack suit almost to the breaking point. Although he knew that breath wouldn't last long, it had become part of his routine whenever he had to visit the morgue.

He stepped inside the whitewashed brick room. More than a dozen tables were neatly arrayed, like display tables of dry goods in Namm's Department Store. They were identical, all draped with white linen sheets, and, judging by the shapes under the sheets, most of them held corpses. Despite the chill air, the smell of death was palpable.

The only living person was a middle-aged man in a soiled black frock coat. He was casually examining a corpse at the distant corner of the room, where a low hanging bare bulb provided a glaring light. He looked up at Morehouse, squinting behind his tiny wire-rim spectacles. "Ah, Bucky. You bring my two bucks?"

"What two bucks?" Although he could see a wisp of steam as he spoke, Morehouse elected to divest himself of his new camel hair greatcoat—he didn't want anyone's entrails getting on it. He kept his battered brown derby on, patting it lower on his bullet head.

"From Saturday's fight, you goddamn welcher." Shannon Elswick, deputy coroner for King's County, twisted his features into what was supposed to be a scowl of anger, but his red, rubbery face instead gave the harmless appearance of a burlesque comic.

"Oh, you know I forgot all about that." Morehouse walked toward him between two rows of tables.

"I'm not surprised." Elswick's features relaxed from the exaggerated frown and he chuckled. "How could you remember a fight that didn't go past the second round? I told you putting money on Billy Shiles was a fool's bet—he never has lasted longer than ten."

"Not only am I a fool," Morehouse replied with mock sorrow. "I am a penniless fool—just a poor, honest civil servant. I'm afraid I'll have to pay you at some time in the future."

Elswick jerked his head toward the coatrack by the door. "Honest, huh? How much did you pay for the new coat?"

"It was a reward." There were some perks that went with being a detective with the Brooklyn Police Department. "Got it from a grateful citizen."

"You mean the citizen knew he gave it to you this time?"

Morehouse shrugged. Perhaps it wasn't a "reward" exactly, but, after all, how could he be expected to protect local businesses if he was too cold to go out and investigate crime? The detective only had to

point this out to a Fulton Street clothing merchant
before the garment was handed over to him.

The coroner glanced back down at the dead man
on the table. "I got a busy day today, Buck."

"Who you got here?" Morehouse scrutinized the
ancient, withered man on the slab. A few wisps of
white hair were pressed against his blotched scalp,
wrinkles hung loose around his neck and throat, and
his purple lips were sucked in where his teeth used to
be. A white sheet covered him below the waist, but all
the visible parts of his body showed the scars and
scrapes of a hard life. What was not apparent was what
had brought that life to an end.

"Dunno," answered Elswick. "I'm just calling him
'Old Caucasion Male Number Four' for now. He was
found dead in an alley in Red Hook last night."

"Cause of death?"

"Who the hell knows? I've only started the examination, but there's no sign of violence." Elswick
pushed at the bridge of his spectacles. "Look at him.
Must have lived more than eighty years, and probably
close to death for at least the last few of them. He's in
a condition where anything at all could have killed
him. Could have been heart disease, consumption,
starvation . . . Hell, when he was found he wasn't
wearing nothing but tattered drawers. Outside in this
weather, wearing just his drawers—bet it turns out
he died of exposure."

Still staring at the old man's gaunt face, Morehouse
thought he saw some dignity there. He answered
softly, "I'll pass—haven't had much luck betting
lately—but don't be so sure about the exposure. Just
as likely he was found dead and stripped of his
clothes." Morehouse didn't like the thought of walking around in a dead man's garments, but times were

hard and winter was cold. Odds were some other poor soul was keeping warm in what had recently covered the body of Old Caucasion Male Number Four.

Elswick shrugged. "I already had two other stiffs this morning who were from exposure." He added, "Like I said, it's been a busy day."

Morehouse took the hint. "Yeah, sorry, but I'm here on business. I was told you had a stabbing victim."

"Oh yes." Elswick looked about the morgue. "Haven't started on him yet. I think he's . . . yes, over here."

Morehouse followed the coroner down the aisle three tables away from the old man.

Elswick lifted the sheet enough to see the corpse's face. "Yeah, this is him." He folded the sheet down to waist level, then referred to a sheet of paper tacked to the head of the table. "No name. Found on the Flushing Avenue side of City Park early this morning."

"'Tony the Hammer.'"

"Huh?"

"His name is Anthony Aspesi, more commonly called 'Tony the Hammer'—he likes—*liked*—to pop out of hiding places and clobber his victims in the back of a head with a hammer. He'd leave them either unconscious or dead and rob them of whatever they had." Morehouse stared with disgust at the dead thug whose coarse features weren't softened any by death.

Elswick dug a pencil from his pocket and made a note on the paper. "Well, we have a name now." Pointing at Aspesi's abdomen with the pencil, he added, "And no doubt about the cause of death."

"Gutted like a fish," said Morehouse. The detective saw several fairly clean stab wounds and tried not to look too closely at the ugly slash that had caused Aspesi's belly to gape open.

This was going to be hopeless, Morehouse thought. He would have to find out who had murdered Aspesi. No, "murder" wasn't the right word, he decided— someone had rid the city of a dangerous parasite, one who had caused others to end up on these very tables but had never been brought to justice.

"Gonna be your case?" Elswick asked.

Morehouse nodded. He was getting all the impossible cases these days. The officers were all politicking for high positions in the new department that would result when Brooklyn and New York completed their consolidation as a single city. Morehouse's captain in particular was delegating all responsibilities that could result in failure and taking personal credit for all successes—including a major murder case that Morehouse had been instrumental in solving last year.

The detective considered his situation, as he found himself doing almost every day lately. He'd spent twenty years working his way from a street cop to his current position. Unlike most of his counterparts, he'd done it without political connections or by buying his rank from higher-ups. He'd *earned* it, damn it, by breaking cases that no one else would make the effort to take on. And now he was being set up for failure. If he didn't clear his cases, he knew there would be no position for him in the new department. And Buck Morehouse had no place else to go. He would simply have to keep his job by clearing every case that was put on his desk—no matter what methods he might have to employ.

The detective muttered, "No, no doubt about what killed this bastard." With a meaningful glance at Elswick he said, "Exposure."

Elswick laughed, then caught the seriousness in

Morehouse's expression. "You've got to be—I can't—
I mean obviously . . ."

Morehouse put out a forefinger and, holding it several inches above the body, traced the belly wound.
"Looks pretty exposed to me."

The coroner was tight-lipped.

"See, if this was murder," Morehouse continued,
"there'd be an inquest, and an investigation . . . I'd
have to spend my time trying to find out what piece
of vermin finally killed *this* piece of vermin."

"He was already reported as a stabbing victim," Elswick pointed out. "How are you going to explain—"

"Turns out they were just old injuries. Everybody
knows what kind of life Aspesi led—they'll buy it."
Morehouse fixed Elswick in his gaze. "So . . . cause of
death 'exposure'?" There was a note of pleading in
his voice when he added, "I'll owe you one."

The coroner thought about it. "Well, it'll save me
some work, too. But you'll owe me *three. And* the two
bucks from the fight."

"Three it is," Morehouse agreed. And they both
knew what was meant. Coroners were paid a fee for
each body they examined, so some corpses, especially
those like Old Caucasian Male Number Four, made the
rounds from county to county so that each coroner
could bill a charge. "I know an attendant in Bellvue; I'll
tell him to send you a few soon as Manhattan's done
with 'em." He dug into his jacket pocket, pulling out a
silver dollar and counting some smaller coins. "And
here's the two from the fight."

Elswick hesitated to take the money. "Another time
is fine, Buck. I don't want to take your last—"

"Ah, take it. I'm gonna win it back on the next fight
anyways." Morehouse always believed he would

recoup his losses "next time," no matter that his belief was rarely borne out.

"There's a middleweight bout in Williamsburg Friday night. Don't remember who's fighting, though."

"Doesn't matter. I'm picking the winner this time, Shannon, so bring your money."

Morehouse left Elswick to continue his work, and headed back to the station house where he now had one less case in his workload.

Marshall Webb was kept waiting twenty minutes past his appointed time before he was finally permitted entry into the elegantly furnished office of his boss, *Harper's Weekly* associate editor Harry M. Hargis.

Hargis thought the decor was elegant. In Webb's view, "ostentatious" was a better description. Most of the furnishings had been purchased by the editor during his frequent vacations abroad, and any comment on a particular piece would prompt Hargis to launch into a lengthy tale about the trip during which it was acquired. A brilliantly colored oriental rug from Persia covered most of the floor, a rather drab French oil painting hung on the wall, a marble reproduction of *David* that Hargis had bought in Florence stood on a wrought-iron pedestal, and a bronze figurine of Hermes from one of the Greek Islands was atop Hargis's carved mahogany desk. All of the items had been purchased at great expense, and Hargis made a point of casually mentioning their costs; he always tried to sound casual when stating the sums, as if money was of no importance to him, but in Webb's opinion the fact that the editor felt compelled to give them at all indicated the opposite.

The dapper editor, whose personal appearance was

in keeping with his surroundings, waved a hand. "Have a seat, Webb."

"Thank you." Webb eased into a green leather armchair that was as soft as a kid glove.

Hargis ran a manicured finger along the waxed tips of his dainty mustache. They both curled up to exactly the same height, and their color matched the silver sheen in his oiled hair. "What did you want to see me about, Webb?" There was little warmth in his voice.

"First, I'd like to thank you for having given me the opportunity to write for *Harper's*," Webb began.

"Perhaps a more productive way for you to show your appreciation would be to spend more time at your job." Hargis reached for the cedar humidor on his desk and took out a long black cigar. "You certainly haven't been very attentive to your duties of late."

The reprimand was deserved, for the assessment was accurate. "No, I haven't," Webb readily admitted. "And that's why I came to see you now. It isn't fair to you, or to *Harper's*, for me to continue in my position here. I am resigning."

Hargis fumbled an attempt to light his cigar. He stretched his head so far forward that his high celluloid collar bit into his neck. "You're *what?*"

"I'm sorry, Mr. Hargis, but I'm leaving. Of course, I'll finish anything I'm working on and give it to—"

"Nobody *quits Harper's.*" Hargis had totally lost his customary composure. "Writers aspire to come here, not leave us." He poked the air with his cigar. "Do you realize how many men dream of having a chance to write for *Harper's?* And here you're telling me—"

"That I'm leaving. Yes."

"You were a freelancer when I took you in, gave you

a nice office, a generous salary—" Hargis slapped the top of his desk as if he suddenly understood. "Is this some gambit for more money?"

"No, you have indeed been generous." Webb wasn't sure that he could make the editor understand. "I simply no longer enjoy my work here. I'd like to pursue other things."

"Oh, that's it! A better offer." Hargis squinted. "Who's it from? The *Times*? The *World*? You know, you'll hate working for Pulitzer."

"No, there is no better offer." Webb had no intention of telling Hargis about his plans to write dime novels again. He felt his statement was honest, though; certainly the arrogant *Harper's* editor would never consider writing for *Pritchard's Dime Library* to be a "better" offer.

"Then I just don't understand."

That fact was becoming clear to Webb.

Hargis then made a visible attempt to regain his composure and adopted a conciliatory tone. "How about a drink?"

Webb didn't want to appear impolite. "Yes, thank you."

"Cognac?"

"Fine."

Hargis turned to the sideboard behind his desk and poured two glasses from a crystal decanter.

After each man had a sip, the editor finally lit his cigar and drew deeply. "I truly do not understand your decision," he said thoughtfully. "But I will accept it. Although perhaps . . ." He slowly blew a stream of smoke, and appeared absorbed in the curling wisps.

"Yes?"

"Perhaps we do not have to completely sever the

relationship. What is it that you dislike about your present position?"

Webb took a swallow of the superb brandy, and decided there was no reason not to tell Hargis what had been troubling him—as well as he understood it himself, anyway. "I am stifled in that office," he said. "Nothing is making news *inside* this building. I preferred when I was *outside*—on the streets, where the people are, and learning new information. Lately, my assignments have been little more than repeats of stories I'd already written."

Hargis leaned back and nodded thoughtfully. "A fair criticism," he finally acknowledged.

Webb had rarely seen Hargis this way. He was usually imperious, and impervious to what others thought.

"I am not accustomed to explaining myself," Hargis said, "but I will make an exception." After another draw on the cigar, he went on. "My goal is to increase circulation. And your stories—on Tammany Hall, on police corruption, on election fraud—have been a major reason *Harper's* has done so well the last few years. I have to give you credit for that."

Webb nodded his appreciation.

"Perhaps we have been repetitive of late, but realize what we're facing: The country is in a depression and every publication is competing to sell papers to a public that is more concerned about buying food and keeping warm. So if revisiting your earlier work continues to sell copies—and it does—then I have to continue with what has been selling."

"But something new might sell, too."

Hargis nodded. "Yes. That's what I was thinking . . . perhaps we can come to another kind of arrangement."

"What kind?"

"The one we had before. You can freelance again.

Of course, you would no longer be on salary, but if you do have a story we can use I'm sure we can pay you better than we did before."

"And I'd work from home? Go where I want to when I want to?"

"Exactly as it was before," Hargis agreed. "And you can choose your own assignments. Submit what you like, and we'll pay you for whatever we can use."

Webb hadn't considered remaining with *Harper's* in any capacity, but he could see no reason not to accept the offer.

"As I recall," Hargis added, "you were interested in the labor movement, weren't you?"

"Yes." Webb wished he could have reported on the Homestead Strike and the Pullman Strike. "And I still am."

"You do have a soft spot for the downtrodden, don't you?" Hargis smiled wryly.

Webb shrugged.

"There've been rumblings that the Brooklyn trolley workers might go out on strike," the editor said. "Probably shut down the entire city if it happened—it would throw everything into chaos."

"From what I've heard, they have some legitimate grievances," said Webb.

"The Knights of Labor is holding a meeting in Brooklyn, Friday night, I believe. You might want to be there in case this turns into a story."

The suggestion sounded a lot like an assignment, but Webb didn't reject it. Instead, he stood and shook hands with the editor. Without saying so, both of them knew that the new arrangement had been accepted.

CHAPTER 5

The fussy young waiter cleared his throat in a sign of impatience. "Perhaps Madame would like me to come back?"

"No," Rebecca said, still perusing the menu. "I've think I've almost decided . . . Yes: I'll have the chicken cacciatore."

The waiter uttered a noisy sigh. "Of course, ma'am." At least he refrained from pointing out that the selection was a foregone conclusion; Rebecca ordered the same dish every time she and Marshall Webb came to the cozy Italian restaurant. The waiter turned his attention to Webb. "And for you, sir?"

Webb made a show of examining his own menu, and Rebecca could tell he was doing so just to get the waiter back for his poor manners. "How is the veal scaloppine tonight?"

"Excellent, sir." The waiter added more emphatically than necessary, "As *always*."

"I believe I'll have that, then," Webb said. "And we'll have a bottle of champagne."

Rebecca chuckled as the waiter walked away with their orders. Enzio's had become their favorite restaurant, and both of them by now had established favorite dishes that the waiters all knew. But she still enjoyed reading the menu each time to see what else they had.

The restaurant itself remained as unchanged as Rebecca and Webb's choices for dinner. Soft candlelight produced a warm glow, fresh flowers in small vases were placed on the checkered tablecloths, and an unobtrusive violinist provided soothing music.

"It is so nice to have the extra help at Colden House," Rebecca said cheerfully. "I do enjoy being able to get out like this."

Webb murmured a noise of agreement, but Rebecca would have preferred a more enthusiastic response. She had been hoping that the two of them would now be able to spend more time together.

While they waited for their food, Rebecca continued to make an effort at conversation. Usually, the two of them spoke easily; there were few people of either gender with whom Rebecca enjoyed sharing intelligent conversation as much as she did with Marshall. But he was clearly distracted this evening.

As the minutes passed, it became clear to Rebecca that the romantic atmosphere at Enzio's was wasted this evening. The only genuine warmth at their table was generated by the dripping candle embedded in a Chianti bottle. Not that Marshall was being cold, just remote.

Rebecca had learned that Marshall seldom expressed verbally what was in his thoughts, and she had also learned that prodding him too directly would rarely open him up. So she studied his appearance, hoping for a sign. His clothes, as always, were impeccable. The expertly tailored charcoal-gray cutaway suit fit his tall frame well, and a black silk Windsor tie was knotted neatly against a wing collar. She knew without seeing them that his boots, no doubt made by one of the city's most skilled shoemakers, were shined to a high gloss. Marshall always dressed with a sense of style, but never in a dandified way. If anything, his choice of apparel tended to run a bit on the stodgy side. She sighed. All too often, the stiff clothing was a match for his personality.

He was handsome, though. Even when, as now, his dark, intelligent eyes seemed to be directed inward, his features were most appealing. She would have to try again to get him to shave off his facial hair. The Franz Josef style he sported—a thick mustache swooping down to merge smoothly into the side whiskers, leaving only his chin bare—was too old-fashioned. He was not yet forty, but the whiskers made him appear older than that, especially since patches of gray had taken root in the brown hair.

With a flourish, the waiter placed the chicken dish on the table in front of Rebecca and served Marshall his veal.

With them left alone again, conversation was still lacking, but at least they could occupy themselves with the meal.

After a lull, Marshall asked with more courtesy than interest, "How's the cacciatore?"

"Delicious. And yours?"

"Very good," was the automatic reply, even though she'd noticed that Marshall had barely tasted his food.

Rebecca put down her fork, looked into Marshall's eyes, and waited until they met hers. "You know, as much as I like the food they serve here, the reason I came was for the company."

He appeared somewhat taken aback; then a

sheepish smile lifted his carefully groomed mustaches. "I apologize. I've been preoccupied."

"With what?"

"I resigned from *Harper's*."

"You did? Why?"

"I suppose that's what I've been trying to figure out." He took a healthy sip of his champagne. "I've been frustrated—working on the same stories again and again and none of it making any difference. All in all, I no longer enjoyed what I was doing; other than a salary, I got nothing out of it." Again the sheepish smile that she found so charming. "Imagine a grown man leaving a good job because he simply doesn't 'enjoy' it—especially these days, when there are so many people who'd be grateful for *any* kind of work."

"You don't owe anyone an explanation," she said. "You can do whatever your heart leads you to."

Marshall cleared his throat, and went on softly, "I spoke with Larry Pritchard. He's eager for me to write some more novels for him."

"Are you going to?"

"Yes. Actually, it was my idea. I think I'd like to write westerns again." There was some sparkle in Marshall's eyes now, and Rebecca was glad to see it. "Something completely different from all that's been going on in New York the last few years. Oh—I'll still write under 'David Byrd,' of course."

Rebecca smiled to herself. She knew he was trying to reassure her that his work for Pritchard would be secret. Dime novelists were considered to be as socially unacceptable as actors, and Rebecca's upper-class family certainly would never approve. But then there were many things that Rebecca was involved with that also garnered their disapproval. "I'll look forward to reading them," she said, picking up her fork again.

The two began eating again; then Marshall said, "Interesting thing is that Harry Hargis offered me the chance to stay on with *Harper's* on a freelance basis. He even had a suggestion for a story: Brooklyn trolley workers might be going on strike any day now."

"Are you going to do it?"

"I'm considering it. I don't see that I have anything to lose but a little time, so I'll probably go over there to cover a strike meeting Friday . . ." Marshall pursed his lips. "Or is it Saturday?" he muttered to himself.

"I'll be going to Brooklyn, too," Rebecca said.

"On Saturday?"

"I'm not sure when." She dug into her chicken, and began to tell Marshall about Vivian O'Connell and her plans for a shelter in Brooklyn.

"Sounds like a fine idea."

"There might be some difficulties with it."

"I'd imagine that there are a great many difficulties faced when trying to establish a new home."

"Vivian O'Connell is—was—a prostitute. She wants to provide a home for other prostitutes who want to start a new life." Rebecca was curious what Marshall's reaction would be.

He answered calmly, "I suppose the neighbors will be unhappy, but no one wants *any* kind of shelter near them, do they?"

Marshall didn't seem taken aback by the news of Miss O'Connell's profession. He always did seem to empathize with the outcasts of society, and although he didn't speak of it openly, she'd come to the belief that he'd had a difficult time surviving himself when he was young. As for Rebecca's own views, she thought of prostitution as an unpleasant occupation, but she'd seen too many girls come to Colden House from hard lives and abusive homes to judge any of them for what they'd had to do to survive.

"This Miss O'Connell," Marshall said, "do you think she's serious? Will she really make the effort or is it wishful thinking on her part?"

Rebecca had wondered the same. "It's too early to tell. But she has been persistent in contacting other homes for information. And she's already begun looking at property. That's why I'm going to Brooklyn—to take a look at some of the places she has in mind."

"Sounds promising."

"I *do* think she's serious. She told me that a friend of hers—another prostitute—was murdered. The police wouldn't even investigate."

Marshall shook his head sympathetically.

"Anyway, I'm going to see what I can do to help Miss O'Connell." The more Rebecca had considered the prospect, the more optimistic she had become. "I'm actually thinking that this might just be the first. There's so little I can do at Colden House—we're always at capacity, with no place to send the girls for jobs. So maybe I can help start other shelters—get more girls off the streets and give them some hope. With more shelters we could share information on education programs . . . job training . . . maybe we can organize in a way that will really bring about some changes in their lives!" Rebecca smiled to herself. She realized that she would be helping Vivian O'Connell as much for herself as for anyone. Rebecca simply *needed* to feel the sense of hope that infused her now.

"More champagne?"

Rebecca glanced up at the young waiter. "Yes, please." She wasn't much of a drinker, but she suddenly felt like celebrating.

* * *

"Another beer?"

Buck Morehouse gave the bartender a baleful stare. "How long have I been coming here, Grady?"

Grady, a burly fellow who looked every bit the ex-cop that he was, gave the bar a perfunctory wipe with his rag. "Oh, must be at least ten years."

"And you ever hear me say no to a beer?"

"Nope." Grady went to the tap and began drawing a brew. "And I don't remember you ever payin' for one, either."

Morehouse chuckled. "Well, I sure ain't gonna break tradition by starting today. Oh, and a shot of rye on the side—it's cold as hell."

"I ain't never gonna make a profit on this place," Grady grumbled good-naturedly.

They both knew the deal—it was the same in every bar in Brooklyn. In fact, it was the same in all of New York and probably in every other city in the country. Police officers ate and drank for free, and in turn saloons were permitted to remain open on Sundays and ignore closing times.

Morehouse looked around the place. Grady's Saloon was in a prime location, in downtown Brooklyn on Myrtle Avenue. It was a decent sort of place, where customers at least aimed at the cuspidors when spitting, the whiskey was decent enough that no one ever went blind from it, and the card games were played with unmarked decks. Even the prostitutes who occasionally worked the tavern were discreet, never performing sex acts in the bar itself. And the atmosphere was inviting; the gaslight was adequate, and the air, although smoky, was breathable. An old iron potbellied stove in the middle of the floor provided adequate warmth and the aroma of burning firewood.

Grady put the beer and whiskey in front of More-house and hoisted a shot glass of his own. "Figured I'd join you."

The two men clinked glasses and downed their whiskeys.

Morehouse exhaled sharply. "Ah, that hits the spot." He looked around again, thinking he might like to have a place like this himself someday. "You glad you opened this joint?" he asked.

"Hell yeah." The bartender ran a sleeve over his wet handlebar mustache. "Especially now." He nodded toward the tables, which were almost all occupied. "I got more customers now than ever. People are out of work, so they got nothing to do but come here and drink. No matter how bad things get—even if somebody don't got money for food or a room, they can scrape together enough coin to come here and drink. For a nickel a beer, or ten cents a whiskey, they get to help themselves to the free lunch counter and stay warm for a while. Now and then I gotta roust some character who thinks his nickel entitles him to stay all night or eat every bite I put out, but that's just part of the job." He grinned. "And I never did mind flexin' a little muscle."

Morehouse returned the smile. Grady had been known for his proficiency with a billy club when he was on the force, cracking numerous heads during his tenure. "And you don't miss being a cop?"

"Hell no!" Without being asked, the bartender poured Morehouse another shot of rye. "It's all crazy now with reorganization."

"That's for sure," muttered the detective. "All the officers are politicking for positions in the new department. And the patrolmen and detectives are all just hoping to still have jobs." Morehouse downed the shot and grabbed his beer glass. "Well, I'm gonna have a bite."

One small round table was open, and Morehouse put his beer glass on it to reserve the spot. He shot a warning glare at those seated near him that the beer had better not be touched, and walked over to the free lunch counter. He loaded a plate with cold ham, a wedge of cheddar cheese, a couple of pickles, a thick slice of indeterminate sausage, a handful of peanuts, and several pickled eggs. The ham was fatty, and all of the food was heavily salted so that customers would buy more drinks with which to wash it down, but it was the kind of lunch that Morehouse favored—especially since the additional beers he would need would be as free as the lunch spread.

Sitting down at the table, where his beer glass had remained full, Morehouse began eating the food and morosely pondering his future. There was no chance of him buying a place like this. In fact, it was a monthly challenge for him just to make his rent payments on time. The detective's modest salary was drained by a tendency to wager on bum boxers and slow horses. If not for saloon proprietors like Grady, he'd have to cut back on food and drink to make ends meet. At the thought, Morehouse smiled to himself, realizing that he could actually stand to lose a few pounds anyway— at the rate he was going, the new coat he'd gotten from the Fulton Street clothier soon would be too tight for him to wear.

Morehouse belched loudly and pushed his unfinished plate aside for the moment. He should have gotten in on the graft that was rampant in the department. Here he was, with twenty years on the force, and not a penny in savings. All because he was too honest to take payoffs.

The goods he received from merchants were one thing, but he had never crossed the line of taking cash. And partly because of that, he wasn't quite trusted by others in the department and had failed to forge the sort of alliances that are forged by cooperative corruption.

Biting hard into a pickle, he thought of the others who would certainly be well positioned in the new department. His captain, for one: Oscar Sturup, who ingratiated himself to his superiors, and made every decision based not on achieving justice but on political and career considerations. That was what it took to get ahead these days, and Morehouse had never developed the knack for operating that way. He looked up at Grady, who was drawing a beer for an old man shivering in a thin overcoat. Morehouse could do *that*, though, he was sure. True, he couldn't buy his own saloon, but maybe he could get a job as a bartender.

The door opened, letting in a cold draft and a wiry young policeman wearing sergeant stripes on his greatcoat and a blue helmet high on his narrow head. Morehouse recognized him immediately as Lonnie Keck, but he made no effort to greet him.

Keck stomped his boots, knocking off snow that melted in the muddy puddles left by previous customers. He then blew on his bare cupped hands and announced to no one in particular, "Goddamn, it's freezin' out there!" Keck took off his helmet, revealing a head of short wavy blond hair. He went over to the bar, put his helmet on the counter, and propped a boot on the brass footrail. "Gimme a whiskey," he ordered gruffly. "And you better make it the good stuff, none of that horse piss you give the regulars."

Grady grimaced but moved to comply.

Keck turned his back on the bartender and looked about the saloon as if he owned the place.

Morehouse grabbed his beer and held it to his mouth, hoping to avoid being seen. Sergeant Lonnie Keck looked to be about sixteen, with a pale straggly mustache and pimply cheeks, but Morehouse knew him to be in his mid-twenties. Keck was young for his rank, but then the rank had been secured by appropriate payments to the right people. Although Tammany Hall and the New York Police Department had been the recent subjects of corruption stories, Brooklyn had its own systemized graft and corruption. No doubt, Morehouse thought, Lonnie Keck was the type of young man who would prosper in the new department.

"Detective!" Keck called cheerfully. He grabbed his whiskey glass and came over to Morehouse's table.

The detective pretended to be pleased to see him, but he was on guard. Keck served as Captain Sturup's toady, and Morehouse thought for sure the captain would now hear that Morehouse was wasting time in a saloon rather than working on his cases.

Before Morehouse could make an excuse for being in the bar, Keck said, "Did you hear the news? We're supposed to protect the damned trolleys. Turnin' police officers into private guards!"

"No. Who said?"

"Captain told me." Keck enjoyed letting other officers know that he was in Sturup's confidence. "The streetcar companies are planning for a strike—gonna bring in scabs to run the trolleys and the mayor says *we* gotta protect 'em!" He shook his head. "Damned if I'm gonna freeze my ass off so the trolley companies can make money."

The mayor. Now Morehouse understood. Brooklyn mayor Charles Schieren was a major stockholder in the streetcar companies. Of course, he'd want to protect his interests.

Keck turned his head and rudely called for another round of drinks. "Make it quick," he added. He turned back and tugged at his thin mustache, as if trying to flaunt the fact that he could grow one.

"If we're ordered," Morehouse said, "there's nothing we can do but obey." He wasn't going risk saying anything that the captain could take to be insubordinate even if he did agree with the young sergeant.

Grady came by and made a show of wiping clean the table in front of Morehouse before putting his beer down; then he put Keck's whiskey glass down hard enough that some of it spilled.

While Keck grumbled about the service, Morehouse considered the effects of a trolley strike. Rails were all over the city of Brooklyn, so much that its citizens were called "trolley dodgers" by other New Yorkers. As bad as the rail companies were—and they were indeed almost universally hated because of their poor safety records, excessive price increases, and unreliable service—the city needed the transportation they provided. Manhattan needed it, too, since so many Brooklynites worked across the river.

"Tell you what *I'm* gonna do," Keck said. "If they go on strike, *I'm* going on strike, too."

The young man was talking nonsense. "You know we can't do that," Morehouse replied.

"Not 'we.' Just me." Keck tugged at his mustache again. "I'm gonna do like you do—just stay here and eat and drink." With a sly look, he added, "It's just a matter of time till I'm outta this uniform anyway."

"You're quitting the force?"

Keck turned his head both ways, peering around him. In a low voice, he said, "I'm moving *up.*" An arrogant sneer lifted his mustached lip. "You might say I put in for a promotion."

"Congratulations," Morehouse responded with complete disinterest.

"Yup. Soon as they reorganize the department, I'm going to be sitting mighty pretty."

Perhaps the ambitious young man was going to buy himself a higher rank, thought Morehouse. But he didn't care enough to ask Keck what he meant. Nor did he want to give him the satisfaction. The boy just loved to run his mouth and show everyone all that he knew, and Morehouse didn't care to hear it.

The young sergeant gestured at Morehouse's plate. "How's the ham?"

"The sausage is better." Morehouse pushed at the plate. "Well, I was actually just here waiting for some-one . . . an informant . . . with information on one of the cases I'm working on." His words were intended for the captain's ears in case they would be related to him. "Got a helluva lot of cases to clear and I been trying to get them all solved."

Keck grunted noncommittally, then picked up a piece of sausage that was left on the detective's plate. He swallowed it after barely chewing. "Not bad, but not all that good, either. I'll try the ham." He moved to rise.

"Well, I think this guy is a no-show," said More-house. "Better head back to the station house and see what I can do there." He was uncomfortable around Keck and eager to leave his company.

Keck's interest had turned to the lunch spread, and he merely grunted at the detective's departure.

CHAPTER 6

Marshall Webb's caped mackintosh, despite its fleece lining, was inadequate to keep him warm. The sputtering coal stove in the middle of the cable car didn't help, producing soot but little heat.

The cars of the New York Railroad were drawn by a thick, steam-powered steel cable that groaned and squeaked as if it, too, was suffering from the bitter cold. Wind blew shrilly between the cable cars as they slowly progressed, rocking and squealing, to the Brooklyn side of the East River.

Webb thought grimly to himself that the return trip would be even worse because he would have to take a Brooklyn-based train, and those were notoriously unreliable and uncomfortable. Transportation was one of the many issues of contention between the cities of New York and Brooklyn. Each city refused to let the other's trains pick up passengers within its limits, so New York cars would travel the bridge, let off their passengers in Brooklyn, and return empty to Manhattan. The Brooklyn trains repeated this wasteful exercise in the opposite direction. It had been one of the arguments in favor of consolidating the cities into a single government and a unified transportation system, but reorganization had yet to become reality.

Once off the train, Webb transferred to a Fulton Street trolley for the remainder of the journey. The car was crowded, and smelled from damp winter clothes and poor hygiene. After only two blocks, there was a loud *thunk* from under the car and it jerked to a halt. When no efforts from the crew were able to get the trolley in motion again, Webb decided to walk the remaining blocks. He also decided to hire a hansom cab for the trip back home.

A soft snow with flakes almost the size of marshmallows began to fall before he'd walked very far. In the waning daylight, Webb noticed how quickly a coating of snow could change the appearance of a city. Grimy gray streets were suddenly cleansed white, and boxy office buildings took on the appearance of gingerbread houses with the snow as frosting. If the snow continued, even a city like Brooklyn could look beautiful by morning.

Webb's walk ended at Canarsee Hall on Joralemon Street, a stone's throw west of City Hall Park in downtown Brooklyn. Named for the tribe of Indians that once occupied the area, and retaining the original spelling, Canarsee Hall was of redbrick construction with white colonnades that made it look like a government office or a bank.

The hall was used for all sorts of gatherings and public meetings. In fact, Webb had been here just last summer to cover a rally against the proposed consolidation of Brooklyn and New York. He paused on the steps leading up to the hall's double doors, recalling that it was on these very steps where a Brooklyn civic leader had been shot to death—while speaking to Webb. It was with what was probably an inevitable sense of foreboding that Webb continued to the door, where men of all ages, most clad in rough work clothes, were briefly stopped and questioned by similarly attired men before being permitted inside.

When Webb reached the door, he showed his *Harper's Weekly* card to a towering young man who wore no overcoat but appeared impervious to the cold weather. "I'd like to attend the meeting, if I may," he explained.

The young man hesitated, then called to another man just inside the hall, "Jim! C'mere!"

It took only seconds before a pudgy fellow of about forty in a tweed suit joined them. He glanced at the card and offered Webb his hand. As they shook, he said, "Jim Pate, Knights of Labor. Always happy to have the press."

"You don't mind if I report on the meeting?"

"Not at all. If this was a secret, we certainly wouldn't be meeting here, would we?" Pate laughed easily. "The only reason we're checking at the door is to make sure we have enough room for our members—we're expecting a big turnout. Otherwise we'd open it up to the public." Adopting a serious tone, he added, "What we're doing concerns every citizen of Brooklyn, and the more they know the more they'll agree with us."

Another voice called for Pate's attention, and with apologies he left Webb to find a seat for himself.

Although Webb had arrived fifteen minutes before the scheduled start of the meeting, there were few open spaces remaining on the hard-backed wood benches. He found one at the end of a row, under a tall side window that was completely steamed over. The heat that caused it to fog over was generated entirely by the five hundred or so bodies that already occupied the high-ceilinged room, for rental of the hall apparently did not include any other form of heating.

By six o'clock, the aisles were crowded and men stood around the walls. Webb was one of the few wearing a suit and tie.

Right on time, the meeting began. A lean, dark-haired man dressed in simple blue work clothes strode full of purpose to the podium. His voice left no doubt as to his Brooklyn origins when he introduced himself. "My name is Scott Berner. I'm a brakeman and"—he paused for effect—"a proud member of the only organization in America that's fighting for the working man"—another pause—"the Knights of Labor."

He was greeted with thunderous applause and yells of encouragement. A man in front of Webb raised a clenched fist and hollered in a raspy voice, "We're wit'cha, Scotty!"

Berner waited until the audience quieted down before going on. "And why do we *need* an organization?" A few answers were shouted but he waved them into silence, answering his own question. "Because there are organizations trying to keep us from living decent lives. Organizations like the Brooklyn Heights Railroad Company—"

The audience erupted in boos and jeers at the name.

"The Atlantic Avenue Railroad Company . . ." Berner named other Brooklyn streetcar companies, each time having to pause for the audience's disgusted reaction. "These companies are considered only with *profit*. Not their customers, not the city, and certainly not their employees—men like you and me who risk our lives every day to keep the trains running." Referring for the first time to a sheet of paper, Berner said, "Let me read you something from the newspaper. Just two weeks ago, January third, 1895, the grand jury handed up a presentment citing the street railway companies for 'willful and deliberate disregard of the interests of the public' and 'improper and unlawful acts.'" He went on to report that those acts consisted of blocking sidewalks with snow removed from the tracks. Looking out over the audience again, he said scornfully, "The grand jury gets involved for snowdrifts that might inconvenience some pedestrians, but is any action taken when a workingman gets killed or injured trying to keep the trains running?"

"Hell no!" and "They don't give a damn about us!" were the most common responses Webb heard.

Scott Berner went on to list a series of tragedies—fires, falls, electrocutions, crashes—with the date and place of each occurrence. After the recitation, he said, "That's a lot of dead and injured workingmen, isn't it?"

The crowd acknowledged that indeed it was. "Too damn many!" some of them cried.

"There've been so many," Berner continued, "that maybe the public doesn't even pay attention anymore. So let me show you what we're really talking about here." He stepped away from the podium and to the front row of seats. From his vantage point, Webb couldn't see what he was doing, but Berner soon was back at the podium ushering along with him two young women and several children. Both women were dressed in black mourning garb.

There was a respectful hush throughout Canarsee Hall.

Berner introduced Jennifer Roque, a pretty young brunette whose husband of three months had been electrocuted in October while working on the Bushwick line. The other widow was Elizabeth Mella; her husband, Steven, was crushed to death in a collision on Vanderbilt Avenue a month later, leaving her a widow and their three children without a father.

Webb wasn't sure that it was appropriate to put these unfortunate families on display as Berner had, but perhaps it was necessary to show the human toll these accidents had taken.

Berner solicitously escorted the young widows back to their seats, then spoke for a while longer. He mentioned that the Knights of Labor would be helping these families get through this difficult time, and that the organization could only do so because of the support of its members.

Finally, Berner announced, "Now let me introduce you to the man who will lead us in our fight for justice." Expectant murmurs filled the hall. "Here he is: Master Workman Mike Coppinger of the Executive Committee of District Assembly Number Seventy-five, Knights of Labor!"

Coppinger came to the podium, a man of about fifty wearing a red flannel shirt and stiff work pants. He appeared tired but determined. The only thing flashy about him was a gleaming gold tooth. After thanking Berner for the introduction, he said in a basso voice, "After what we've just heard, I don't think anyone can believe that our cause is unjust." He looked around the hall, slowly scanning from row to row, man to man, as if able to see into each one's heart. Then he demanded, "How about *you*? Are you with us?"

The answers were a resounding affirmative.

"Good." Coppinger nodded. "Then let me tell you what we're going to do." He proceeded to give a short speech, but a detailed one, listing the union's specific demands and giving reasoned explanations for each one. Most of the demands were related to safety issues and the need for increased wages. He made it all sound eminently sensible—so sensible that it left little doubt that their goals could be achieved. He concluded by repeating, "So, my friends . . . Are you friends of the working man?"

"Yes!"

"Are you with us?"

"Yes!"

"Are we all in this together?"

"Yes!"

Coppinger nodded with satisfaction at the enthusiasm of the answers. "The owners say they won't give in."

The owners were loudly cursed.

"They say they'll keep the trolleys rolling even if the Knights of Labor does call a strike. Will they?"

"No!"

"Are we going to bring them to a stop?"

"Yes!"

"What will we do to stop them?"

"Whatever it takes!"

"How long will we fight?"

"As long as it takes!"

Coppinger's voice dropped to an even lower register. "And who will ultimately win this fight?"

"We will!"

He smiled. "You're damned right we will."

Berner again briefly stood and told the assembled men to await instructions from their local union leaders, and the meeting adjourned.

After jotting down a few more notes on what had transpired, Webb moved toward the front of the room where a number of men were milling about the union leaders. He found Jim Pate, the fellow who'd let him into the hall, and Pate agreed to bring him to Coppinger.

They edged their way toward him, past a cordon of well-wishers. "Mike!" Pate called. When he had Coppinger's attention, he jerked his head toward a less crowded corner of the room.

When the three men met there, Pate made the introductions.

"Webb . . ." Coppinger said thoughtfully. "You the one who wrote the stories about Tammany Hall?"

Webb admitted that he had authored them.

"And you wrote about the consolidation fight last year, too."

Webb again said that he had.

Jim Pate excused himself to answer another call for attention, leaving Webb and Coppinger in relative privacy.

Coppinger smiled, exposing his gold tooth. "I admire your work—and I can tell from what you've written that your sympathies are with honest working people. Means you'll be on our side in this fight."

"I'm just reporting," answered Webb. "I don't have a side."

Coppinger's voice rumbled from deep in his belly. "Better yet—an *objective* reporter who's on our side!"

Webb had to fight back a smile of his own. The union leader was probably correct in his assessment, but it wouldn't do for Webb to admit it. "May I ask you some questions?"

"Of course."

Webb's pad and pencil were poised. "Is it definite that there will be a strike? Has a final decision been made?"

"No, a formal strike vote hasn't been taken yet. The Executive Committee will make that decision."

"So there's still a chance to negotiate?"

"No." Coppinger's easy smile suddenly had a hard

edge. "There's still a chance for the railroad companies to meet our demands."

"Do you think they will?"

He shrugged. "No sign of it so far."

A burly man in bib overalls passed by them. As he did, he slapped Coppinger on the back and said, "I'm with you, Mike."

Coppinger turned his smile to the fellow and replied, "No, I'm with *you*. We're all in it together."

When he had his attention again, Webb asked, "If you do go on strike, do you believe you'll get public support? There are working people who need the trolleys to get to work."

Coppinger laughed. "If they *need* to get someplace, Brooklyn trolleys aren't the way to go anyhow! Everybody knows how bad they're run, and everybody knows it's because of the owners—they won't pay for reliable equipment, the power lines are inadequate, the horse-drawn lines are pulled by nags who should be sent to a glue factory . . ." Adopting a more serious tone, he said, "I know a shutdown will be inconvenient for some, but once they realize how much better things will be once we get the railroads to change, the good people of Brooklyn will support us."

"Can you really achieve a shutdown? You don't think the owners will hire scabs?"

"They might try. But we have seven *thousand* men prepared to walk off the job—conductors, motormen, machinists . . . everyone from the car cleaners to the electricians who run the power houses. Where can the railroads find replacements for all of us?"

Since Webb's business was to ask the questions, he made no attempt to answer. "Did you mean it about the union doing 'whatever it takes' to stop the cars from running?"

For the first time in the interview Coppinger hesitated. "Let me just say that the trains *will not run.*"

"The owners are already saying that you're planning sabotage—and that they'll pursue criminal charges if it happens."

"So they're accusing us of *future* crimes?" He smiled wryly. "Leave it to the owners to complain about things that *haven't* happened."

"Mayor Schieren says he's drawing up contingency plans to keep the trains running. You might be up against both the railroad companies and the city of Brooklyn."

"Not the city of Brooklyn," Coppinger corrected. "Only its mayor. And in this case, the mayor and the railroad companies are already in bed together. The mayor is a major stockholder in them, so he's protecting his personal financial interests rather than the interests of his citizens."

"You believe that even if the city tries to operate them, you can bring the trolleys to a stop."

Coppinger repeated emphatically, "The trains *will not run.*"

Webb paused before continuing the questioning to glance about the hall. Only a few dozen men were left in the place and the conversations were winding down to a low hum.

"Anything else I can tell you?" Coppinger prodded.

"Even if your demands are just," Webb said, "is this the time to strike—with the country in a depression? There are thousands of people desperate for work, and here your men are going to *stop* working."

"A fair question," Coppinger replied. "And it's one union men get all the time. Here's my answer: The politicians and the bankers and the bosses will say we just don't want to work. But working people will support us because they understand that a job ain't worth anything if it leaves you dead. A workingman is supposed to be able to make a *living*, not end up dead because of his job. In this job, we face risks that can kill us all at once and we earn wages that can leave a family on the road to slow starvation." He shrugged. "I'd rather go quick." Then he looked into Webb's eyes. "Believe me. This is a matter of life and death."

Webb stopped writing. He thought back to the young widows who'd been brought up to the podium, and decided that Mike Coppinger probably wasn't exaggerating.

CHAPTER 7

"Care for some more tea?"

"Yes, please." Rebecca couldn't remember the last time she'd traveled in such comfort. Her winter outing to Brooklyn was proving to be quite comfortable, and Vivian O'Connell was a gracious companion.

O'Connell poured another cup from a large engraved silver flask, and Rebecca received it gratefully.

The two of them were seated in O'Connell's elegant brougham, kept warm by a buffalo robe draped over their laps and brandy-laced tea that Vivian O'Connell had thoughtfully brought.

It had been a busy morning. Miss O'Connell, along with her liveried driver, had picked Rebecca up at Colden House, although Rebecca had suggested they simply meet in Brooklyn. Rebecca appreciated O'Connell going out of her way; it boded well that she was willing to make the effort.

The two of them had then traveled snow-packed streets on their way to possible sites for O'Connell's proposed shelter. They visited a vacant brick warehouse in an industrial section of Williamsburg, which was quickly determined to be unsuitable; although the building was spacious, it reeked of death from the slaughterhouse next door and there was continuous, hammering noise from the power plant across the street. A wood-frame hotel near the Wallabout Docks was also ruled out; the dilapidated three-story structure was a flophouse that had probably stood since before British forces occupied the city and didn't look like it could possibly stand a week longer.

Now, after a stop to replenish the flask with hot tea, they were off to Flatbush to view a property there.

Rebecca found herself enjoying the trip, and staring out the window of the brougham. Although not quite warm enough to break the cold spell, the sun shone brightly in a high clear sky. Yesterday's snow had left a white blanket over the city that had yet to turn to the inevitable grimy gray. The hooves of the chestnut mare that drew their carriage padded softy in the packed snow and kicked up sparkles of the fluffy stuff with each step.

They traveled around the fountain at Prospect Park Plaza, past Mount Prospect Reservoir, and finally along Frederick Olmsted's beautiful Prospect Park itself. Rebecca watched children at play in the park, some building snowmen, others making snow angels, and some using the material as projectiles.

When she spotted a tot being pulled on a small sled, she recalled one of her own childhood memories of winter. After a heavy snow, Rebecca's father would order one of the servants to take Rebecca and her sister, Alice, for a sleigh ride. The two of them would huddle under a pile of fur blankets in the back of the horse-drawn sleigh and travel all over the paths and roads through Central Park. Riding now in similar fashion, Rebecca could picture the old scenes vividly, and almost wished that she could go back to the carefree time when she was a girl.

Rebecca glanced at Vivian O'Connell; the bright sunlight beaming through the window highlighted both the coppery tint in her brown hair and the powder on her full, round face. She looked nothing like young Alice, and Rebecca's reverie ended. The two of them had serious work to do, and so far they had gotten nowhere in finding a suitable shelter.

They continued south down Flatbush Avenue nearly to Flatlands. The area was almost rural, and of so little commercial value that the village of Flatbush had only last year been incorporated into the city of Brooklyn, and Flatlands was still an independent town.

Slowing down on the tricky roadway, O'Connell's driver turned the carriage off of Flatbush Avenue onto a narrow lane. Houses here were rustic and sparse, set back from the road amid large old elms and stately oak trees.

The brougham drew to a stop at a two-story farmhouse on a sprawling lot bordered by a split rail fence.

The liveried driver opened the carriage door. "I believe this is the place," he said, as he assisted the two ladies from their seat.

"Thank you, Daniel." O'Connell smoothed her sealskin cape and adjusted her stylish fur hat. To Rebecca, she asked, "Shall we?"

Rebecca had already begun evaluating the place as a possible shelter. The rambling clapboard building was not a new one. Its Dutch doors and overhanging roof were of an earlier style, and over the years several additions had been made to the structure with little regard for architectural aesthetics. The house had once been whitewashed but probably not since the Lincoln administration, and some of the peeling green shutters sagged on their hinges. As a private home, its appeal was limited, but Rebecca thought she saw a lot of potential as a shelter.

O'Connell had to repeat her knock before a man's voice yelled from within, "I'm comin', damn it!"

The top half of the door opened and a grizzled old man in a stained flannel undershirt peered at them suspiciously with bloodshot eyes. "Yeah, what?" He hooked a thumb under his one suspender, and Rebecca felt relief that he must be wearing pants.

"Mr. Patterson?" O'Connell asked.

The old man hesitated. "I'm Gregory Patterson. Who are you?"

"I'm Vivian O'Connell. I contacted you a few days ago . . . about possibly buying your home." O'Connell maintained a courteous tone and a cheerful smile. She added, "And this is Miss Rebecca Davies. She's come to help me look at the property. I hope you don't mind."

"Are you the whore?" Patterson appeared to brighten at the prospect.

Rebecca flinched. O'Connell's blue eyes sparkled with humor when she answered that she was indeed a whore but that Rebecca was not.

The lower half of the door swung open and Patterson stepped aside. "Well, come inside. I tell you, it'll be nice to have whores here."

O'Connell stepped inside and Rebecca followed with a growing sense of apprehension. She didn't feel any better when she noticed the double-barreled shotgun in the corner of the hallway where most people might keep an umbrella.

Patterson didn't offer to take their coats, nor did he offer a seat or refreshments. He rubbed a palm across his unshaven chin, making a rasping sound that nearly matched his voice. "Ha! Wait till the neighbors learn I sold my place to whores!" He erupted in a fit of laughter.

Rebecca resisted the impulse to remind him that there was only one here, and a retired one at that.

"So you *are* selling?" O'Connell said.

"Oh yes. Can't stand living hereabouts no more. Goddamn neighbors are givin' me fits."

"What's wrong with the neighbors?" Rebecca asked.

Patterson jerked a thumb toward the east. "It's mostly the damned Burchfields over there. They have *cats.*" He spit out the word as if it were the vilest of profanities. "Damned critters run all over my property, messin' my gardens, killin' the songbirds, mewing at all hours of the night . . . I *hate* them cats."

That was certainly clear. "How many do they have?" Rebecca asked, imagining an infestation of felines.

"Three." Patterson idly scratched himself under an armpit. "But I'm doin' my damnedest to get it down to two." He motioned the ladies into the parlor, muttering, "Wish I could exterminate every one of them critters."

The parlor was devoid of furniture except for a single armchair with torn upholstery and a misshapen ottoman. A couple of oily rags tacked above the windows served as curtains.

"Are you already moving out?" O'Connell asked him.

Patterson nodded. "My brother left me a cabin upstate. Nobody around for miles. Soon as I get this place sold, that's where I'm headin'—and I ain't never comin' back."

O'Connell smiled. "Well, I might be interested in buying. Could you show us around?"

Patterson shrugged. "Show *yourselves* around. I got some work to do out in the barn."

"You don't mind?"

"Nah. Take a look at whatever you want. Ain't got nothing left here worth stealin' anyways."

He left them alone and the two ladies smiled at each other, both no doubt amused that Patterson could even think that they'd come to rob him.

"Well, let's see what the place is like," O'Connell said.

The two of them went through the downstairs rooms, carefully examining the kitchen fixtures and one bathroom, and then proceeded upstairs to the bedrooms. The structure seemed sound, although in need of minor repairs and a major decorating effort. One bedroom was sparsely furnished and had a pile of dirty clothes on the floor; the others were almost entirely bare.

After exploring the additions to the farmhouse, one of which was a bedroom and a couple of others that were used for storage, the two women returned to the parlor. Neither of them took the one chair.

"What do you think?" Rebecca asked, having noticed that the more they saw of the place the less enthusiastic O'Connell appeared.

"Well, it certainly isn't much to look at. I don't think a woman has been in here for years—did you see that bathroom?"

Rebecca was actually pleased to see that it *had* an indoor bathroom; she suspected that here in the wilds of Flatbush not many homes did. "It would need some work," she replied. "But remember, you have to look at this place for its potential as a shelter. And it does have some."

"Well, that's why I asked you to come," said O'Connell with a small smile. "I'm used to a different kind of house. So, what do *you* think?"

"There's plenty of room—you could probably have forty girls living here. And it's in generally good repair." Rebecca had looked closely for structural problems because she'd had experience with a bad roof at Colden House. "The kitchen will need more equipment, of course, including a couple of new ranges and an icebox or two. Another bathroom will have to be added also. But that would be true for almost any property you'd look at—not a lot of homes are equipped to handle the number of girls you might have staying here."

O'Connell nodded thoughtfully. "Well, I'm also thinking that this place is awfully remote."

"That can be a plus," answered Rebecca. "Fewer temptations for the girls to get in trouble, and less chance of police coming around and harassing them." Colden House was a favorite place for Manhattan police to seek "suspects" when they had a crime that they wanted to pin on someone.

"But what about getting supplies? Or what if a girl needs a doctor? This is just so far . . ."

"That's true . . . but you can stock up on supplies. And I'm sure you can find a local doctor. A local doctor might even be happy to have a home like this—lots of prospective patients in one place, so he doesn't have to drive his buggy all over the area."

"Hmm. I suppose that *could* work out."

Rebecca took a few steps around the room, starting to picture what it might look like. "You could turn this into a cozy home for the girls. And there's plenty of room to expand if need be." She looked at O'Connell. "Let's see what the other buildings are like—perhaps the carriage house and the barn could be used for teaching classes or setting up some kind of training programs."

They went out through the kitchen door, stopping briefly for Rebecca to point out how the kitchen might be modernized.

Outside in the crisp air and bright sunshine, O'Connell glanced up at the house. "I'll have to hire a carpenter and a painter to get the exterior in shape."

"No, you won't. Well, the carpenter, maybe, but you can have the girls do the painting."

O'Connell laughed brightly. "The girls who'll be staying here have never painted anything but their faces."

"Isn't that the point?" Rebecca asked. "They have to learn new skills. Besides, they'll have to have something to occupy themselves with while they're here. They can fix up the house—it will help give them a sense of pride in the place—and they should all share in the daily chores—the cooking, laundry, cleaning."

Vivian O'Connell scanned the house again, and her bright blue eyes widened a bit more than usual. Rebecca thought she was starting to see what the house could eventually become. "I think I'll take it," she announced.

"We haven't even seen the other buildings yet," Rebecca reminded her with a smile.

They stopped in the carriage house, which contained the remnants of some unidentifiable vehicles and a few broken tools, and they agreed that it might be put to use as a school.

Before they reached the barn, Gregory Patterson emerged from it carrying a wire trap large enough to catch a raccoon. He put it down in the snow and wiped his hands on his stained coat. "So, what do you think of the house?"

"I'm seriously considering buying it," answered O'Connell.

Patterson grinned broadly, showing a number of gaps where teeth used to be. "Well, won't that be something? Wait till the Burchfields find they got themselves a whorehouse next door!" He seemed convinced that a house full of retired whores was still a "whorehouse."

"Shall we discuss price?" O'Connell suggested.

"Come inside." Patterson, still carrying the trap, led them into the kitchen.

There were only two spindle-back chairs at the small pine table, so Rebecca stood while O'Connell and Patterson discussed a selling price. O'Connell was a capable negotiator, and Patterson was clearly eager to sell, so the price was quickly whittled down to under a thousand dollars.

"I'd like a day or two to make a final decision," said O'Connell, "but I expect you just made a sale."

"Sure, you can take a couple days." Patterson looked thoroughly pleased. "Just let me know." He picked up his trap. "Gives me a little more time to catch one of them damned Burchfield cats."

On their way back to the brougham, where Daniel was patiently waiting, O'Connell nudged Rebecca in the side. "You know, I think the neighbors might *like* having whores living in the neighborhood if it means getting rid of that grouchy old bastard."

While the coachman held the door open, O'Connell said, "I feel like celebrating. Would you care to join me for dinner? It's the least I can do to thank you for coming with me today."

Rebecca promptly agreed. It appeared that there would soon be a new shelter and that was indeed something to celebrate.

* * *

Vivian O'Connell's plush suite in the Fields Hotel was furnished in blond wood and lustrous blue upholstery. Thick oriental rugs covered most of the floor and heavy drapes were tied back at the windows.

Rebecca and O'Connell sat at a dining table in front of the double window that overlooked Fulton Street. Two of the hotel's kitchen staff served them a fine meal of roast duck accompanied by an excellent champagne. The china and silverware were as fine as those that could be found in any Fifth Avenue mansion—including that of Rebecca's family.

As they ate, they talked enthusiastically about the possibilities for the home in Flatbush.

After the main course, O'Connell dabbed at her lightly rouged lips with her napkin. "I do have a question. I don't know how to ask it without seeming to pry, but it's something I've been wondering about."

"Ask," prompted Rebecca.

"How do you fund your home? You see, I can buy Patterson's place and probably keep it going for a while. But I've been doing some calculations, and housing thirty or so girls will be *expensive*. I don't know that I can keep it going for very long on my own."

Rebecca didn't mind answering. Although it was obvious that Vivian O'Connell lived well, running a shelter certainly would be a major financial drain. "My family established Colden House before I was born; it's been a family charity, and they still provide regular support. Over the years, we've also developed some donors who've been a tremendous help. Perhaps you can find local philanthropists here in Brooklyn who can help."

"The difficulty," said O'Connell, "is that not all

Brooklynites will be as enthusiastic as Mr. Patterson about having a house full of whores." She laughed. "It was never a problem when I ran an active brothel— the city's leading citizens were happy to have the services available to them and paid me enough to keep the place running at a nice profit. Now that the girls *won't* be working the trade anymore, I'm afraid no one will want them."

Rebecca gave a nervous glance at the waiters who could hear every word of their conversation.

O'Connell caught the look. "Oh, don't worry about them. They know all about me, and they're tipped well to keep it to themselves."

Both waiters smiled, bowed, and then served a selection of rich desserts and cups of hot tea. O'Connell appeared delighted at the selection and dug into a thick slab of chocolate cake.

"You *never* had a problem with the brothel?" Rebecca asked.

"Mmm, delicious." O'Connell swallowed and took a sip of tea. "Only minor problems—customers getting out of hand now and then, girls quarreling with each other . . . but nothing I couldn't manage."

"That experience should help you with the shelter— it's not always easy having twenty or thirty girls under one roof."

"Oh, I'm not worried about that. I've dealt with all types of people. The problem is that I'll be on my own."

"You had partners before?"

O'Connell lifted another piece of cake on her fork. "No, not partners exactly. But as I said, the community was happy to have us." She smiled. "*Everybody* was well taken care of."

Rebecca didn't want to hear the details of how they were taken care of. She asked, "Have you thought of what you'll name the house?" She knew that once it had a name, it would seem more of a reality.

O'Connell's smile faded and she put down her fork. "Yes, I have." She glanced up at the servers and dismissed them with thanks. When she and Rebecca were left alone, she said, "I'd like to call it 'Sayre House.' I'm doing this because of Frenchy, and I think it should have her name." She gazed out the window for a moment. "When she was killed, no one but me cared, as if she'd never existed. Now at least her name will live on in the house." After another moment, she turned back to Rebecca with teary eyes. "I suppose that sounds awfully foolish."

"No. Not at all. I think it's a fine way of honoring her memory."

"It's just over two years ago she was killed," O'Connell said in a voice thick with emotion.

It sounded as though she wanted to talk about her friend's death, so Rebecca asked, "And there were never any suspects?"

"There was never any investigation, so there was no chance to find suspects. The morning of November seventh, 1893, Frenchy was found in an alley a couple of blocks from the brothel—beaten to death sometime during the night. The police acted as if she was nothing more than a dead dog to be carted away."

Rebecca began to wonder if it would be too late to find out what had happened to Frenchy Sayre. Marshall had a way of prodding the authorities into action; perhaps they could still get some justice for the young woman. Rebecca didn't want to suggest it to O'Connell—no sense raising any hopes—but wanted to know more about her friend. "How old was she?"

"Just turned twenty-two."

"'Frenchy' . . . Was she from France? Did she have an accent?"

Vivian O'Connell smiled for the first time since the discussion had turned to her late friend. "She was fluent in the French arts, but didn't speak a word of the language." Her eyes sparkled with amusement.

It took a few moments for Rebecca to understand and she felt herself blush when the realization hit her.

O'Connell didn't let her discomfort last long. She went on, "Since the police didn't investigate, I tried to—asked the girls who knew her if they were aware of anything and talked to some of Frenchy's customers. I didn't learn anything useful." She paused for a sip of tea. "I kept the house going for a while, but the place was never the same. So I decided to close the house and open a place to help girls like Frenchy, who are trying to start new lives. I couldn't help her, so I'm hoping maybe I can help someone else."

"'Sayre House' would be a fine name and a fine tribute," said Rebecca. But she was still thinking that more might be done. If Frenchy Sayre's murderer was still at large, he could kill again. There were men, she was aware, who preyed on prostitutes, and opening a shelter might not be enough to protect them. Could a two-year-old murder still be solved? she wondered.

CHAPTER 8

The radiator was whistling like a teakettle and Marshall Webb couldn't stand it any longer. He pushed himself away from his desk and went to the radiator under his parlor window.

Webb tried to bleed some air from the noisy contraption, which added some gurgles and gasps to its watery noises. Eventually he succeeded in getting the radiator to whistle at a lower pitch, but realized that if he wanted the feeble heat that it generated he would have to tolerate the sounds that went with it.

He stood and paused to look out the window of his second-floor apartment. No matter the occasional battles with the plumbing, he much preferred being able to work here at home than in the cramped, sterile confinement of the *Harper's Weekly* offices.

Webb lived in a brownstone on East Fourteenth Street near Union Square. The area had once been the heart of New York City's entertainment district, and although many of the old theatrical houses had moved up Broadway to Herald Square, the neighborhood retained a strong theatrical presence. The attractions covered the cultural spectrum from Huber's

Dime Museum and Tony Pastor's Variety House to
Steinway Hall and the Academy of Music. Among the
theaters were numerous dining and drinking establishments, most of a German flavor. It was a diverse
neighborhood much livelier than the publishing
houses and financial institutions that dominated the
area near *Harper's*

Having left full-time employment with the publication, he was now able to work in the comfort of home,
the same place where he had written so many dime
novels over the years. His "office" consisted of a combination parlor, library, and dining room. A massive
rolltop desk, stained dark, was the largest piece of furniture, with matching glass-door bookcases on either
side of it. A small dining table and a pair of bent-back
chairs were near the windows, and an oversized
leather easy chair dominated the parlor area. There
was little decoration, but Webb preferred not to have
his home cluttered with artwork or knickknacks.

Webb returned to his desk, where numerous sheets
of foolscap covered with his meticulous handwriting
were spread out. None of it was prose, merely background notes related to the likely trolley strike. He was
thorough when doing a story, providing all the facts
and figures necessary to support it. In fact, it was
largely due to his detailed reports that New York
State's Lexow Committee was able to make cases
against the police and politicians involved in a corruption scandal orchestrated by infamous Tammany Hall.

So far, Webb had spoken with representatives from
most of the Brooklyn railroad companies; they were
as emphatic in stating that "the trains *will* run" as the
Knights of Labor's Mike Coppinger had been when
he avowed that they would not. The only point of
agreement between the two sides had to do with the

elevated trains; these were independent from the trolley companies, and had maintained good relations with their employees. Workers on the els received better wages than their earthbound counterparts and their trains were better maintained, resulting in fewer accidents. It seemed that if a strike was to occur, only streetcar lines would be affected. But that would still be devastating to the Brooklyn transportation system.

Webb had begun checking his notes for the different types of accidents that had occurred on the tracks in the past year, when the harsh ringing of his telephone interrupted him. He grumbled at the annoying device; generally, he found the invention to be more of an annoyance than a convenience.

His annoyance vanished immediately when he recognized Rebecca's voice on the line.

"Do you know what today is?" she asked.

Webb moved a few papers aside to see his desk calendar. He hesitated briefly; working at home often left him unsure what day of the week it was. "Yes. January thirteenth."

"*Sunday,* January thirteenth," Rebecca answered.

"Yes . . ."

"I take it you won't be coming to dinner?"

"Oh! Was I supposed to—" Webb looked again at the calendar; this wasn't a holiday. Rebecca's parents held a formal family dinner at their Fifth Avenue mansion every Sunday. Webb used to go with her fairly regularly, but he had excused himself more and more often until he now went only on major holidays and special occasions. Having gone for Christmas and New Year's, he assumed he was free from the obligation for a while. "I could, if you—"

Rebecca burst out laughing, and Webb thought there was a musical sound to her laughter as it came through the receiver. "I'm just teasing you. You're probably exempt until . . . probably Easter."

"Whew! I was worried there for a minute." Webb realized it was impolite to sound so relieved. It wasn't that he disliked her family; he simply didn't fit in with them. The Davies were already prominent in the city when it was still Dutch, and they tended to be preoccupied with wealth and social status. Webb had neither, and they always subtly made him aware that although he might dine in their home and spend time with Rebecca, he wasn't one of them. Trying to sound as if his relief had nothing to do with avoiding her family, he quickly explained, "The trolley strike might be called for tomorrow, and I'm trying to do as much writing as I can before it hits—because I think once it does, everything is going to be crazy."

"That's why I'm calling," Rebecca said.

Webb was puzzled. "About the strike?"

"You'll be going to Brooklyn again soon, right?"

"Very likely tomorrow."

"You have that detective friend over there. I was wondering if you could talk to him."

"You mean Morehouse?" Webb had worked with Buck Morehouse to solve a murder last summer, but they weren't really friends. They hadn't been in touch once since the case was wrapped up.

"Yes! That's his name . . . I was trying to remember." Rebecca drew a deep breath. "Anyway, here's what I'd like to ask him. . . ." She then told him of a prostitute named Frenchy Sayre who'd been murdered a little over two years earlier. "It was never really investigated," she concluded, "and I was hoping you could ask Detective Morehouse to look into it."

"I doubt that he'd—"

"It's up to him to say yes or no, but could you please ask him?"

Webb thought it was a preposterous notion, but he answered, "Of course. As soon as I get a chance to see him."

Rebecca thanked him and kept him on the line a while longer describing her visit to Flatbush with Vivian O'Connell and ideas of how the two of them could work together with their shelters. Webb had the sense that she'd taken a liking to the former prostitute. Rebecca chatted brightly for some minutes before she told him to get back to his writing. The last thing she said was, "You *will* try to convince Detective Morehouse to look into Frenchy Sayre, won't you?"

Webb promised that he would and hung up the receiver smiling. The odds of Morehouse taking on a two-year-old murder case were low and the prospect of solving it almost zero. Rebecca often had unfounded bursts of optimism, but it was one of the many qualities he admired about her.

After going to the kitchen to brew a fresh pot of coffee—which provided far more warmth than the radiator—he returned to his desk and looked over the pages of notes again.

There were too many numbers, he thought. He had accident totals arranged by category, charts of wage scales, and numbers of employees on the various lines. All of it made for cold, dry reading.

Webb had to admit that sometimes he got lost in facts and details. People were what mattered; he needed to cover the *personal* side of the labor dispute. Perhaps he could speak with the young widows he'd seen at the Knights of Labor meeting.

He picked up his pen to make a note to himself and was struck by the realization that Rebecca never seemed to lose sight of the personal side of things. It was why she could treat every girl at Colden House as an individual who needed personal attention. And it was why she could actually believe that someone else might care about the murder of a prostitute.

Webb silently repeated his promise to her that he would speak with Buck Morehouse.

The station house of the Second Precinct was housed at 49 Fulton Street, a stone's throw from the King's County Courthouse, in the heart of downtown Brooklyn. It was one of the busiest police stations in the city, but Buck Morehouse toiled in a very different atmosphere from that of the bustling squadroom.

The detective was slouched forward in his wobbly, straight-backed chair, his elbow resting on the scarred surface of his old oak desk and his head propped up on his palm. The cramped office was sparsely furnished with beat-up furniture that would have been rejected by most secondhand shops; its only redeeming quality was that it was so small and shabby that Morehouse had it all to himself.

"Hard at work again, Detective?" The clipped voice behind him dripped with contempt.

Morehouse twisted around. "Just thinking, sir." He didn't mention that the topic of his thoughts was resentment at being called into the station house on a Sunday. The fact that most of the police force had been told to report was of no consolation to the weary detective.

Captain Oscar Sturup stood tall and straight in the doorway of Morehouse's office, his arms crossed behind his back. His blue uniform was stiff and the insignia of his rank shimmered brightly. Sturup's tight lips and trimmed black beard appeared rigid, and his dark, deep-set eyes were equally hard. "'Thinking,'" he repeated. "You mean resting, don't you, Detective?"

Morehouse knew he couldn't win this argument with the captain. When he was out of the station house, Sturup accused him of not being at work; when he was in the office, he was often reprimanded for not being out investigating crimes. But then, Oscar Sturup was a politician who fancied himself a military commander; in Morehouse's opinion, his captain had no concept of what police work really involved. "No, sir," he replied in a resigned voice. "I was thinking about a new lead in the, uh, Higgenbotham case—you know, the shoeshine boy who was beaten to death out by City Hospital."

Sturup snorted with disdain. "Right now, we need to be concerned with more important matters than shoeshine boys."

That was fine with Morehouse, who actually had no leads at all in the case. "Yes, sir," he said, with no idea what he was saying yes to.

"We expect that the trolley strike might be called for tomorrow. And the mayor—I've met with him personally . . ." Sturup paused for Morehouse to be suitably impressed by this fact. When the detective's only response was to scratch his unshaven cheek, Sturup continued briskly. "The mayor is *determined* that the trolleys run as normal."

Morehouse could tell that Sturup was determined to comply with Mayor Schieren's wishes. If he succeeded, Morehouse thought wryly, perhaps the mayor would see to it that Sturup was rewarded with some railroad stock.

"I've also spoken with the police commissioner," Sturup went on, "and I've been given complete discretion on assigning manpower for the Second Precinct."

Probably not a wise decision on the commissioner's part, thought Morehouse.

"Of course, there's no need to concern yourself with the overall plan, only your particular assignment." Sturup unfolded his arms and handed Morehouse a roster of names. "If the strike hits, these officers will be in your charge. And your assignment is the Atlantic Avenue line, from Carlton to Grand."

"To do *what* on the line?" Morehouse didn't quite understand.

"To keep it clear." Sturup sniffed. "I should think that a detective would be able to deduce that." He went on, "Those three blocks of Atlantic Avenue are to be kept clear for the trolleys to run without impediment."

Morehouse counted the names on the roster. There were twelve, including Sergeant Lonnie Keck, who had vowed to him that he wouldn't put himself on the line for the railroad companies. Twelve men to cover both sides of three long blocks. The task was clearly impossible, but Morehouse knew that argument would be futile. "Yes, sir." He sighed.

"Good." Captain Sturup did a crisp about-face and left Morehouse to contemplate if there were any saloons in the area that might have an opening for a bartender.

CHAPTER 9

Buck Morehouse didn't care that according to the clock and the calendar it was technically Monday morning. Four a.m. was still the middle of the night, damn it—the middle of a bitter cold, dark night.

Adding to the sense that it was still nighttime, and something from which he might awake at any moment, was the eerie scene in which he found himself. Or rather, the scene to which he'd been assigned.

Atlantic Avenue was one of downtown Brooklyn's busiest thoroughfares, a broad boulevard with a pair of trolley tracks running through the middle of it. This three-block stretch, from Carlton Avenue to Grand, was a commercial district. Streetlights weren't numerous enough, nor bright enough, to clearly see the advertsisements, but Morehouse knew his precinct and he knew that the three- and four-story buildings bore signs for everything from shops like DAIGER MILLINARY and ABRAHAM BEATES, FURRIER to the HILBERT GUARANTEE & TRUST CO. and the TUTTLE HOTEL—ROOMS TO LET BY THE DAY OR WEEK.

Four o'clock in the goddamn morning, when the entire city, except for cat burglars and drunks, would

ordinarily be fast asleep, and here Morehouse was in
the middle of a dark street that was as crowded as if it
were five o'clock on a Friday evening.

The Knights of Labor had chosen this day and this
hour to launch its strike on the city's streetcar lines. And
strikers and supporters were out in force, filling the
sidewalks. Some stood along the curb, facing the tracks
as if ready to dart out at any trains that dared try to roll
past them. Others stood in groups, attempting to warm
themselves, near ash cans that were being used as
makeshift heaters. The cans were spaced along the sidewalks, and although the flickering fires burning within
provided a soothing orange glow, they did little to warm
anyone but those who stood nearest to them.

Although Captain Sturup, who had condescendingly
said there was no need for Morehouse to concern himself with the overall plan, never did reveal anything
more to him, Morehouse had heard enough from
other officers to get a picture of the department's overall strategy for handling the strike. Like so many admin-
istrative decisions, it made little sense to Morehouse.

Brooklyn's entire police force, including the re-
serves that had all been called up, totaled fifteen hundred officers. A full thousand of them were being
assigned to strike duty. Little of that manpower, however, was assigned to the streets. Large squads of officers were stationed within the powerhouses to prevent
sabotage of the electrical plants, and smaller squads
were assigned to the stables used by the horse-drawn
lines that operated outside the downtown area. Those
precautions made sense to Morehouse; the decision
that puzzled him was placing a police officer on every
single car of every single train. It left far too few available to patrol the streets, and the police were badly
outnumbered.

The Knights of Labor alone had more than five thousand men on strike. With their wives—Morehouse was surprised at the large number of very vocal women on the street—children, and a sympathetic public, they had an overwhelming advantage over the police officers. It was certainly true on Buck Morehouse's three-block stretch of Atlantic Avenue. He had twelve officers—reluctant ones at that—to control a restless crowd that the detective estimated to be in the hundreds.

Still, given the directive to keep the rail lines clear with no instructions on how exactly to implement that order, Morehouse did the best he could with the meager resources at his command.

He positioned four men on each side of the avenue, spaced out evenly. He told them to stand at the edge of the curb, facing the road, with the crowd behind them; that way, they could keep an eye on any trolleys passing by and rush to their aid if there should be any trouble. A minor difficulty for these officers was in finding a spot on the curb that didn't have an obstructed view. As usual, dozens of unharnessed and abandoned trucks and wagons had been left alone parked along the avenue. Although they constricted the flow of traffic during daylight hours, the city had never addressed the parking problem since the trucks also provided makeshift shelters for unfortunates who had no place else to spend the night.

To watch for potential mischief from the throngs of people on the sidewalks, Morehouse had a pair of men patrolling each side with orders to walk swiftly in order to cover the long blocks as often as possible. With the bitter cold, he was confident that they'd obey if only to keep warm.

Morehouse thought it was the best he could do under

the circumstances: keep the rails under watch, maintain a visible police presence in front of the crowds, and monitor for trouble with the patrols. He tried not to think about the fact that his fine arrangement would be of little use if the mobs got out of control.

The detective covered a great deal of ground himself, checking that his officers remained in proper position, nervously watching the crowd, and keeping an eye out for the first trolley that appeared. During the first hour, all was peaceful although tension was simmering.

The only action Morehouse had to take was to prod Sergeant Lonnie Keck back into his position. The headstrong young officer, who had groused about "freezing his ass off to protect the trolley companies," seemed determined to keep his posterior warm by standing close to one of the burning ashcans. He grumbled again when Morehouse told him to get back to the curb, and did so slowly like a recalcitrant teenager. Morehouse had to resist the impulse to slap him.

By the second hour, there was some light traffic—a milk truck, a coal wagon, a couple of hansom cabs—but all of the vehicles were confined to the roadway. Not a single train had yet to appear on the rails. Of course, at this time of day—or night, as Morehouse still thought of it since the sun had yet to rise—few trains were scheduled to run. But the Monday morning rush of commuters should be under way shortly, and Morehouse thought the trains must try to start rolling soon.

Apparently some in the crowd thought the same thing. From the middle block, between Vanderbilt and Underhill, a mob of men rolled one of the wagons that had been parked at the curb out to the rails. Morehouse didn't even see them start out;

he was alerted to the action by the cries of encouragement from the crowd.

There were at least twenty men moving the wagon, some pulling by the shafts to which a horse would normally be harnessed and others pushing from the rear.

"Stop them!" bellowed Morehouse.

There was no response to his command. His call was inaudible above the roar of the crowd, and his men too dispersed. He began running along the street, stopping to tell each officer to join him in going after the wagon. By the time he'd completed his run, however, only one officer was with him, a wild-eyed rookie patrolman named Schneider. The rest still lingered back at their original positions.

Morehouse stopped to catch his breath and looked out at the wagon. It was now positioned so that it blocked both tracks, and the men who'd moved it out were knocking off the wheels so that it couldn't be rolled away again. They left it there to the wild cheers of the crowd.

Morehouse realized there had been no chance of stopping the wagon anyway; the mob had the advantage of numbers. But he did have enough men to get the obstruction off the tracks.

He retraced his steps along the street, and pulled four officers from their positions to go out to the wagon with him. When the five men got there, they saw it had been weighted with cobblestones. "Just get it off the tracks," Morehouse ordered. "Shove it into the road."

They first attempted to push the disabled wagon but failed to budge it. Then they began the laborious task of emptying out the cobblestones, a task made more difficult when some in the crowd began pelting them with hard-packed snowballs.

It was almost half an hour before the wagon was dragged off of the rails. The officers were sweating from the exertion and young Schneider's helmet had been knocked off his head by a thrown rock.

As if by a signal, as soon as that obstruction was cleared, two more wagons were rolled out, one at each end of Morehouse's stretch of Atlantic Avenue, and left on the tracks in a similar manner.

Morehouse sent the first men back to their positions and ordered others to remove the new obstructions. He didn't lead them this time, but watched their efforts and assessed the situation. The officers were reluctant, making so little effort that they could easily be mistaken for a city road crew. There weren't even many snowballs thrown at them since the crowd clearly recognized that the cops weren't at all eager to help the trolley companies. By now, the mood of those massed on the sidewalks had shifted from one of tension and determination to more of a holiday atmosphere as they watched the entertaining spectacle before them.

With two carts still on the tracks, a third was suddenly moved by another group of men. This one had been loaded with wood, and to the vocal delight of the crowd the men set it ablaze.

Morehouse felt a pang of panic as the flames sprang up. He grabbed Sergeant Keck, who was once again warming himself by one of the makeshift heaters. "Come on! We've got to get that out of there."

Keck shook him off. "Hell no. I ain't going nowhere." So far, Keck had done nothing but remain on the sidelines.

"That's an *order*," said the detective.

The young sergeant sneered, pulling his wispy mustache crooked. "Watch yourself, old man. You might be in charge today. We'll see who's giving the orders when this thing is over."

"*You* watch yourself," Morehouse snapped. "Talk to me like that again and I'll shove a billy club down your throat."

Keck slammed his lips shut and gave Morehouse a vicious look that appeared absolutely demonic in the glow of the firelight. He then looked out to the wagon, where flames were climbing high. "Can't do nothin' about that anyways. You oughta call the fire department if you want that put out."

Morehouse paused to consider the situation. It was true that the wagon couldn't be moved while it was burning. It was also true that since it was in the middle of the trolley tracks, there was nothing else near it that could catch fire. The sensible thing to do was let the fire burn itself out.

As he watched the flames die down, Morehouse decided it was best to let this whole matter die out. Dawn was breaking and road traffic was picking up. It made no sense to pull obstructions off the tracks and into the roadway—not when there were no cars attempting to travel the rails anyway.

Morehouse didn't know why no trains had come, but he felt his assignment had thus far been a success: Not a single trolley had been blocked on his little stretch of Atlantic Avenue.

Marshall Webb had gotten the telephone call shortly after two in the morning, which meant that he'd had less than three hours of sleep. And by the time he hung up, he knew that was all that he'd be getting on this night.

The caller who'd put an end to his slumber was

Scott Berner, of the Knights of Labor, who told Webb that the union had just authorized a strike for four o'clock in the morning. Webb knew that he'd gotten the advance notice because the union men assumed him to be sympathetic. He thanked Berner for the information and made himself ready to go over the river.

Fortified with a quick breakfast of cold sausage and hot coffee, Webb dressed warmly, put some extra cash in his wallet, checked that he had a notebook and pencils, and went out to hail a hansom cab.

On the slow ride over to Brooklyn, Webb considered where precisely he should go to best cover the events. Berner had told him that workers were planning to close down the city's four main surface systems: Atlantic Avenue, Brooklyn City, De Kalb Avenue, and Broadway. The Atlantic and De Kalb lines originated within a few blocks of each other, in the downtown area, so Webb decided that should be his immediate destination.

Webb also thought about the information he should try to gather. Writing for a weekly periodical put him at a disadvantage compared to the daily newspapers. They would have reporters and contacts all over Brooklyn, whereas Webb was entirely on his own. And they were geared to publishing the latest news with short lead times. If Webb tried to report the same information, it would be old news by the time it appeared in the pages of *Harper's*. His best bet usually was to gather all the material he could, but with an eye to providing a broader perspective than the more detailed daily reports.

After crossing the East River, the hansom headed southeast through the darkness and the cold, the old mare's hooves clopping along Fulton Street. Despite the hour, a number of people were on the streets, many of them moving in the same direction as Webb's cab.

At the westernmost terminal of the De Kalb line, a large crowd had gathered, and Webb ordered his driver to stop. Webb stepped down from the hansom and walked among the poorly dressed men, women, and children who milled about outside the station. No action seemed imminent, and it was still some minutes before four o'clock, so Webb returned to the hansom and resumed the journey.

Half a dozen blocks farther along, they came to the Fifth Avenue terminal of the Atlantic Avenue system. Here the crowd was at least double the size of the one at De Kalb and there was a greater police presence. It was obvious to Webb that this was the place he should start, so he paid and dismissed his driver.

Webb first wandered among the crowd, listening for their comments and trying to get a sense of their mood. It didn't take long for him to realize they were determined that no trains would emerge from the terminal. He also drifted close to the helmeted police officers who were bunched together in groups of two and three and kept darting nervous looks about them. They were virtually silent, and all Webb could discern about their collective mood was that they were scared and would prefer to avoid conflict with the citizens who had them so overwhelmingly outnumbered.

Well, Webb decided, *if the trains are going to roll they have to get out of the terminal,* so he walked to the structure itself. The wood-frame building was like a large barn, and its high double doors were closed. The terminal's purpose was to house and service the trains, and only railroad employees were permitted inside; passengers didn't board except at designated stops.

Webb approached a pair of police officers standing what was obviously guard duty at a single door on the north side of the building. He introduced himself, handed his card to the older of the two officers, and asked who was in charge.

"Why? What's it to ya?" The cop tilted the *Harper's Weekly* card and squinted, trying to make out what it said. Several electric lights attached to the terminal's exterior were on, but their illumination was inadequate for reading—and Webb suspected the officer might have difficulty even in the best of light.

"Because I'm a reporter. I'm covering the strike for *Harper's.*"

The officer gave up with the card and grunted. "Inspector Johnstone's in charge."

"May I speak with him?"

"He's inside." The officer made a show of shuddering in his greatcoat, obviously resenting the senior officer.

Webb repeated his request.

"Ain't supposed to let nobody in. We got our orders."

A silver dollar was enough to remand the order, and Webb proceeded through the door.

Inside were at least ten trolley cars, several of them coupled together. Each one had a uniformed Brooklyn police officer seated inside and a dozen more were near the front doors. There were also a number of railroad workers, almost all in suits and ties rather than work clothes; the companies were trying to operate with administrators at the controls. Even if the railroads did manage to run some of their trains, Webb couldn't imagine how any passenger would feel safe with an administrator for a motorman.

After an inquiry, Webb was directed toward two men, both wearing plainclothes, in an intense discussion next to a two-car train positioned on the track right at the front door. It looked like the train was poised to burst out the doors.

Webb introduced himself and learned that the two men were Inspector Alexander Johnstone of the Second Precinct, in charge of the police officers at the terminal, and Mr. Ryan Akin, Associate Director of Operations for the Atlantic Avenue Railroad Company. They both agreed to permit Webb to observe, but couldn't take the time to speak with him until later. That was fine with Webb, who soon found there was plenty to hear and see.

Akin, whose squat body was cloaked in a fine Chesterfield coat and wore a beaver hat low on his head, had the eyes of a bassett hound and a mournful mustache. He said to the inspector, "Damn it, Johnstone, we will *not* cave in to those Knights of Labor radicals. We *will* run the trains today."

Johnstone's overcoat wasn't nearly as fine as Akin's and it rumpled as he shrugged. "Alls I'm saying is I can't guarantee to protect you if you do." He had ginger-brown whiskers that obscured most of his face and deep-set eyes that were difficult to read.

"It's your *job* to protect us," Akin snapped. "You just do your job." He pulled out an enormous watch from his pocket and aimed one droopy eye at its face. "Five minutes to four." He looked back up at Johnstone. "In five minutes, we open those doors and this train goes out. You make sure it's not blocked."

Johnstone shrugged again and stepped away to speak with a few uniformed officers. Akin called over several of the railroad men and told them they would be rolling in a matter of minutes.

When the five minutes was up, the double doors were unbarred and pushed slowly open. Webb noticed that not one police officer helped open them.

There was an electrical hum and the waiting trolley nosed forward at a crawl.

There was a roar from the crowd outside and a pressing swarm of men pushed the two doors closed again. The trolley nearly rammed into them before braking to a halt. Cheers outside greeted this quick victory for the strikers.

Ryan Akin waved his hand at the motorman. "Back her up. We're gonna make another run."

As the train eased backward, Akin said to Johnstone, "Why are your men even here if they're going to stand by and do nothing?"

The inspector answered, "No one's been hurt and nothing's been damaged. Seems to me we're providing adequate protection."

"Should have hired some Pinkertons," grumbled Akin. "*They* know how to handle strikers."

Before the next attempt, Akin consulted with some more of his men and urged them to do all they could to keep the doors open until the train was through. They then put their manpower in position and within half an hour made another attempt.

This time one car made it out before the doors were closed again, pinching it where it was coupled to the second car. With the train stuck, some in the crowd pelted it with broken cobblestones, others smashed it with sticks and metal pipes.

Seeing his property under assault, Akin screamed shrilly, "Bring it in! Bring it in!"

The officers did join in at that chore since one of their own was in the exposed front car. It took some ten minutes of hard effort before the terminal doors were pushed open enough to allow the cars to back up into safety. Once they were inside, the doors were immediately shut and barred.

"Look at that car," groaned Akin. It had taken quite a beating from the mob. "That is the property of the Atlantic Avenue Railroad Company." He spun on Johnstone. "I demand that you go outside immediately and arrest those hooligans."

"Which hooligans?"

"The ones who caused the damage, you oaf!"

"Sure. You come out with me and point out which ones they are."

"It's—it's *all* of them."

"Yeah. I got less than thirty officers and we're gonna go out and arrest a few *hundred* citizens."

"Then what do you propose to do?"

"I proposed that *you* stop trying to take the trains out. Nobody's trying to bust in here, so just keep the cars inside and they should be safe."

"Oh, this is preposterous. Who's your captain?"

"Captain Oscar Sturup."

"I demand to speak with him. Where is he?"

"You can demand all you want, but to speak with him you gotta find him. I don't know where he is."

"You don't know where to contact your superior?" Ryan Akin clearly didn't approve of the way the Brooklyn Police Department ran its operations.

Johnstone hitched his shoulders. "The captain said he's gonna be out all over the precinct observing."

The two of them continued arguing for some time. Although entertained, Webb didn't expect to learn much. It seemed certain that the trains wouldn't be venturing out of the terminal again and that neither man would be available to speak with Webb for some time.

Webb left the terminal by the same door through which he'd entered and again mingled with the crowd. From what he saw and heard, Inspector Johnstone's advice was sound: if the trolley had succeeded in making it completely out of the terminal, it would never have made it one block before it was derailed and turned into a pile of scrap metal.

Walking slowly east along Atlantic Avenue, jotting notes in his small book, Webb noticed that a red sky was dawning. It reflected orange off the snow and made icicles on the buildings look like dripping flames.

Just after crossing Vanderbilt Avenue, Webb spotted a familiar face. Detective Buck Morehouse stood at the curb, hands plunged in the pockets of a camel hair coat that was a size too small. He had a brown derby topping his head and a hopeless expression on his rubbery face.

Webb wasn't going to bother the detective, but he noticed that he seemed to be engaged in nothing but staring at a burnt-out wagon on the trolley tracks. So he went over to the officer. "Detective," he said.

Morehouse turned to him slowly, as if unable to pull himself away from the sight of the burnt wagon. Recognition dawned on his face and it brightened considerably. "Marshall Webb. I'll be damned." He shook the writer's hand enthusiastically. "How the hell are you?"

"Doing fine, thanks. And you?" Webb had enjoyed working with the detective before and was genuinely glad to see him again.

Morehouse gestured toward the track. "Not so good. I got three blocks of track I'm supposed to keep clear, and right now I got three wagons sitting on it that I can't get moved."

"I don't think you'll need to," said Webb. He told Morehouse how things were at the terminal.

The detective's relief was visible. "Thanks, Webb. You're a better source of information than my own department—they don't tell me nothing."

"I only know what happened at the Fifth Avenue Terminal," said Webb. "There could be trains coming from the other direction."

"Oh, that's right." Morehouse frowned.

"But my guess is that the strikers have all the terminals blocked." Webb then said, "I know you're busy right now. Can we talk sometime later?"

"*Any* time," agreed the detective.

Rebecca Davies walked into the kitchen of Colden House. Young Stephanie Quilty, the only person in the room, greeted her with a shy smile.

"I thought you could use some help," said Rebecca.

"I can manage, Miss Davies."

Rebecca slipped on an apron. "I know you can. The truth is I need something to do." She went over to the preparation table. "Do you mind?"

"No. Of course not."

The two women stood side by side, chopping vegetables for dinner and chatting sporadically. Rebecca found herself enjoying the effort. She always enjoyed Stephanie Quilty's company, but she also needed to be doing something constructive like this.

It had been weeks since she'd even had the prospect of a job for one of her girls, and Colden House hadn't had an open bed in a long time. None of Rebecca's efforts had achieved anything, so even cutting carrots and celery seemed more rewarding than her other efforts.

Rebecca had just pulled a couple of chickens from the icebox when she heard the hall telephone ring. Several minutes later, Miss Hummel came into the kitchen and announced, "It's Miss Vivian O'Connell for you, ma'am."

Rebecca wiped her hands and hurried out to take the call.

O'Connell's smoky voice was cheerful. "I did it! I bought the place from Patterson!"

"That's wonderful!" Rebecca had thought often about O'Connell and Sayre House. With so little progress at Colden House, she had found herself planning all the things that might be done with a new shelter in Brooklyn.

"Yes. Now it's definite. But with the property paid for, now I have to see about getting more funding."

"That's always a problem."

"Well, I was hoping you might help me with that."

Rebecca didn't have any extra funds available. "Help in what way?" she asked cautiously.

"Could you come with me again in a few days? I'm planning to visit some people to ask for their support."

"Oh! Well, certainly I could—but didn't you hear? The trolley strike is on. Getting around Brooklyn will be awful."

"We'll take my carraige."

"But the traffic—"

"Might slow things down, but I'd really like to get started."

A traffic jam was a small inconvenience, Rebecca decided. It was important to get the new shelter open as soon as possible.

Chapter 10

Buck Morehouse was better prepared for the second day of the strike. He had no more officers at his command, nor did he have any new plans for employing them, but he was fortified with a hearty breakfast from Grady's Saloon—washed down with a couple of hot toddies—and had peanuts in one pocket and gumdrops in the other to help get him through the morning.

Getting through was all he intended to do. Mayor Schieren had announced late yesterday that he would request the militia to come into city and protect the trains. Morehouse figured that if the mayor was already conceding that the city needed help, how could the detective and his meager contingent of officers be expected to accomplish what armed troops were needed to do?

So at four a.m., Morehouse and his men were back on their stretch of Atlantic Avenue. Other than having a full belly, it was no more pleasant than it had been the day before. A freezing mist was in the air, making the night darker and colder. By four-thirty, the hot toddies had worn off, and the sting of the chilly mist on his cheek was biting.

Morehouse's men were in the same positions they'd taken yesterday, but the detective wasn't paying them close attention, having learned from experience that there was so little they could do. More than one of the officers was now following Sergeant Lonnie Keck's example and keeping close to the makeshift stoves that had been set up on the sidewalks by the strikers.

The crowd itself was even larger than the first day of the strike, and flush with power. Morehouse had learned that in all of Brooklyn, only one train had run yesterday, a mail car in Flatlands. The strikers had completely shut down every other line.

The tension was at a higher level than yesterday, too. Railroad owners, embarrassed at losing round one, had vowed the trains would run today and implied having hired what they called "private security guards"—known to workingmen as "strikebreakers." The rhetoric from the Knights of Labor was heated in reply, promising that the strikers would hold their ground and keep every streetcar line tied up.

As the first hour of the second day came to a close, Morehouse tried not to dwell on the prospect of more trouble today. Instead, he reflected on his personal success of the day before.

Captain Oscar Sturup had gathered together a number of the officers like Morehouse who had been assigned strike duty at the end of the day. In addition to relating the mayor's request for troops, Sturup gave his perspective of the first day's events. The captain claimed that he'd been spot-checking all around the precinct on "observation detail"—knowing Sturup, Morehouse took that to mean that the captain wanted to remain mobile so that he could avoid trouble areas that could reflect badly on his command and quickly show up wherever there were successes that could reflect glory.

The important thing was that, although Sturup pointed out mistakes made by several of the officers in carrying out their assignments, he didn't say a single word about Buck Morehouse. And that was the highest praise the detective had ever received from him.

The sky was imperceptibly starting to lighten when several groups of men again dragged wagons from the side of the street out to the tracks. The crowd egged them on, and women and children did their bit, tossing sticks and rocks onto other areas of the rails.

Buck Morehouse popped a licorice gumdrop in his mouth and watched, but barely moved and gave no orders to his officers. There was no sense expending energy on a hopeless cause.

When a couple of boys dragged an overflowing ash barrel to the tracks and dumped it over, leaving a mound of refuse on the rails, Morehouse chuckled to himself. Let the militia come in and take care of this crowd, he thought. It would be a political disaster to bring armed troops to face civilians, the detective believed, but at least the police would be off the hook.

A sudden chatter of small explosions caused Morehouse to miss the gumdrop he'd been chewing and bite his tongue. He looked around and saw the people around him ducking down, many of them falling flat on the icy sidewalk. The thought went through his head that the troops might already have shown up— the noise sounded like a volley of gunfire.

He quickly started walking toward where the sounds had come, on his side of the street, a little to the east. As quickly as they had started, the explosions were over, and people were cautiously getting up again. It took only a few steps, the sounds echoing in his mind, for

Morehouse to realize that the sound had been the same as what could be heard every Independence Day and at festivals in Chinatown—somebody had set off a pack of firecrackers.

Morehouse relaxed after the false alarm, and reprimanded himself for being so jumpy.

"Hey! Somebody come over here!" came a man's cry. "This guy ain't gettin' up!"

Morehouse couldn't see, but walked quickly toward the cry. He was soon blocked by a group standing near one of the makeshift fireplaces. They were looking down, and the detective had to elbow his way through them to see what they were staring at.

Lying facedown on the sidewalk, motionless, was a man in a dark greatcoat. A Brooklyn Police Department helmet was askew on his head.

Morehouse crouched down and turned him over. The light from the fire in the ash can wasn't much, but it was enough to see the straggly mustache of Sergeant Lonnie Keck.

Did he faint from fear at the sound of the fireworks? Morehouse wondered. He grabbed the young officer's face to see it better, but it felt lifeless. Could he have been actually scared to death?

In the meantime, Patrolman Schneider had also arrived. He grabbed a burning piece of wood from the barrel and held it like a torch so that Morehouse could examine the fallen sergeant.

The wet stain on the dark cloth of the greatcoat was now visible. Morehouse unbuttoned the double-breasted coat and opened it. There were two distinct, ragged holes in the dead sergeant's chest. At least two of the explosions they'd heard had been gunshots.

* * *

This strike had the makings of a historic one, Marshall Webb knew. It was the first trolley strike in Brooklyn history, the first strike on an electric system anywhere in the country, and with Mayor Schieren calling for reinforcements from the militia it would be the first time armed troops had been called in to confront citizens anywhere in New York.

Having seen all he could in the streets on the first day of the strike, Webb decided to start the second day with those in command. And judging by the results of the first day, command of the city's transportation system was in the hands of the Knights of Labor.

Even before four a.m., Webb was in a large office in the rear of Mugge's Hall on Bridge Street, headquarters of District Assembly Number 75, Knights of Labor. The union men had granted Webb's request to report on their activities and had agreed to provide interviews as time permitted.

The large, stark office was strictly a workspace, with no luxuries. A small potbellied stove provided just enough warmth to keep the room temperature above freezing. Enormous maps of the city and rail systems were tacked to the otherwise bare walls. A few wooden chairs were around the room with no sense of order and there was one chipped file cabinet in a corner. In the middle of the room, covered with layers of papers, was a long rectangle table that actually consisted of two tables of slightly different heights butted together.

Men stood around the table shuffling papers, discussing the latest reports from the streets, and making plans that seemed to be constantly evolving. The men gathered there changed, too, as there was a steady stream going in and out the door into the main hall.

One who never left the room was Master Workman Mike Coppinger of the Executive Committee.

Coppinger wore the flannel shirt and work pants that seemed to be his trademark, and his basso voice was the loudest of the bunch. He was obviously in charge but usually solicited the opinions of the others and made decisions that sounded as if they'd been reached by consensus. Exhaustion was in his eyes, but excitement was in his voice, no doubt due to the exhilaration of the first day's success. He smiled often, his gold front tooth gleaming.

After a flurry of discussions and decisions, Coppinger finally said, "Good. That's the plan, so let's do it."

Several of the men left the office and Coppinger stepped back away from the table. Catching sight of Webb seated nearby, he walked over to him. "Sorry to keep you waiting." The gold tooth gleamed. "Seems like there are a million things going on."

"Quite all right," said Webb. "I appreciate you letting me be here. Do you have a minute for some questions now?"

"I hope so." Coppinger sat down next to him, the first time Webb had seen him sit all morning.

"Are you satisfied with how the strike is going so far?" Webb began, his pencil poised.

"Of course! They're better than expected. Our support is strong, our members are unified, and the trains aren't running."

"How long can you keep them shut down?"

"As long as it takes." Coppinger poked the air with a forefinger to make his point. "The decision is really up to the railroad owners—if they let it go on, they're foolishly hurting everyone."

"The union isn't the one causing the pain?"

Coppinger took no offense at the question. "No. We don't *want* to hurt the railroads. To hear some people, they say we're trying to put the trolley companies out of business. That's nonsense—without the companies we won't have jobs. All we're after is for the bosses to negotiate a fair deal—livable wages and safer conditions. Is that asking too much?"

Webb didn't answer; he wanted to maintain a position of objectivity, although he thought to himself that it didn't sound like the union was asking for too much at all. "No doubt you've been effective so far," he said. "But what about the mail cars? It's a federal crime to interfere with delivery of the mail."

Coppinger hesitated. "A mail car got through in Flatlands yesterday. How can that be 'interference'?"

"One car," said Webb. "Six others were blocked. Will you still block them? Risk federal criminal charges?"

The gold tooth flashed, and Coppinger seemed impressed that Webb was on top of the facts. "It's a questionable situation," he admitted. "We've decided to leave the mail cars alone—but we'll stop any Brooklyn trolleys that are pulling them."

It was Webb's turn to smile at the union's maneuver. He wondered if federal authorities would see the distinction.

"What about the elevated railroads?" Webb asked. "You've shut down the surface trains, but the els are still running."

"True." Coppinger seemed unhappy about that fact. "The els are operated by different companies—companies that have treated their workers better than the streetcar companies have. But we're working on that."

"You think they'll strike, too?"

"Perhaps. We're hoping the el workers will walk off in sympathy with us—they must realize that we're really all in this together."

Scott Berner poked his head in the doorway.

"Mike! Just heard from the men on De Kalb—all the terminals are blocked. No trains are gonna move on that line."

"Good!" Coppinger replied. "Any word from Atlantic Avenue?"

"Not yet, but we expect a good crowd." At Coppinger's nod, Berner left the room again.

"I was on the Atlantic Avenue line yesterday," Webb said. "And at the Fifth Avenue terminal. I thought the mob was going to tear that train apart when it tried to go out."

"We have to do whatever we can to keep the cars from rolling."

"Including violence?"

"What violence?"

"There were some officers who had rocks, sticks, and snowballs thrown at them. I heard one in Flatbush was knocked out from a rock."

"We're not looking to attack the police. Most of them are in solidarity with us. And considering how little they did to help the trolley companies yesterday, I see no reason why any of our members would want to harm them." Coppinger shrugged. "Of course, we can't control everyone. If somebody gets excited and wants to throw a rock, is there any way we can stop him?"

"What about the militia?" Webb asked. "Do you think *they'll* be in solidarity with you, too?"

Coppinger looked grim. "No, I don't. But I think it's an idle threat on Mayor Schieren's part. Do you really believe a mayor will call in troops against citizens of his own city?"

"He also owns shares in the railroads. He wants this strike over and the trolley companies making money again."

"That may be, but—"

The office door was flung open and Scott Berner pushed through. "Mike," he said breathlessly. "Just got a phone call. A cop's been shot on Atlantic Avenue—he's dead."

"Damn it, *no*." Coppinger looked as if he'd just been shot himself.

CHAPTER 11

It took a long time for Vivian O'Connell's brougham to negotiate its way through the heavy traffic. With the streetcars shut down, Brooklyn residents found other means of transportation, some hitching rides on delivery wagons, others swarming toward the elevated stations that were still operating, and many more simply walking—so many of them that they overflowed the sidewalks and filled the roadway, making it difficult for carriages like O'Connell's to get through.

Still, Rebecca found the journey a pleasant one. She and O'Connell were in relative comfort and they occupied themselves by talking endlessly of plans for Sayre House.

It was two o'clock, an hour later than their appointed time, that the brougham reached their destination, pulling up to a double brownstone on Montague Street, just off fashionable Clinton Street. The home was that of Mr. Matthew Anderson-Smith and his family. This part of Brooklyn Heights was where the city's oldest and wealthiest families made their homes, and some of the mansions were as fine as those on Fifth Avenue where the Davies family lived.

Rebecca noted that the broad streets and sidewalks were cleared—just like across the river, the wealthy received special services from the city government.

Before stepping out of the carriage, O'Connell took a hand mirror from her purse and checked her face. Rebecca could tell that her hair color had been freshly touched up; it was lustrous with just a hint of copper that gave it extra shine. Not a hair was out of place and her face powder and rouge had been applied in moderation and with artistry. She had obviously made an extra effort at her appearance today, an effort that extended to her clothing—a fine fox coat with matching hat and elegant kid leather boots.

The oak door of the brownstone swung open on massive hinges, and the ladies were greeted by a diminutive butler in a stiff black suit.

O'Connell handed him an engraved calling card.

He held it in a white-gloved hand and read aloud, "Miss Vivian O'Connell." He cleared his throat. "I believe a Miss *Rebecca Davies* is expected."

"I'm Miss Davies," Rebecca promptly said.

"Yes, well, you've been expected for some time." It was a reprimand for their tardiness. He looked again at O'Connell with some puzzlement; apparently her presence had come as a surprise to him. "Please come in, ladies." He opened the door wider and stepped aside to let them into the foyer.

The foyer, which had an exquisite tiled floor, was as large as some apartments, and had more chairs, side tables, and sofas than some parlors. The furniture was of the richest wood and the upholstery luxurious. Expensive tapestries covered most of the wall space, a marble bust of Shakespeare was on a pedestal, and a crystal chandelier sparkled above.

Rebecca was reminded of a story she'd heard that in

Colonial days, iron nails were so expensive that people who could afford them would hammer them into their front doors as decoration to advertise their wealth—even if the rest of the house was held together by wooden dowels. She wondered if the Anderson-Smiths were putting up a similar facade of affluence.

The butler called for a uniformed maid who took the ladies' outer clothes; then he led them to a study in the rear of the house. Rebecca noticed that O'Connell's ample form had been squeezed into an emerald-green skirt trimmed in black braid and a crisp white Russian blouse-waist. Underneath, there had to be a remarkably strong corset to maintain her shape.

The study was similar to the one where Rebecca's father spent much of his time, probably similar to all of those men in his position—leather armchairs, bookcases with ornately bound volumes that were rarely cracked open, thick carpets, and dark polished wood. It was a place for men to drink, smoke, and doze in comfort.

The butler announced the ladies, presenting them to Mr. Matthew Anderson-Smith, a trim man of about fifty with whiskers similar to Marshall's, except they were a bit grayer and hung down at his jawline like an upside-down collar. He was seated behind a magnificent carved desk with rosewood inlays, and appeared to be reviewing a ledger book. He also appeared to be even more surprised at Vivian O'Connell's presence than the butler had been.

Anderson-Smith rose when the ladies entered, and after the introductions offered them a couple of comfortable chairs. He also said to the butler, "Zachary, I'm sure the ladies will appreciate some refreshments. Please see to it."

The servant gave a small bow and backed out of the room, leaving the three of them alone.

"How is your father, Miss Davies?" Anderson-Smith asked.

"Very well, thank you. Do you know him?"

"I've had the pleasure of making his acquaintance. At the Union Club, I believe."

If so, Rebecca knew, Anderson-Smith had been there as someone's guest. The exclusive Manhattan gentlemen's club would never permit a Brooklynite to be a member. Even the newer Knickerbocker Club, formed by those who couldn't crack the Union Club's waiting list, had similar standards.

"I hope that I shall have occasion to see him again," said Anderson-Smith, trying to sound casual.

"I'm certain my father would enjoy that. I'll mention it to him."

Anderson-Smith waved a hand as if it was of little matter. But the smile that twitched at his thin lips indicated that it was important to him.

The butler, followed by two other servants, brought in silver trays laden with a variety of beverages and plates of dainty sandwiches that had the crust trimmed off of the bread.

While they ate, Anderson-Smith continued to chat about New York families, and Rebecca continued to encourage him in his notion that he could consider himself one of them. Brooklyn's aristocrats, no matter how wealthy or how prominent, were always of lesser importance than their counterparts across the river. Manhattan socialites were like those of Boston, barely acknowledging the existence of anyone outside their elite circle. It was sad, Rebecca thought; she'd encountered many men and women similar to Matthew Anderson-Smith who were like street urchins pressing their faces against the windows of places that wouldn't allow them inside instead of enjoying their own lives.

Throughout the lunch and the pleasantries, Vivian O'Connell said almost nothing and Anderson-Smith barely looked at her. Rebecca assumed it was because of the Davies name—Anderson-Smith was doting on her because she was a member of one of New York's most prominent families, and he viewed such people as an American form of royalty.

Rebecca dabbed at her lips with a napkin and leaned forward. "Do you play chess, Mr. Anderson-Smith?"

He tentatively shook his head no.

"Because my father is absolutely enamored of the game, and is always looking for new opponents."

"Oh, chess, yes. Marvelous game." Anderson-Smith spread his hands in a self-deprecating gesture. "I'm no master, but I'm sure I can give Mr. Davies a good match."

"I'll be sure to mention that to him," said Rebecca. She was also sure that Anderson-Smith would soon be spending considerable time trying to learn the rudiments of the game.

Having suggested that she might offer Anderson-Smith something of value to him, Rebecca then moved to the purpose of the visit. She glanced at O'Connell and said, "Miss O'Connell and I don't want to take up any more of your time, but we have come here on a matter of some importance."

His eyes never ventured to O'Connell. "Yes, I understand you're involved in a charity—some sort of home, is it?"

"Yes. Colden House. But we're here today because Miss O'Connell is opening a new shelter here in Brooklyn. It's going to be called 'Sayre House.' We thought that as one of the city's leading citizens you would like an opportunity to contribute to getting it established."

Anderson-Smith didn't appear that he liked the opportunity at all, but he remained gracious. "If I can, I'm sure I'll make a *modest* contribution. Terrible time to be starting anything, what with the economy the way it is. And I'm heavily invested in the rail companies—with this accursed strike, I don't know that I can really afford to make any donations right now."

"I understand that money is tight," said Rebecca, "but the fact that so many young women are without jobs and on the streets is what makes a new shelter necessary."

"Ah, it's for women, is it?"

Rebecca glanced at O'Connell again. Should she mention whom the shelter was intended to house? "Yes," she began. "It's for—"

O'Connell broke in with her smoky voice. "It's for young ladies seeking to get out of a life of prostitution."

At least she didn't refer to them as "whores," thought Rebecca.

Anderson-Smith didn't give O'Connell any more than a glance from the corner of his eye. "You mean you want me to help support a home for"—his voice dropped—"*soiled doves?*" He sounded appalled at the notion.

"Yes," Rebecca said. "These young women—"

He shook his head tightly, causing his side whiskers to flutter. "I don't see how I can have my family name involved in such a thing." Even his skin seemed to tighten up in an effort to block the notion from his thoughts.

"If it's your name you're worried about," said O'Connell, "we can always keep your donations confidential."

Anderson-Smith appeared puzzled, and Rebecca thought she understood why. Some society people only gave money to charities so that their good deeds could be publicized and they could accrue some prestige for their good works; anonymous donations would reflect no glory on them.

"Mr. Anderson-Smith," Rebecca said, "isn't it a good thing that these young ladies want to change their lives? Shouldn't we support them in their efforts, and think of what they want to become, not what they used to be?"

"I'm sorry," he said. "As I mentioned, with the economy being uncertain, I must limit my charitable donations to a few select causes. And this one . . ." He shook his head with distaste.

Vivian O'Connell spoke up again. "My, that's a lovely portrait." She was looking at a gilt-framed painting of a middle-aged woman with rather plain features who was draped with expensive jewelry. The painting hung in a place of prominence near Anderson-Smith's desk. "Would that be *Mrs.* Anderson-Smith?"

Anderson-Smith hesitated. "That is my wife, yes." He still had yet to look directly at O'Connell.

O'Connell's eyes were sparkling and her voice almost seductive. "I understand she's very involved in charitable work herself."

"Well, she's, uh . . . I don't know that she, uh . . ."

To Rebecca, O'Connell said, "I think we've taken too much of Mr. Anderson-Smith's time already." To their host she said, "Perhaps we can come back and speak with your lovely wife sometime. *She* might find our proposal to be of interest."

He started. "I don't think—" Then he looked at O'Connell for the first time and his eyes were pleading. "There's no need to contact my wife—she's quite busy with other matters." He nodded toward Rebecca. "If Miss Davies believes your home to be worthy of support, that's good enough for me. What was the name of this place, again?"

Both women answered, "Sayre House."

He reached into a drawer and wrote out a check. After blowing the ink dry he handed it to Rebecca.

"That's very generous," she said, reading the value.

"We *shall* keep this confidential, correct?"

O'Connell answered cheerily, "Of course. And thank you—we're really very grateful."

Back in the carriage, Vivian O'Connell looked at the check herself. "A few more like this and we'll be off to a good start!"

"There won't be any more like this," Rebecca said emphatically.

"Why? Whatever do you—"

"You knew him, didn't you? A customer of yours?"

O'Connell smiled. "Of my house. I never had the misfortune to entertain him personally."

"I won't be part of blackmail. He gave you this money because you said you'd talk with his wife. That's extortion."

"It *negotiation*. I never said I would tell his wife that he frequented my brothel—that was his assumption." She turned her blue eyes on Rebecca. "Just like he's *assuming* that you'll introduce him to your father."

Rebecca hesitated. It was true that there had been an implied quid pro quo. "I *will* tell my father about him." Not that her father would remember; he rarely paid attention to anything she said.

"I don't see—"

Rebecca put a hand on O'Connell's arm. "I don't mind you using my family name to arrange meetings with potential donors. I do the same. And although I might play along with their hopes that there could be some social advantage to them donating, I never threaten anyone for refusing. That's what you did. It was a threat, and I won't be part of that."

Chastised, O'Connell said that she understood.

"Is there anyone else to visit today?" Rebecca asked.

"No. But I've spoken to several other possible donors. Some I'll see on my own. There are a few society types who might benefit from you being there, too—if you're still willing."

"I am. Now that we understand each other."

They rode back to O'Connell's hotel, again chatting about Sayre House, through the heavy traffic. Rebecca wasn't planning on going back to Manhattan until much later, since Marshall had told her he had checked into the Fields Hotel— the same place O'Connell was staying—while covering the strike.

CHAPTER 12

The King's County Hospital morgue now seemed positively balmy compared to the temperatures Buck Morehouse had had to endure during his duties on Atlantic Avenue. Morehouse almost thought it was *too* warm, and doubted that the deep breath he'd taken before coming in was nearly enough to sustain him against the smell of decomposing bodies.

The detective closed the door behind him and took another step inside the whitewashed room. "Looks like you got a full house, Shannon." Every one of the tables was topped by a human form under a white linen sheet; one of the ones nearest the door appeared to hold only half a human, and Morehouse had no intention of looking under that sheet.

Shannon Elswick looked up from the corpse he'd been cutting open. "Ah, Bucky. I've been expecting you." The deputy coroner wiped some gore from his hands onto his soiled black frock coat, and squinted at Morehouse from behind his tiny wire-rim spectacles. "Yeah, it's been busy in here. People just don't seem to die at a regular rate—it's really quite inconvenient sometimes." The features of his red rubbery face were twisted with sadness that people's lives could end with so little consideration for his work schedule.

Morehouse hung up his coat and patted down his derby. "You examine Keck yet?"

"Of course! As soon as he came in." Elswick sounded mildly insulted that Morehouse could think he might not give a murdered police officer immediate attention.

"Where is he?" Morehouse noticed that he could see his breath, and was relieved that the room was indeed cooler than he had first thought.

"Over here." Elswick led him to a table near the back wall. "Looks straightforward."

The coroner folded the sheet down to the waist. Sergeant Lonnie Keck, divested of his uniform and all other clothing, looked like a little boy, Morehouse thought. His fair hair and that vain wisp of mustache were limp and his eyes were closed peacefully in death. The peaceful appearance ended there—in Keck's chest were two large ragged bullet wounds.

Elswick coughed. "I gather this one will be a tough one for you to solve, what with him being killed by a mob."

Morehouse grunted, staring at the two wounds, so close to each other that there was but a strip of flesh between them.

"Anyway," Elswick said, "I won't be able to call this one 'exposure.' Everybody already knows about him being shot."

"No need," said Morehouse. "Just tell me what you found."

Elswick cleared his throat and reported clinically, "Two bullet wounds. Got him in the lung and heart. Probably died instantly." He grabbed Keck's shoulder and shifted him onto his side like a butcher maneuvering a side of beef. "As you can see, he was—"

"Shot in the back," Morehouse finished. The holes in the back were much smaller and cleaner.

"Yes." Elswick appeared miffed again; he was a man who didn't like interruptions. "Two entrance wounds in the back; both bullets exited the front." He let the body drop onto its back again, exposing the larger wounds.

"So no bullets."

"No. I dug around in case there might be a fragment, but nothing. Doesn't really matter; the bullet wouldn't tell us anything other than caliber, and from the size of the entry wounds, I'd say it was a thirty-eight."

"Looked like that to me," Morehouse agreed. He actually hadn't seen nearly as many fatal bullet wounds as Elswick, but he wasn't about to have the coroner draw all the conclusions.

"Maybe a thirty-two." Elswick had to have the last word.

Morehouse continued to stare at the body thoughtfully.

Elswick apparently interpreted his silence as sorrow. He said in a kindly tone, "I'm sorry, Bucky. Losing a fellow cop must be terrible for you."

The detective replied evenly, "Lonnie Keck was a whining son of a bitch who made a career out of kissing the captain's ass." He shrugged. "But—he's dead. And he *was* a cop. And him getting killed in the strike is all over the news. So I got to figure out what happened."

"Wasn't it one of the strikers who shot him?" Elswick pushed up his spectacles. "That would mean you got a few thousand suspects to choose from."

"I don't think so," Morehouse muttered. He recalled that the crowd near him had appeared shocked and mournful at the young officer's death. And a couple of strikers had helped carry Keck's lifeless body to the ambulance when it had arrived to take it away. "Where's his clothes?"

"Over . . ." Elswick looked around. "Over there." He led the detective to a table next to his desk. There were several pasteboard storage boxes stacked on it. He pulled one out of the pile, removed the lid, and put it on his desk.

Morehouse took out Keck's helmet, giving it only a cursory study before placing it on the desk. He then removed the dead officer's greatcoat and examined this closely, particularly the two holes in the back. Morehouse fingered the openings, lifted the garment to sniff the material, and then brought it near a bare electric bulb hanging from the ceiling to look at the cloth more clearly. No doubt about it: The weapon that killed Lonnie Keck had been fired at close range, probably no more than a few inches from his back.

The detective proceeded to examine the rest of the uniform, then put it all back in the box. "Thanks, Shannon."

"That it?"

"Unless you can tell me who shot him."

Elswick appeared to consider for a moment. "No. I think I told you everything I know."

"Then that's it." Morehouse walked over to the coat-rack.

"Say, Bucky, I want to thank you."

"For . . . ?"

"I already got a couple stiffs from Bellevue—and I appreciate you taking care of that."

Oh yeah. The bodies that Morehouse owed him for

that "exposure" case. "I always pay my debts," said Morehouse.

"I know. And I know you had a few of those lately. So I thought I might do you a favor—maybe get you out of the hole a little."

Morehouse paused from buttoning his overcoat. Although he was preoccupied with the circumstances of Keck's death, his financial circumstances were never far from his thoughts, either. "Whatcha got?"

"A tip. There's a boxer—Robbie Moore—fighting on Saturday. He's a lightweight, and he looks like a goddamned scarecrow, but the kid's got a right hand like a bolt of lightning. You put your money on Robbie Moore and you'll make yourself a nice little bundle of cash."

Morehouse nodded. He hadn't seen a bundle of cash in some time. Not of his own, anyway. "Thanks, Shannon."

He left the morgue and debated briefly whether to go to the station house or Atlantic Avenue. He decided on Grady's Saloon.

Marshall Webb waited patiently in an outer office at the Brooklyn Hall of Records, a formidable building that also housed the headquarters of the Second Brigade of the National Guard.

Webb had had plenty of time to think while he sat alone in an uncomfortable straight-back chair. One of the things he considered was the reason he was being granted access to the general for an interview at this busy time. All of the Brooklyn newspapers and almost all of the New York papers—with the exception of the conservative *Times*—were siding with the workers in their strike against the railroads. *Harper's Weekly* had yet to publish, so it was one of the few hopes that the streetcar owners had for favorable coverage—and Webb had done nothing to dissuade them in those hopes.

Webb's thoughts then drifted to Rebecca, who had surprised him with a visit the evening before. He had to smile at the thought of how enthusiastic she had been about Vivian O'Connell and their plans for the new shelter. And he had to smile again, more wryly, at her reminding him to ask about the death of the prostitute Frenchy Sayre—with virtual warfare breaking out on the streets of Brooklyn, she was still concerned about one girl who'd been dead for two years.

"Webb?"

He looked up to see a large round man with magnificent black whiskers and an even more magnificent uniform. The blue cloth was swathed in gold and silver braid and bedecked with medals and ribbons. A red sash and a sword with an exquisite hilt were secured at his waist. His black boots were polished to a high gloss and a plumed helmet was tucked under one arm. Webb thought the extravagant garb was more appropriate for a European monarch than a state militiaman.

The writer stood. "Marshall Webb, *Harper's Weekly.* General?" The uniform couldn't possibly belong to a lesser rank.

The officer pulled himself as tall as his bulk would allow. "General James McLeer, commanding officer, Second Brigade, New York National Guard." He looked as if he expected Webb to salute.

A more modestly uniformed young aide said in a loud whisper, "We have to leave for the armory in fifteen minutes."

McLeer nodded, then jerked his head toward the door of the inner office. "Come," he said to Webb.

Webb followed him into a plain office with spartan furnishings. Most prominent were an enormous map of Brooklyn on the wall behind the general's desk and a desk chair the size of a throne. "I appreciate you seeing me," Webb said. "I won't take up much of your time."

"That's correct." McLeer lowered himself into the throne. "You have ten minutes."

"The mayor has officially requested troops, is that correct?" Webb sat uninvited on another hard chair and took out his notebook. If he only had ten minutes, he was going to make the most of it.

"Yes." McLeer squinted myopically and found a paper on his desk. He held it out for Webb to read.

There was some legal language—"pursuant to" and "amended by"—but Webb quickly found the important statement in the typed letter:

> *It appearing to me that there is imminent danger of a breach of the peace, tumult, or riot, I, Charles A. Schieren, as Mayor of the City of Brooklyn, hereby call for aid upon the commanding officer of the National Guard, stationed in Brooklyn.*

"You agreed?" Webb asked.

"I don't have the option not to agree." The general found another sheet of paper and read aloud, "The mayor of any city may call for aid upon the commanding officer of the National Guard stationed therein or adjacent thereto. The commanding officer upon whom the call is made shall order out in aid of the civilian authorities the military force or any part thereof under his command." He stopped reading and looked up at Webb. "It's the law."

"How many troops will you be ordering out?"

"Every single one under my command—four regiments and one Gatling battery." He squinted at another paper. "As of this morning's count, that's 2,838 armed men who will soon be patrolling the streets of Brooklyn."

"A *Gatling battery*?" Webb repeated. Gatling guns were for mowing down large numbers of enemies; he hated to imagine what they would do to civilians on city streets.

"Oh yes. And a hundred fifty of my men are officially classed as sharpshooters—they'll be positioned on rooftops and at windows." He went on to summarize where the various regiments and companies would be deployed. Troops would be on every car and at every station—with bayonets at the ready.

"You do realize this information may be published, don't you?" Webb was incredulous that General McLeer was revealing his plans so openly.

"I hope it will be. I want those filthy strikers to know exactly what we're going to do."

"And exactly what is that?"

"We will take whatever steps necessary to get the trains running again."

"Including the use of force?"

McLeer scowled. "We are the *militia*, Mr. Webb. We are called upon when other options have failed. Of course we will use force. In fact, my men will be given a standing order: shoot to kill." He sniffed. "The strikers will soon find that they are dealing with a very different organization from the Brooklyn Police Department— we don't wait for someone to shoot us first."

His aide appeared at the door and General McLeer informed Webb that his allotted time was up.

Webb thanked him for his time and left, wondering

whether McLeer had told him all this to intimidate the strikers who read about his plans, or as a way of giving his opponents fair warning. He suspected that it was because General James McLeer was simply proud of the plans he'd made and wanted the world to know what a fine military tactician he was.

"Captain Sturup wants you in his office. *Now.*"

Buck Morehouse looked over his shoulder at the young patrolman who stood in the doorway of his tiny office. "You mean *right* now?"

The young man seemed perplexed by the question. "I think so," he answered. "But he just said 'now.'"

Morehouse stood and stepped past him thinking that this slow-witted young man would someday likely become the police commissioner.

On the way to Sturup's office, Morehouse also thought that he must be in serious trouble—Sturup came to his office for the routine reprimands; he only summoned the detective when he was most angry.

Morehouse knocked on the open door of an office that was well furnished with creature comforts, including a sideboard that the detective knew held a selection of fine liquors. "You wanted to see me, sir?"

Oscar Sturup glowered at him from behind his desk. "No, actually I *don't* want to see you. But I *am* seeing you. That's why I called you here." His face was as rigid as his posture.

"I don't understand." And he truly didn't.

"I *don't* want to see you in the station house and that's where you seem to be for some reason. You *should* be on strike duty."

"But, sir. The shooting . . . I've been looking into Lonnie Keck's murder. I think—"

"You've already botched that."

"I just started—"

"You left your post after he was shot."

"Yes. I—"

"You left a *rookie* patrolman in charge."

"Schneider, yes, sir. He's a good man—the only one who really did his duty on the first night."

"So you—without authorization—decided to abdicate your responsibilities to him the second night?"

Morehouse wasn't sure what "abdicate" meant. He answered, "I started investigating the shooting immediately. I spoke to those who were standing near Keck and—"

Sturup scowled contemptuously. "What's to 'investigate,' Detective? There was a vicious mob in the streets. The night before they assaulted our officers with sticks and rocks. Any surprise that one of them decided to take a shot?"

"Two shots," Morehouse corrected. "In the back."

"Fine. *Two* shots. The point is Sergeant Keck was killed by a striker and the chances of you finding which one are just about zero."

"It might not have been—"

"Damn it, Detective! This is a time for you to *listen*, not talk." He paused to be sure that Morehouse would say nothing. At his silence, he went on, "I've spoken with my superiors. Sergeant Lonnie Keck will be accorded a hero's funeral, as befits a police officer killed in the line of duty. He was protecting the citizenry of Brooklyn when he was brutally killed by radicals engaged in an unlawful strike."

"The strike is unlawful?"

Sturup's eyes gave him a silent reprimand for speaking again. "You are to return to your assignment on

Atlantic Avenue immediately. As soon as the National Guard takes over, I will reassign you."

"But what about finding out who killed Lonnie Keck?"

"You *are* a dense one, aren't you, Detective? Tell me: with hundreds of people on the street, in the dark, with violence brewing all around the city, how do you propose to deduce exactly which one of those people pulled the trigger?"

Morehouse could think of no immediate response.

"I thought so. You have five minutes to get back to your assignment." With that, Sturup nodded toward the door.

CHAPTER 13

Marshall Webb permitted himself to sleep in, not rising until six a.m. It was still much earlier than he was used to, but it was the latest he'd slept 'since the trolley strike began.

After getting out of his comfortable bed in the Fields Hotel, he made use of the washstand, picked up the new issue of *Harper's Weekly* from the lobby newsstand, and had a hearty breakfast in the dining room while reading over the publication.

The paper included his first article on the strike, and Webb was glad to see that his editor, Harry Hargis, had barely touched it—but then Hargis didn't do much actual editing at *Harper's*, other than to insert mentions of his friends in the society stories. The information on the militia was too recent to make this issue, but the article did provide a thorough background on the causes of the strike. Although Webb did try to be objective in his reporting, no reader could fail to see that the Knights of Labor grievances were portrayed as reasonable, and their recourses limited. Webb thought the facts of the labor dispute justified a strike, and he saw no reason to pretend otherwise in his article.

Webb left the hotel to see for himself the current status of the strike, not from the leaders of either side, but from those in the street. With the National Guard troops assembling in four armories, he knew the odds of the Knights of Labor prevailing would soon be plummeting. He had the sense that today would be the calm before the coming storm.

Stepping out onto busy Fulton Street, Webb was startled by the bright morning light and had to squint until his eyes grew acclimated to it. The sky was high and clear, and the sun, not far above the horizon, was changing from orange to a lemon yellow. There was no longer a brittle feel to the air; it was still cold, but winter seemed to be loosening its grip on the city. It was still the middle of January, though, so Webb was aware that the loosened grip might only be in order to get a fresh hold and squeeze the city even harder in an arctic chill.

From Fulton to Flatbush Avenue, Webb simply enjoyed the reprieve, feeling the sun upon his face and noting how the buildings sparkled from the melting ice and snow that glistened in the sunshine.

The crowds on the sidewalk were large, but there was little tension in the air. They exuded a sense that the streets were theirs, and that they were prepared to hold their ground no matter what came.

There was reason for them to feel that way. Trolley cars still weren't running and the police officers posted along the street were doing nothing to get the trains through. A few wagons and ash barrels blocked the rails, groups of strikers were ready to swarm any cars that did try to come through, and Webb heard that some of the electric wires that powered the lines had been cut.

Webb turned east on Atlantic Avenue. The mob so

far had only been up against a skeleton crew of railroad administrators and the lackadaisical patrols of an indifferent police force. He wondered how all these men, women, and children would react when faced by troops armed with Gatling guns and bayonets. Their sticks and stones and snowballs would be of no use to them in combat.

A few blocks up the avenue, Webb again spotted Buck Morehouse. The detective looked as rumpled as ever, his posture was slumped, and his expression baleful.

Webb edged his way through the crowd and walked up to Morehouse, who didn't seem to be focusing anywhere in particular. "Morning, Detective. Good to see you again."

Morehouse's expression brightened. "Hello, Webb. What are you doing out here?"

"Still reporting on the strike."

"Quite a story you have in *Harper's* this week."

"You read it?" Webb didn't think Morehouse was the reading type.

"Nah. Heard some of the strikers talking about it—sounds like you came out on their side."

"I don't have a side. I just think the facts are on their side."

Morehouse scratched his nose. "Well, I'll pick up a copy later. If I ever get off this damn strike detail."

From what Webb knew of the detective, he literally meant that he'd pick one up at a newsstand, not buy one. "How much longer are you out here?" he asked.

"I think my captain would just as soon I stayed out here forever," Morehouse grumbled. "From what I hear, though, we might be off the streets pretty soon. Just trying to hold the fort until the militia takes over." He fidgeted in his camel hair coat. "And hope nobody gets hurt in the meantime." He added softly, "Nobody else, I mean."

"I heard you lost one of your own the other day," said Webb sympathetically. "I'm sorry."

Morehouse pulled a meaty hand from his pocket and gestured a short distance away. "Lonnie Keck. Got himself shot right over there."

Webb repeated that he was sorry about the officer's death.

"Keck was a no-good son of a bitch, and I never did like him." The detective shrugged again. "But still . . ."

But Keck had still been a cop, and Webb understood that there was a bond among police officers, much like that among soldiers in battle—if the man's wearing the same uniform as you, he's one of yours.

Morehouse said, "You told me the other day you wanted to talk to me."

"Yes, but it was nothing urgent." Webb had only intended to talk to the detective about the death of Frenchy Sayre because he had promised Rebecca that he would do so.

"Well, I'd like to talk to *you*."

"I'd be glad to. When—"

"Can't talk out here," said Morehouse. He frowned. "And I don't get a break until noon."

"I'm staying at the Fields," said Webb. "Shall we get together there and talk over lunch?"

Morehouse hesitated.

"It's on me," said Webb.

The detective accepted.

The Fields Hotel was once one of the city's most elegant establishments. Although it was beginning to show its age, time had only taken a toll on the building's structure, not on its reputation. The lodgings were still chosen by visitors wanting comfortable accommodations, attentive service, and a convenient location. And the dining room was still in demand for business lunches and social events from those who appreciated fine food and an extensive wine list.

Buck Morehouse was looking foward to this lunch ever since he'd run into Marshall Webb that morning. A meal at the Fields would be a most welcome change from the free lunch spreads at places like Grady's Saloon.

Morehouse walked into the hotel lobby and stomped his boots trying to knock off the grimy slush that had accumulated on them because of the thaw that had begun that morning. The leathers of his boots were soaked and moisture had seeped through to his socks and his feet were uncomfortably wet and cold. His only regret about dining at the Fields Hotel was that this was the classy kind of place where he would have to leave his boots on—at Grady's no one would have cared if he'd dried his bare feet by the potbelly stove.

He walked past the polished long bar, where derby-topped men stood shoulder to shoulder, glasses in hand, and through to the dark, richly furnished dining room. Webb was seated at a table for two near the fireplace, a tumbler full of amber liquid in front of him on the white linen tablecloth. The writer was dressed expensively, the same as Morehouse remembered, but he was by no means a dandy.

Morehouse joined him, and wondered briefly if he could slip his boots off under the table and give them a chance to dry.

A schooner of beer was Morehouse's first order; then he took a minute to review the menu. While

Webb ordered roast chicken, Morehouse opted for pork chops with gravy, potatoes, and turnips.

While waiting for the food, the two of them chatted casually, catching up on what each of them had been doing since they worked together to solve the Joshua Thompson murder the previous summer. Morehouse found the talking made him more than usually thirsty, and by the time his lunch came he needed another beer.

Once they'd both made a significant dent in their food, Webb prompted, "It sounded like you had something important to talk to me about."

"There is. Damn—" Gravy had dribbled onto the lapel of Morehouse's suit. He wiped at it with his napkin, which just smeared it into the brown fabric. No matter, he decided—at least it matched the color of his coat better than some of the other stains that were already there. He took a deep swallow of beer. "Can we keep this just between ourselves? I don't want nothing I'm gonna tell you appearing in *Harper's* or any place."

"Understood," said Webb with a nod. "Now, what is it that you don't want appearing in print?"

"It's about the officer who was killed."

"Lonnie Keck."

"Right."

"What about him?"

"I think he was murdered."

Webb looked puzzled.

"What I mean," said Morehouse, "is that I think he was singled out."

"From what I read in the papers, the prevailing idea was that someone in the mob must have got carried away and took a shot at a cop."

Morehouse put down his fork. "It doesn't seem that way to me. In the first place, why would any of the strikers kill a police officer? We were hardly doing anything out there—most of the people on the street knew that the cops were in sympathy with them, so what does it gain?"

"I don't know." Webb ran a fingertip along his thick mustache. "I was with the union leaders when they heard the news, and they were terribly upset. I'm sure they realized that killing an officer would only hurt the strikers' cause."

"And even if it was a striker," said Morehouse, "it wasn't somebody who got carried away and just fired off a couple of shots."

"How do you know?"

"It was planned. He set off a string of firecrackers—the sound had everyone ducking for cover *and* it covered up his shots. Two shots, with a thirty-eight probably, and the gun was pressed right up to Keck's back."

Webb mulled it over. "You're sure that's how it happened?"

Morehouse nodded. "It's all I'm sure of at this point."

"Any suspects?"

"No. I talked to everyone who was around when he got shot, but no one noticed anything unusual—and once the firecrackers started going off, everyone was too scared to notice anything."

"What's your next step?"

"That's the problem." Morehouse again drank deeply of his beer. "My captain ordered me *off* the case. Says Keck is going to get a big funeral and be treated as a hero for protecting the streets from the strikers."

"So you want to investigate a case that isn't yours?"

Morehouse smiled; he could tell that Webb was surprised that Morehouse would be willing to take on any task that he wasn't required to do. It was something that the detective had wondered about himself. He certainly didn't care anything about Lonnie Keck personally, but the officer's death was nagging at him. Perhaps because it had occurred on Morehouse's watch. Or maybe because he just had a gut feeling that there was something wrong about how it happened. Or—also likely—he just felt like being as contrary as Captain Sturup always accused him of being. Whatever was driving him, he knew that he wanted to discover the real motive for Keck's murder and track down whoever so gutlessly shot him in the back.

Webb asked, "How do you go about investigating a murder when you've been ordered not to?"

The detective smiled. They'd come to the reason he was here. "I thought I'd ask somebody to help me out—somebody I know I can trust and who's been successful at this sort of thing before."

Webb returned the smile. "What do you want me to do?"

"I'm not sure yet. I don't think I have a starting point—but if I do, would you be willing to look into it?"

"Yes," the writer answered simply. He frowned for a moment. "If you don't have a starting point, perhaps start at the end."

"Huh?"

"You have no idea who shot Sergeant Keck, correct?"

"Right."

"Then start at the other end of the bullet: start with Keck. Who would want him dead?"

Morehouse shrugged. "I don't know."

"Well, from what you said, it seems unlikely that he was killed randomly by the mob."

"That's right."

"Then it was either somebody who wanted Lonnie

Keck in particular dead, or who was simply determined to kill a police officer and Keck was the most
convenient target."

"He was *that*," said Morehouse. "Keck never moved,
not even when I needed him to. He kept himself nice
and warm by that barrel."

"What do you know about him?"

Morehouse had to think. "Not much, to tell you the
truth. He bought himself a sergeant's rank and was
never really much of a cop. Mostly just an errand boy
for the captain."

"See what you can find out and let me know," said
Webb.

"Very good. I will." Morehouse dug into the potatoes eagerly.

"Perhaps I could impose on you for a favor, too,"
said Webb.

"Anything I can do," Morehouse answered around
a mouthful of potatoes. More gravy dripped, this time
landing on his necktie.

"Two years ago a prostitute named Frenchy Sayre
was murdered. From what I understand, her death
was never investigated."

"The name doesn't ring a bell."

Webb referred to his notebook. "She was killed
during the night of November seventh, 1893. Beaten
to death."

It still didn't register with Morehouse. He shook his
head.

"She worked for a Vivian O'Connell at the time."

That name rang a bell. "O'Connell ran a place on
Willoughby—one of the best brothels in the city."

"You, uh . . . ?"

"Not me. Her girls were too expensive for me."

Webb smiled. "I didn't think police had to pay."

"Nah, not my type." Morehouse chose not to explain that to him "expensive" was more an attitude than a cost. An expensive girl, even if she's free, has the attitude of an expensive girl. Morehouse preferred his women easy and comfortable.

"Anyway," Webb said, "can you look into the Frenchy Sayre death?"

"I'm willing, but I got to tell you honestly that there's not much hope. A whore murdered two years ago—that's about as cold as it gets."

"I understand. But I'd appreciate anything you can tell me."

Morehouse wiped his lips. "I'll see what I can do." He cast a longing look at his empty beer glass. "Well, I got to be getting back on duty."

"Another beer before you go?"

Morehouse nodded. One of the things he liked about Webb was that they understood each other.

CHAPTER 14

The going was slow, as the horse had to tread carefully over the rural road. Most of the ground was still frozen, but there were spots where it had thawed into treacherous patches of mud and muck. The horse's hooves and the wheels of the carriage frequently bogged down; often, only one wheel would stick and Vivian O'Connell's coachman had difficulty keeping the vehicle directed in a straight path.

When they arrived at the remote part of Flatbush where Greg Patterson had his farm, Rebecca looked at the place differently than she had during their previous visit. No longer was she looking for possible flaws in the weathered, two-story clapboard farmhouse. Patterson was gone, presumably to his cabin upstate where he'd be free from neighbors and their cats, and the property was now owned by Vivian O'Connell. In her mind's eye, Rebecca already saw the place freshly painted, its shutters repaired, and signs of life behind the grimy windows. This was already Sayre House, and Rebecca was focused on its potential rather than its problems.

"Shall we begin?" asked O'Connell.

"Let's."

Inside, the women shucked their heavy coats. Both were dressed simply, in clothes that could hold up to work. It was the first time that Rebecca had seen Vivian O'Connell not make an effort at appearing elegant.

They started with the parlor. O'Connell went to the window and yanked down the oily rags that Patterson had used for curtains. "Getting rid of stuff like this will already make the place look better," she said. "I came out yesterday, and cleared out some of the garbage—it's amazing how much trash Patterson had in a place that looked so empty."

Rebecca was relieved to hear that O'Connell had done that; she had wondered whether the former madam was up for doing manual labor and getting her hands dirty. Running a shelter would certainly require a lot of that.

The two of them embarked on a room-by-room tour through the house. In each room, they made a detailed examination; in a new ledger book, O'Connell wrote down every fixture that needed to be replaced and every repair that needed to be made. Then she and Rebecca discussed how each room should be laid out and furnished. They weren't extravagant in their plans, trying only to equip the place so that it could begin functioning as a shelter as soon as possible. Rebecca drew on her own experience, both for what was required and where the goods might be obtained most inexpensively.

Near the staircase was a pile of dry goods, a disassembled iron rail bed, and a couple of serviceable chairs. "I bought a few things that I knew we'd need and had them delivered yesterday," O'Connell explained. "Probably should have waited until we had the complete list, but . . ."

"No, that was a good idea," said Rebecca. She could understand O'Connell's eagerness to start getting the new home ready.

Upstairs, they continued making their plans and recording their needs. In addition to the existing rooms, they tried to imagine where they could add facilities for toilets and bathing.

When they came to what had been Greg Patterson's bedroom, Rebecca was surprised to find it the cleanest of the house. "That was nice of him to leave this in such good shape," she commented.

"He left it a pigsty," said O'Connell with distaste. "Filthy clothes all over, and a mattress crawling with vermin. I took it all outside yesterday and put it with the rest of the trash."

She'd also swept the floor and washed down the walls, Rebecca noticed. O'Connell's stock again rose in her estimation.

Back downstairs, they ended their inspection in the kitchen, and sat down in rickety spindle-back chairs at a small pine table next to the window. There, they had a long discussion about all the appliances that would be necessary to cook for a house of forty girls.

When they'd finished, O'Connell said, "I don't know about you, but I need to get the taste of dust out of my mouth."

Rebecca agreed. The entire house needed a thorough scouring of the kind that O'Connell had given Patterson's former bedroom.

O'Connell went to the icebox—another item that was in need of replacement. "Like I said, I brought some essentials yesterday." Those included a heavily frosted chocolate cake and a bottle of grape juice.

She dug through a box, and came up with plates, glasses, and utensils, laying them out on the small pine table. O'Connell seemed delighted to be serving her first meal in Sayre House, and Rebecca was happy to see her enthusiasm.

As the two of them ate, O'Connell continued to study the ledger and ask Rebecca about this item or that. Her enthusiasm seemed to wane as she looked over the long lists on each page.

"It just seems overwhelming." She suddenly sighed. "To go from an empty old place like this to a home for forty or so girls . . ." She shook her head. "It's just overwhelming," she repeated.

Rebecca couldn't help much with that. Colden House had already been in operation when she'd taken over the running of the shelter, so she had no experience getting a place going from scratch. "Well, I think you have the right idea," she said, trying to be encouraging. "One room at a time, and one load of supplies at a time. And before you know it . . ." An idea struck her. "You know, you don't have to get the place ready for forty girls all at once."

"What do you mean?"

"Get a few girls at first. It will be easier to feed and shelter them. And they can help you get the rest of the place ready. As you get more bedrooms available, and the kitchen facilities built up, then you can take in more girls. Plus, you can set up systems for doing things—the cooking, laundry, cleaning—much easier with a smaller household."

"That makes sense." O'Connell brightened, then looked again at the open ledger book. "I don't look forward to adding up what all this will cost, though. I'm definitely going to need more money—and soon."

"Have you had any lucky getting donors?" Rebecca knew there was little she could do herself to get funds for the new place; she had only recently begun receiving adequate support for Colden House.

"I've talked to a few more people." She shook her head at the book. "But I'm going to have to talk to a lot more."

"Funding is always a problem," Rebecca said. "What's listed there are onetime expenses for getting the place set up. Wait till you see how much it costs every week to keep a home operating." She didn't want to discourage O'Connell, but it was necessary for her to have a realistic picture of what she'd be facing if she wanted the shelter to remain open for any length of time.

"I'll get the money." O'Connell had a determined fix to her mouth. "I can be very persuasive—and persistent."

Rebecca believed her. She only hoped that O'Connell wasn't going to try to persuade many men in the same way she had persuaded Matthew Anderson-Smith into giving her a check.

Over the next few minutes, O'Connell took a couple more bites of cake, but she didn't seem to relish their flavor as she had before. Holding up her fork to stress her point, she announced, "Here's what I'm going to do: I'm going to get this place ready to house four or five girls and have them move in. Then all of us will keep working on the place, just like you suggest. And we'll take in more girls only when we have rooms ready and money coming in. For now, I'm not going to worry about what it takes to house *forty* girls."

"That sounds sensible," Rebecca agreed.

O'Connell's blue eyes sparkled. "To tell you the truth, I don't even know how many whores will want to give up the life and come here anyway. Maybe there *aren't* more than a few."

From her experience, Rebecca was sure that there would be plenty, but she said, "You needn't restrict Sayre House to former prostitutes. You could make it open to *any* young woman who needs shelter."

"'Sayre House,'" O'Connell repeated. "It's becoming real. I only wish Frenchy was here to see it."

"At least the shelter will be a lasting tribute to her," Rebecca said.

"And it keeps her alive," said O'Connell. "When I talk to people about donating to Sayre House, almost every one of them asks me who 'Sayre' is. Gives me a chance to tell them about her." She added wistfully, "Brings back a lot of memories for me—most of them good ones."

Rebecca briefly debated with herself, then said, "I hope you don't mind, but I've spoken to someone about Frenchy, too."

"Why would I mind?"

"I told him about her murder and asked if he could look into it—maybe it's not too late to find her killer."

"I've given up hope of that. But who—"

"A friend of mine. He has connections with the police department and has done some investigating before."

"I told you, I already asked about her and didn't get anywhere. I don't see what can be done after two years."

"Perhaps it is too late," Rebecca admitted. "But here's what I'm thinking: If her killer is still at large maybe he'll kill again. There *are* men who target prostitutes and maybe he already has more victims."

"I hadn't thought about that. I only thought about poor Frenchy."

Rebecca went on, "What you're doing here—providing a place for girls who want to leave prostitution—

is important and it might save some lives. But what about the others—the ones who don't leave? Any one of them could end up killed by the same man who murdered Frenchy Sayre."

"It's worth a try," O'Connell said.

They were interrupted by a polite knock at the front door. Both of them left the table to answer it, and O'Connell opened the top half of the Dutch door.

Standing there was a plain, stout woman with a wool shawl wrapped about her shoulders. The faded collar of a gingham dress was visible at her neck. "You the new neighbors?" she asked.

O'Connell introduced herself and Rebecca.

"My name's Mrs. Burchfield," the woman said. "Live next door to ya." She squinted at them. "Old Patterson said you're openin' a whorehouse here."

"No," O'Connell said. "We're opening a shelter for young women. Some of them—*most* of them, probably—will be former prostitutes."

"Have anything against cats?"

O'Connell laughed brightly. "No, not at all."

"'Cause I got some cats."

O'Connell again assured her that she had nothing against felines.

"Glad to hear it—Patterson was always after them. And my feeling is *every* creature got a right to live." She held up a cake box. "Made you a cherry pie." For the first time she cracked a smile. "Welcome to the neighborhood."

CHAPTER 15

Marshall Webb was happy to leave the city of Brooklyn and its trolley troubles for a while. It was unlikely that he would miss any important developments, anyway. This was the last day before the militia was due to take over the streets, so it seemed probable that the stalemate between the union and the railroads would continue with little excitement.

Back in Manhattan, shortly before noon, Webb was traveling north on the Ninth Avenue El, which rocked precariously on the rails that ran high above the city streets. It moved in squeaky fits and starts that jostled the passengers throughout its slow journey. The train, as usual, was crowded enough that everyone was cushioned by the other passengers packed around them. The New York rail lines were generally not much safer, more reliable, or comfortable than their counterparts across the river—but at least they were still running and New Yorkers knew they would eventually arrive at their destinations.

Webb's destination was the American Museum of Natural History, a colossal building like a medieval castle, dominating its entire neighborhood. The el finally got him there, screeching to a halt at Seventy-seventh Street. Webb checked his pocket watch; he was only ten minutes late. He hustled from the platform, stopped at the main entrance to pay his two bits admission, and went up four flights of stairs to the museum's library.

The cool, somber room was as quiet as a tomb and about as sparsely occupied. Webb spotted only three patrons in the hushed room. Two of them were ancient old men hunched over some even equally ancient tombs; one of them whistled through his nose as he breathed, making it sound as if a wind were blowing through the place. The other man was the one Webb had come to meet.

Webb quickly passed along one of the dark wood shelves that lined the walls of the room and plucked out a volume at random. Without looking directly at the man he'd come to see, he took a seat across from him at the reading table and opened the book, which turned out to be in Latin.

"Late again, Webb," the man whispered. He had a mouth like a gaping wound and a pug nose, and spoke from behind a large picture book on big game hunting in Africa.

"Sorry." He glanced up at Danny Macklin, a man built like a fireplug and with a face nearly as red. Macklin's cloth cap was tilted low over his forehead and the collar of his overcoat was turned up. It wasn't because of the chill, Webb knew, but to avoid being recognized.

Danny Macklin, a product of the slums of Five Points, had spent thirty years fighting and scheming his way up in the world—specifically the cutthroat world of New York politics and patronage. Macklin was one of the thirteen sachems who ran the Tammany

Society, the notorious political club that chose candidates for city office, determined political appointments— with particular attention to getting sympatic judges on the bench—and sold city jobs so routinely that there was a set price list for the most common positions. And the Tammany bosses ensured that their wishes were carried out through intimidation, election fraud, and bribery. It was this scheme that Webb had exposed in the pages of *Harper's Weekly*, leading to an investigation by the state's Lexow Committee and the eventual downfall of a number of crooked politicians and graft-hungry police officials.

Some of the evidence Webb had unearthed about Tammany operations had been provided by Macklin. The sachem wasn't seeking to clean up city politics, Webb knew, but was tired of being only one of thirteen bosses. He wanted a bigger piece of the pie—more influence, more clout, more money—and by his helping Webb bring down others, his own position was enhanced. If Macklin's betrayal was discovered, however, it would mean a certain death sentence. So the two men had taken to meeting in the library of the museum; the location was remote, on the northern frontier of the city, and a library was not the kind of place that a Tammany henchman would likely wander into.

"So whaddaya want from me?" asked Macklin.

"The usual—information."

"Not sure what I can tell ya." He turned a page in his book. "Things are a little, uh, unstable these days."

Webb knew what he meant. Ever since the vote to consolidate into a Greater New York, every politician, civil servant, and Tammany hack was jockeying for a position of power in the reorganized government. Macklin would be careful in what he would tell Webb since he didn't yet know how the ramifications could work to his benefit in the new order of things.

"It's not about New York," Webb tried to reassure his informant. "It's about Brooklyn."

Macklin snorted. "Who the hell cares what goes on over there? Nothin' but a bunch of goddamn trolley dodgers."

"As I recall, you were in favor of consolidation—one of the few at Tammany who was."

"Yeah, I *was*," Macklin said morosely. "But things ain't exactly turnin' out like I expected."

"Why? What's the problem?"

Macklin put his book down flat on the table, and slowly looked around the room with suspicion. Satisfied that no one was spying on them, he said, "The idea was that we could expand our system into the new turf—take over their penny-ante operations and start generatin' some good profits." His wide mouth twisted. "Problem is them two-bit hustlers in Brooklyn are tryin' to move into *our* turf." He sounded appalled at their audacity. "And right now, it looks like we might have a little difficulty defending ourselves."

Webb felt some pride at that statement. Tammany was indeed the weakest it had been in many years, in no small part due to his reporting. He also felt some amusement—Danny Macklin hadn't seemed to catch on to what Webb was ultimately after. Blinded by his own quest for power, Macklin was willing to reveal anything to Webb that might harm his rivals and leave him an opening to enhance his own influence. But what the ambitious sachem didn't appear to grasp, and what Webb would never point out to him, was that if Webb and other reformers succeeded in their efforts to clean up city government the entire corrupt system would collapse—and Macklin would be out of business right along with those he had helped Webb to expose.

As to Macklin's question about who cared what went on in Brooklyn, Webb did. Specifically, he was wondering about the shooting of Sergent Lonnie Keck. Not only because of what Buck Morehouse had told him, but because Keck's death was being used to justify the call for National Guard troops. Most of the newspapers, even those that had initially been sympathetic to the union, portrayed Keck as a hero, killed in a violent strike while protecting the citizens of Brooklyn. It seemed awfully convenient for the streetcar companies, Webb thought. And knowing the circumstances of his death—that he hadn't been killed by somebody taking a potshot, but rather by a cold-blooded killer who stuck a pistol in his back and covered up the sound of the shots with a string of firecrackers—it was especially suspicious.

One thing in particular that Buck Morehouse had mentioned caught Webb's attention: that Lonnie Keck had *bought* his sergeant's rank. To Danny Macklin, Webb said, "These 'two-bit hustlers in Brooklyn you mentioned—how do they operate over there?"

"Whaddaya mean?"

"How much control do they have over Brooklyn government? Is it anything like here in Manhattan?"

Macklin grinned, displaying an incomplete set of very bad teeth. "You going after them now?"

Webb didn't answer but lifted his eyebrows, as if that was a distinct possibility. He could already see Macklin calculating how an exposé of Brooklyn corruption could leave an opening for Tammany.

"They don't got nowhere near the power we got here," Macklin said, "but they got a lot of little hands in a lot of little pies."

"What about the mayor? Do they own him?" Webb wondered if Mayor Sheiren's actions were being dictated to him.

"Nah. He's owned—but it's by *businessmen*." Macklin sounded as if businessmen were far lower on the social scale than crooked political bosses like himself. "Especially the railroad companies. He ain't indebted to the political bosses as much as he is to the railroad men."

"What about other city jobs?" Webb continued. "Are they controlled in Brooklyn like they are here?"

"Nothing's run as good as we run things here," the Tammany sachem said with pride.

"I heard about a sergeant who bought his rank," Webb said. "*That's* the same as how it's run on this side of the river."

"Yeah, but what the hell is he gonna get out of it? It's a lousy investment—no payoff."

"What do you mean?" Webb knew that in New York the police officers who bought high ranks profited quite nicely from the graft to which their ranks entitled them. A policeman's salary was considered a minor source of income compared to the regular payoffs he collected. Of course, many of them were now without any jobs thanks to Webb and the Lexow Committee.

Macklin shrugged. "Brooklyn's small potatoes. Sure, they got their illegal saloons and whorehouses and gambling joints, but not near as many as we got here. Hell, they call the place 'the City of Homes and Churches,' so that's got to tell you something. Whereas we got the Bowery and the Tenderloin—'Satan's Circus,' as the reformers call it. Anyway, buying a sergeant's rank will only get you the crumbs—whatever real money there is goes to the captain."

"A captain would be for sale, too?" Webb didn't

know why he should be surprised, but he had assumed that systemic corruption was peculiar to the
well-organized operations of Tammany's New York;
he hadn't heard about such a system functioning
across the East River.

"Sure. Hell, you know in New York it goes all the
way up to the police superintendent—*everybody* can be
bought and sold."

A *captain*, thought Webb. Buck Morehouse had also
mentioned that Keck had acted as his captain's
"errand boy." "How does that captain get the 'real
money'?" Webb asked.

"Same as he does here. Same as he would in probably any city in the country: A local businessman
wants to keep his place operating without the cops
shutting him down, so he makes a regular payment to
the local precinct captain."

In New York, Webb was aware, legitimate businessmen often had to pay protection to criminals—it was
the criminals who paid graft to the police to protect
their own enterprises.

"But they don't pay the captain directly," Webb
said, again drawing on his knowledge of the New York
system.

"Of course not. Somebody else carries the bag—
collects what's owed and brings the take to the captain."

"Somebody like a sergeant."

"Usually. And he gets a cut for doing the pickups.
But like I say, in Brooklyn that wouldn't amount to
much." Macklin added, "The free drinks he'd get
from the saloons, and havin' his pecker polished in
the whorehouses, would probably be worth more
than whatever cash he'd make."

And apparently the relationship between sergeant

and captain didn't garner the junior officer much in the way of loyalty, either. Lonnie Keck had been Sturup's "errand boy," but upon the young sergeant's death, Sturup was willing to have him used as martyr for the railroad companies rather than let Buck Morehouse do a proper investigation.

Webb's thoughts turned again to the strike. "These fellows who run the Brooklyn rackets—you think they'd have any involvement in the trolley strike? Take sides in the conflict?"

Macklin rubbed at his pug nose. His eyes appeared to be searching inward. "I dunno. Not that I heard."

The answer was likely an honest one; Webb had learned that Macklin was embarrassed to admit that he didn't know something. "Well, you're a smart man," Webb said. "If the strike was going on here, could you see a way how *you* could get involved to your advantage?"

Macklin accepted the flattery as a matter of fact. He gave the question some thought—judging by the intense scowl that creased his forehead—and finally said, "I can see a couple ways."

"Such as?"

"I always figure to look who got the money. And in this case it's the railroads, not the workers—hell, the reason the poor saps are strikin' is 'cause they don't make enough money." He twisted his lips contemptuously of those who were too honest to make a livable wage. "So we go to the railroads. Maybe we provide some manpower to clear the tracks . . . or ship in some scabs to run the trains . . . or bust the heads of the union leaders so they call off the strike. Anyway, we get the trains to running, and collect from the railroads."

"You wouldn't go to the union and try to work with them?"

"Nah, they ain't got no money."

"The workers may not, but the union collects dues from every one of them."

Macklin shook his head emphatically. "I don't see there's any real money in unions." The direction of his head movement changed to vertical. "I'd go to the railroads."

There was no need for that, thought Webb. The railroads already had the mayor and the state militia to do their dirty work for them.

Macklin hunched his shoulders. "We about done? I got business to attend to, ya know."

"One more question. If somebody wanted to buy a job on the Brooklyn police force, who would he see?"

"You *are* gonna go after them bastards on the other side of the river, ain't ya?" Macklin was smirking.

"Perhaps."

"Jason Ward. Keeps outta the spotlight, but in Brooklyn he's the boss. Operates a saloon in Red Hook—the Four Aces."

"Thanks." Webb stood to go.

Macklin laid a hand on his arm. "Ward wants to stay outta the spotlight—and that means stayin' outta the newspapers. He gets wind you're interested in him, and things could go rough for you. Everybody knows what you did to business in New York with your stories, and Ward ain't gonna want you doing the same thing to his operations in Brooklyn."

Webb smiled wryly. "Thanks for the warning, but I'm not going to be scared off."

"I don't *want* you scared off. I just want you to be careful—at least till after you put Ward out of business." Macklin had greed in his eyes, no doubt already contemplating how he could profit from whatever Brooklyn turf might become available to him.

Webb smiled more broadly. There were two reasons why he considered a schemer like Danny Macklin to be such a reliable source. One was that he had a track record of providing Webb with information that proved to be accurate. The other was that he made no secret of what he hoped to get out of his cooperation.

There was another stop Webb wanted to make while he was in Manhattan, this one a courtesy call at the other end of the city.

After another crowded streetcar ride, this one in a southerly direction, Webb arrived at a seedy, low-rent office building in the heart of New York's publishing district. Walking through dimly lit hallways, across warped plank flooring, he made his way to the third floor. Between the offices of a bail bondsman and a theatrical agent was the door of Pritchard's Dime Library, which was so advertised in chipped black paint on the frosted glass window. He knocked gently, since the rickety door didn't appear that it could withstand much of jolt, and hoped that his editor wasn't out at one of his marathon lunches.

"Come in!"

Webb stepped inside the cramped office, pausing to wipe his wet boots on the threadbare mat. "I thought it was about time I came to see you," he said, holding out his hand. Fortunately, the temperate spell was still holding, for the office didn't feel much warmer than outside.

Lawrence Pritchard, having stood from behind his battered pine desk, shook it enthusiastically with a clammy grip. A smile creased his drawn face, causing him to look like the picture on a Jolly Roger. "I should say it is." He gestured at one of the two old kitchen chairs that served as office furniture. "Sit, sit. It's good to see you again, Marshall."

Larry Pritchard really needed to make a point of eating something at his lunches, Webb thought. The middle-aged man looked positively emaciated, giving the impression of a skeleton, an impression that was added to by his pale complexion and sunken eyes. And his severe black suit hung loose on his bony frame. The publisher spent most of his lunch times reading, though, preferring to work in a restaurant to this cubbyhole of an office.

"I know I've been out of touch," said Webb. "I just wanted you to know that I'd still like to write novels for you again."

Pritchard blinked rapidly behind his pince-nez and ran a hand over his nearly bald scalp. "I was wondering about that—although there was no real obligation, of course. I thought perhaps when you came here a couple of weeks ago you'd just had a bad day at *Harper's*. And then I saw . . ."

That was why Webb had come. He thought Pritchard might have seen his article in the latest issue of the weekly and wanted to explain. "I resigned from *Harper's*," he said.

Pritchard began blinking again. "But I just read—"

"About the trolley strike?"

"Yes."

Webb nodded. "My editor at *Harper's* asked me to look into the situation. I did, and it interested me, so I've been covering it."

"It was a good article," said Pritchard. "Fine job of research—as always—and a clear presentation."

"Thank you." Webb could tell Pritchard meant

what he said. "And I am sticking with the story. With the militia coming in, this is going to be historic—and I don't think in a positive way."

"I think it's an awful thing that's going on over there," said Pritchard. "The mayor of Brooklyn calling in troops to take arms against his own people. Unconscionable, if you ask me." He sighed, as if he regretted that no one actually did ask him his opinion on the matter.

"But once this story is finished—and with the troops coming in I don't see how the strikers can hold out very long—then I'm free. I'm already out of my office at *Harper's* and I'll be under no obligation to them. An occasional freelance article will probably be it." He smiled. "And that will only be as time permits from writing westerns for you."

"I am happy to hear that," said the editor. He looked as if he was already tallying sales figures. "And to tell you the truth, I'm happy you're covering the strike. It *is* important, and I can't think of another writer who could possibly do as good a job of reporting on it."

"So you don't mind waiting awhile longer?"

"Not at all. But . . ." Pritchard reached behind him to a crooked bookcase that overflowed with books and manuscripts. He pulled down a small stack of periodicals and rifled through them. "Ah, here we are." He withdrew a magazine. "I have a good friend in London, Miss Linda James, who is also in the publishing business over there. We send each other publications from time to time. She might find something in England that I would like to obtain the American rights to publish, and vice versa. Anyway, this was in the last batch she sent me." He pushed the magazine across his desk to Webb.

Webb looked at the pale green front cover of the slim publication. It was a copy of the *Strand Magazine*, dated February 1892. He didn't know why Pritchard wanted him to see a three-year-old magazine. "There's something in here you're interested in?"

"Yes. There's a Sherlock Holmes story in there— 'The Speckled Band.' Very clever, I thought."

"*Harper's* already publishes Arthur Conan Doyle in America." Webb had read several of the stories and didn't find them very realistic. He couldn't picture the supercilious Sherlock Holmes taking on the toughs of New York's powerful underworld.

"Oh, I realize that." Pritchard smiled. "But it got me to thinking. Why should I buy rights to a British author, when there's an American who can do at least as good a job and write a series set right here in the U.S.A.?"

"You mentioned something about detective stories the last time I was here," Webb pointed out with little enthusiasm.

"I realize you're interested in writing westerns again," said Pritchard. "But have you given any thought to detective stories?"

Webb admitted that he hadn't.

Pritchard pressed on. "You know this city, you've certainly had experience with the criminal element, and you know how to put together a story." He beamed optimistically, as if hoping he could project his enthusiasm onto Webb. "It's all the ingredients for a successful new series!"

But Webb wanted the escape of another genre, far removed from the discouraging reality of everyday life. And he liked the code of western justice, where justice wins out and evil is punished. In New York, he knew all too well, all that was necessary to win was wealth and power. All one had to do was look across the river, where the railroad companies were about to crush their workers with the help of state militiamen.

Despite Webb's lack of a response, Pritchard was still smiling. "And, of course, these stories will be *novels*."

"Yes . . ." Of course they would be novels, otherwise why would a dime novel publisher be interested in them? Webb couldn't see what Pritchard was driving at.

"That means you can take liberties. The stories don't have to be real crimes; you can have anything happen that you want. I know you like a neat ending, where the bad guy gets his just desserts." His smile took a mischievous twist. "You can have every story end the way that it should."

Webb thought about that, and agreed to consider the proposal. There could be some satisfaction in that kind of writing. But he still wished that he could bring out the right kind of results in the real world.

CHAPTER 16

Overhead, the King's County Elevated Railroad was running, with every car packed to capacity and some passengers precariously holding on to the doors. But below on Fulton Street all was still. The only railroad transportation available in the city was on the el, whose workers were still resisting pleas from the Knights of Labor to join the strike, and so anyone who needed to get anywhere did so by traveling above the streets.

Buck Morehouse walked along commercial Fulton Street, normally one of the busiest sections of the city with landmark destinations like Namm's Department Store, the imposing Arbuckle Building, the Germania Savings Bank, and the Park Theatre. Nearby, around the fountain in City Hall Park, vendors usually pushed carts hawking everything from oysters to peanuts; they were gone now, with no one interested in purchasing their fare.

This had been his city for years, Morehouse thought. Patrolling the streets as a foot cop, investigating crimes as a detective, visiting the ballparks and the boxing arenas, eating and drinking in the saloons, meeting the people of all walks of life who populated this marvelous, vibrant city.

Today, he barely recognized his hometown. Oh, the landmarks were still there, such as the stone cupola atop City Hall and the clock tower that climbed so high above the Fulton and Flatbush Storage Company that it was visible from almost every part of the city. And the names of the streets hadn't changed, of course, but the people weren't the same. In particular, there were now more than two thousand armed troops of the New York state militia who had taken over the city in response to Mayor Scheiren's request for military assistance.

The only upside to the arrival of the National Guard was that many of the police could be reassigned to their normal duties. For Buck Morehouse, reassignment came as a welcome relief. Instead of his freezing among the mob on Atlantic Avenue, Captain Sturup assigned him to stakeout duty at Wallabout Market where there had been a string of recent robberies. Morehouse had the sense that Sturup's main objective was for the detective to remain far away from him. And since Morehouse knew a tavern near the market, he planned to do most of his staking out from within its well-stocked barroom.

He was technically off duty at this hour but felt compelled to come out and see how the militia would be greeted by the citizens of Brooklyn and the strikers whom the soldiers had been ordered to subdue. He wasn't the only one who was curious, judging by the faces he saw peering tentatively from the windows and doorways of the building that lined the route.

The detective drew out a couple of licorice gumdrops from the bag in his pocket; he popped them into his mouth and chewed slowly as he walked along

Fulton Street. This was where the railroad bosses had decided to break through the obstacles set up by the strikers. If no other surface train ran in the entire city, they were determined to get the trolleys running on the Fulton line. Having hired hundreds of scabs to operate the trains, and with the soldiers to protect them, success for the streetcar companies seemed certain.

Equally determined to keep the trains from getting through, however, was the Executive Committee of the Knights of Labor. The railroads had made no secret of the fact that they would be going all out on the Fulton Street line; in fact, they'd boasted of their plans as if daring the union men to do anything about it. Today would be a show of strength, and the railroads believed they were now strong enough to crush their opposition.

Like Morehouse, many other Brooklyn citizens had come to Fulton Street this morning, some to see the peculiar sight of soldiers on the city streets, others members of the union and their supporters, and many more simply curious as to what might transpire. It had the feel of a crowd expectantly waiting for a parade to pass by, and Morehouse was reminded of a similar scene the day before, when there was a funeral procession through the downtown area for the late Sergeant Lonnie Keck. It was strange—and perhaps no coincidence—that on one day Keck was being lauded as a heroic protector of the citizenry, whose death provided evidence that greater force was needed, and on the next day that force was about to be unleashed on the streets of Brooklyn.

The similarity to the funeral march was strengthened by the sudden arrival of blue-uniformed troops marching in tight formations in the middle of the street, alongside the rails. Instead of the double-

breasted greatcoats and tall helmets of the Brooklyn
Police Department, however, these men in blue wore
the uniforms of the Forty-seventh Regiment of the
New York National Guard. Each carried a rifle on his
shoulder, and cartridge boxes and bayonets were secured to each belt. Sunlight glinted off their brass
buttons and the gold braids of the higher-ranking officers. Morehouse noted with a touch of amusement
that the soldiers' leather-visored caps were similar to
those worn by streetcar conductors, making them
look like the scabs they were supposed to protect.

The crowds on the sidewalks were hushed, absorbed in the display of military might, so it was easy
to hear the officers bark orders to their men. They
were called to a halt and then ordered to take up
their positions. The soldiers were spaced along the
tracks, making two long lines, one on each side of the
rails. They were at attention, each line of men with
their backs to the tracks and their eyes directed
toward the sidewalks.

Then came a sight that hadn't been seen on a
Brooklyn streetcar line for days: A single trolley car
rolled slowly along the track, its wheels making a
metallic squeal. There were no passengers, only a uniformed conductor and motorman, both no doubt
scabs brought in to replace the striking union men.
The railroad companies knew they would have no
paying fares until the lines were secured; all they
wanted at this point was to show that they could suc-
cessfully get the cars moving along their scheduled
routes again.

The first car did make it through, crawling along
cautiously but steadily, at least until it got to the point
some blocks away where it turned out of Morehouse's
sight. The crowd seemed to have been stricken numb

and silent, and no attempt was made to interfere with the train.

Ten minutes later, a second car came along, manned like the first and also with no paying passengers. The crowd began to rouse itself now, shouting at the car and throwing stones and brickbats. Some of the soldiers, many of them young, began to look distinctly nervous. And some of the union sympathizers along the sidewalks began to move around, shifting their positions. The trolley suffered some minor damage from the projectiles as it ran the gantlet, but it kept going without losing any speed.

There was some quiet again as all seemed to brace themselves for the third car that was sure to follow.

When the third trolley came into view, the shouts rose to a thunderous level and projectiles rained on it so thickly that many struck the militiamen. One soldier jumped as a thrown bottle broke on the ground behind him, causing the crowd to jeer him for his nervousness.

The car was almost directly in front of Morehouse when about twenty brawny men, in a coordinated move, broke away from the crowd on the sidewalk and ran out to the train. Moving quickly, they rushed past the surprised militiamen and to the near side of the car. It screeched to a halt and the two crewmen aboard jumped off the other side.

Some of the strikers pushed against the side of the car while others lifted at the bottom. They got it to rocking, and then with a final strong effort overturned the trolley with a smashing sound of broken glass, crushed metal, and splintered wood. The sound of destruction was almost drowned out by the immediate cheers from the crowd.

It was so loud that Morehouse barely heard the order from a Guard officer to "Fix bayonets!"

A squad of twenty or thirty militiamen had formed a well-ordered line and promptly obeyed the command, attaching the blades to their rifles and holding them at the ready.

The next order was clearly audible: "Charge!"

The celebration of the strikers was cut short—literally. Soldiers ran into the men who'd turned over the car, stabbing and jabbing ruthlessly with their bayonets. Shrieks of pain mingled with cries of horror from the crowd.

The strikers tried a quick retreat, backing away from the car and tripping over themselves as they fled the blades of the militia. Some were too wounded to move and tried to fend off further attacks by holding up their hands—hands that soon dripped with blood.

A young man who'd been standing near Morehouse raced out. The detective wasn't sure if he was going to try to stop the soldiers or pull one of the wounded to safety.

A gunshot split the air, penetrating through all other sounds, and the young man fell motionless in the street.

Morehouse looked around him quickly, instantly reminded of Sergeant Keck's death. He saw nothing but terror in the eyes of the people standing with him.

Someone else in the crowd spotted the gunman before the detective did. Soon a number of fingers and eyes were directed to a rooftop across the street, and curses were launched impotently in the same direction.

Morehouse was looking about, seeking another patrolman to join him in going after the perpetrator, when he saw the gunman stand up from his crouched position. He was a militiaman and smoke was still curling from the muzzle of his gun. Instead of trying to flee, he calmly reloaded and crouched back down, his rifle again directed to the street.

No one else had the nerve to venture off the sidewalk, however, and there was no more rifle fire.

Morehouse scanned the rooftops and saw a number of additional troops similarly positioned. The Guard had obviously stationed sharpshooters to cut down any troublesome strikers.

Without even waiting to see if someone would remove the young man's body from the street, Morehouse left the scene. He didn't have the stomach to see anything more. The militia hadn't merely taken over his city. They had declared war on its people.

"That's very good," Rebecca said. "But try pronouncing this word again." She pointed to one of the words in the McGuffey's Reader.

Michelle Burton, a fourteen-year-old girl who'd been in Colden House for more than a month, struggled to pronounce the word: "Croak-a-dilly?" she ventured tentatively.

"Crocodile," Rebecca corrected.

Burton screwed up her button nose. "Miss Davies?"

"Yes?"

"What *is* a crocodile?"

"Well . . ." The creature was actually difficult to describe, Rebecca suddenly found. "It's like a giant ugly lizard . . . it lives in the rivers . . . in Africa . . . and it's quite ferocious."

"In Africa," Burton repeated.

"Yes, I believe so."

"So there aren't any in New York?"

Rebecca laughed. "No."

"Then I don't have to worry about them."

"Of course not."

"Good. Then it doesn't matter if I know what to call them." She smiled. "Can I go on?"

Rebecca laughed again. "Yes, go ahead."

She listened to the girl read aloud for a while longer. Rebecca could understand why young Miss Burton wasn't about to worry about what to call an animal she would never encounter. She had come to Colden House almost two months ago, an orphan who had supported herself sewing frocks in an East Side sweatshop—until she was fired because she caught her hand in a sewing machine and could no longer work fast enough.

After encouraging Miss Burton to continue reading on her own, Rebecca excused herself and went downstairs. She enjoyed having a chance to work with the girls, teaching them reading and basic arithmetic—it was one of the most satisfying aspects of a job that had become so frustrating lately.

Back at her desk, she glanced at the two measly letters that the morning mail had brought. She hadn't even bothered to open them yet, putting off the inevitable bad news.

With a hopeless sigh, she sat down and sliced open the first envelope. It was a terse letter from a friend in Hartford who reported that there were no jobs available, and hinted that it would be appreciated if Rebecca didn't inquire about possible employment so frequently. Rebecca's first impulse was to write back immediately, but she knew that she would simply have to comply with her friend's wishes; no help would be forthcoming if Rebecca antagonized the people she had to depend on for assistance.

She held off another minute before opening the second letter. This was longer, and she read it three times before believing the news. There was a job available for one of her girls in Syracuse.

Such a response had become so rare that Rebecca almost choked up with gratitude. She wanted to yell, and announce the good news to all. Again she restrained herself—so many of the young women in Colden House would *not* be leaving for some time, that it would seem cruel to celebrate the good fortune of only one of them.

Rebecca did hurry back upstairs, though, and found Miss Hummel alone in the infirmary sorting through the linens.

Holding out the letter, Rebecca walked up to her longtime assistant. "Look at this."

Miss Hummel looked at the page, squinted, then held the sheet at arm's length. "It looks lovely, ma'am, but I'll be needing my spectacles if you want me to actually read the words."

Rebecca couldn't wait for her to find her glasses. "There's a job available for one of the girls," she said in a loud whisper.

"That's wonderful news, ma'am!"

"It's in Syracuse, as a salesclerk in a ladies' hat shop—should be nice clean work. And there's room and board available nearby, in a reputable house that my friend recommends."

Miss Hummel ran a finger back along her hair as if a lock might have fallen out of place. As always, her iron-gray hair was pulled tightly back in a shape that resembled a helmet, and Rebecca suspected that not even a single strand had had the temerity to come loose in more than twenty years. "Which of the girls will be moving out?"

That was often a difficult matter for Rebecca to decide. She always tried to be fair, considering how long a girl had been staying at the house, what skills she might possess, and what kind of environment was most likely to work out for her. "I'm thinking of Becky Forbes," she answered. That young woman had been in Colden House for almost six months, after spending years in a tenement room stripping tobacco. Inhaling tobacco dust in a room with no ventilation had left her with a chronic breathing problem.

"Good choice," Miss Hummel agreed, nodding. "She needs to be getting out, and clean work might help with her lungs."

Rebecca glanced again at the letter, thinking how much this would do to help one girl's life and trying not to think about how many more were still in need of opportunities like this one. "I'm going to tell Stephanie," she said. Rebecca wanted to include her young new assistant in the news; Stephanie Quilty lacked for self-confidence, and Rebecca always made a conscious effort to share information with her so that she wouldn't merely feel like hired help.

It seemed Rebecca floated downstairs, still buoyed by the rare good news, on her way to see Miss Quilty in the kitchen. Just as she reached the foyer, there was a hard knock at the front door.

Rebecca veered off her course to the kitchen and pulled the door open to see a large man in coachman's livery. He seemed familiar.

The man took his hat off. "I'm sorry to trouble you, Miss Davies," he said in a mournful voice.

Oh! Vivian O'Connell's driver, Rebecca remembered. "It's no trouble at all, Daniel." Rebecca looked past him to the carriage. She could not remember having an appointment with O'Connell, and in the past the former madam had always come to the door herself, leaving Daniel at the coach. "Is Miss O'Connell expecting me?"

"No, ma'am. That's why I'm here." He appeared thoughtful for a moment. "No easy way to say this, I suppose: Miss O'Connell is dead."

Rebecca was speechless. Disjointed thoughts ran through her head, but none of them took a coherent enough form to be turned into anything worth saying. She finally uttered, "What . . . how?"

"Miss O'Connell was killed, ma'am. Last night in Washington Park." He hesitated again. "That's all I know for sure, ma'am."

An odd question came into Rebecca's head: With O'Connell dead, who had told the driver to come here with the news?

As if able to read her mind, Daniel said, "I am sorry, ma'am. Miss O'Connell was a nice lady—always treated me well—and I think the two of you were trying to do something good. That's why I came to tell you; I just thought you should know."

"Thank you," Rebecca whispered. She was starting to realize that as much as she was sorry for Vivian O'Connell, she was also disheartened by the fact that the "something good" the two of them had been trying to do might also have been dealt a fatal blow.

CHAPTER 17

It was late afternoon by the time Marshall Webb got the message Rebecca had left him, returned her telephone call, and found a hansom cab willing to fight through the Brooklyn traffic and get him back over the bridge to Manhattan.

He went directly to Colden House, where Rebecca answered his knock so promptly that he thought she must have been waiting near the door.

"I'm sorry it took so long to get here," he said. "And I'm so sorry about Miss O'Connell."

She bit her lip and silently nodded her thanks. Webb could tell she'd been twisting her honey-blond hair around her fingers, a habit she had when she was worried or upset; while most of it was in a chignon, long unruly locks framed her face. A red flush colored her fair cheeks and her lips were tight. He wasn't sure, but her eyes looked like she might have been crying.

"What can I do?" Webb asked.

"I need to get outside for a while," she said. "Can we take a walk?"

"Of course." He got her walking coat and bonnet

from the hallway coat stand and helped her on with them. "It's getting cold again."

"I don't care. I need some air."

They stepped outside onto State Street, where the sky was crystalline and so was the air. The mercury had fallen during the day and there was a brittle feel to the weather, as if any creature or object could crack at any moment. Gusting winds had kicked up to the point where they seemed to bite viciously at any patch of exposed skin.

Rebecca suggested they go to the Battery, directly across the street, so Webb carefully escorted her through the snarled traffic—not bothering to return the invectives hurled at him by a particularly cantankerous teamster who seemed upset by nothing more than the fact that they were walking faster than he could drive his barrel-laden wagon—and led her into the park.

The Battery was at the southernmost point of Manhattan, bordered by the choppy waters of New York Harbor. The traffic there was almost as heavy as on the streets, and tugboats, ferries, and barges sounded horns, whistles, and bells as they navigated their courses.

In the spring, the park would be an attraction. Now, as Webb and Rebecca strolled one of its paths, it was bleak, with leafless quivering trees, bare ground, and surrounded by slate-gray water. The two of them had almost complete privacy as they walked and talked.

"I can't believe Vivian O'Connell is dead," Rebecca said.

"Do you know what happened?"

"The driver told me she was beaten to death, but all he heard was from the hotel staff. Somebody there told him it was a robbery."

"But how—" Webb glanced down at Rebecca's bare hand resting in the crook of his arm. "Where are your gloves?"

She shrugged. "I didn't think to put them on."

Webb removed his own and despite her protests slipped them on her. His gloves looked like oven mitts on her small hands.

"It could be that I'm right," Rebecca said.

"About . . . ?"

"That somebody is going around killing prostitutes. Frenchy Sayre and Vivian O'Connell worked together and both were beaten to death. Maybe it was by the same man."

"Could be," Webb replied, although he didn't seriously believe so. He had the sense that Rebecca was simply sounding out ideas as they came to her, that she was not completely thinking them through. He figured the best thing was to let her speak, and not try to discuss things seriously until she'd recovered from the news of O'Connell's death.

Rebecca went on, "It was only a few years ago that that killer was going around London killing prostitutes—Jack the Ripper. And the police never did catch him, did they?"

"No, they didn't." Webb decided that her thinking was going far enough astray that he should make the effort to reason with her. "Two prostitutes being murdered in two years doesn't mean there's a connection," he said. "It's a dangerous line of work and many of them are hurt or killed—in fact, I'll wager that there have been more than them killed in the last two years. They don't get a lot of publicity—unless the murders are particularly grisly—and they often don't get more than a token investigation by the police."

"As happened with Frenchy Sayre."

"Yes." After a moment, another thought occurred to Webb. "How would anyone even know that Vivian O'Connell was a prostitute? She wasn't plying the trade anymore, was she? Looking to pick up customers in that park? And she didn't dress like a prostitute, did she?"

Rebecca shook her head. "No. At least she told me she was retired. And I believe her."

"So then it could have been simply a mugging. A city park at night is not a safe place for a woman."

"Especially if somebody followed her there."

Webb shot her a glance. "Why would you think that?"

"Because maybe somebody wanted *Vivian O'Connell* dead, not a random prostitute or a random robbery victim."

"I don't understand." And he didn't. Webb truly couldn't follow Rebecca's thought processes today.

"Maybe somebody didn't want her opening a new shelter for former prostitutes. She'd told me she'd had trouble getting any cooperation when she began pursuing the idea. Perhaps someone thought that killing her would kill the shelter. Or . . ." Rebecca bit her lower lip again. "She also told me that lately she's been approaching more people about getting donations to fund the house—people she used to know from her days as a madam. Maybe somebody didn't want her making contact with them again."

"If it goes back to when she was a madam," Webb said, "there could be all sorts of things that were going on. More goes on in some of those places than simple, uh, vice. Some houses of prostitution make extra money robbing their customers, some blackmail them, some—"

"Oh!" Rebecca had turned to him sharply.

"What is it?"

She hesitated. "No. It's nothing. Just a thought."

"Tell me," he urged in a soft voice.

She shook her head no, and Webb noticed her bare throat was turning red in the cold air. "You're freezing," he said. "We should go back to the house."

"It's okay. The cold feels good."

Nevertheless, she didn't object when he took off his wool muffler and wrapped it around her neck.

By now, they were close to the Barge Office, at the foot of Whitehall Street in the east end of Battery Park. The granite Roman Revival structure, with a tower that could be seen from much of Lower Manhattan, was the arrival point for immigrants ferried over from Ellis Island. The stream of newcomers to America didn't abate with the winter weather; around the building, people and vehicles milled about with little apparent sense of direction or organization.

Webb and Rebecca continued to walk in the direction of the Barge Office, close enough to hear the voices of the people who surrounded it. Immigrants, speaking a dozen tongues, huddled together or walked around looking for relatives. Vendors tried to sell them their first American meals—popcorn, peanuts, fried oysters. Money changers offered to convert foreign currency to dollars. A small army of newsboys hawked the city's major papers—the *World*, *Herald*, *Sun*, and *Tribune*—as well as foreign language newspapers like *Il Progresso Italo-Americano* and *Yidisher Tageblatt*. Hackmen and railroad agents loudly advertised the availability of transportation, while other men who billed themselves as "agents" tried to entice the newcomers with promises of jobs and housing.

Rebecca was staring at the people, and Webb now believed that he could read her thoughts.

Both of them knew from experience that most of the "agents" were no better than vultures, preying on the hopes and inexperience of the immigrants. Many of the newcomers would end up toiling in sweatshops, most would live in filthy tenements—if they could find housing at all—and many of the young women would be lured or forced into the vice industry.

Rebecca, Webb knew, was thinking that some of the girls would eventually need the help of Colden House and she was no doubt fretting that she would have no room to accommodate them.

Without saying anything, Rebecca turned back the way they had come. The two walked together in silence for a while.

"I'm determined to make sure of two things," Rebecca abruptly announced. "One is that Vivian O'Connell's killer be caught—I'm not going to let the police get away with ignoring her death the way they did Frenchy Sayre's."

Webb nodded in agreement, although he wasn't sure how the Brooklyn police could be told to do anything they didn't want to. "And the second thing?"

"Sayre House is still going to open. I'll get it started myself, if I have to."

Webb nodded again, and promised he would do what he could to help.

CHAPTER 18

Although grateful for Marshall's promise to help, Rebecca was determined to start looking into Vivian O'Connell's murder on her own. So the next morning, she again left Colden House, this time alone and this time toward the eastern end of the Battery.

There, at the foot of Whitehall Street, she caught the South Ferry for Brooklyn. She told herself that it made more sense than facing the traffic over the bridge, but she also knew that her choice of transportation was in part because she still wanted to be out in the cold air.

It wasn't long into the ferry's journey across the mouth of the East River that she decided she had her fill of the winter cold. A leaden sky promised snow; ice crystals were propelled through the air by gusts that blew over the ferry and stung Rebecca's skin like darts, and the craft rolled uncomfortably in the choppy waters.

During the ride, Rebecca thought about Vivian O'Connell, realizing that she actually knew very little about the woman. She'd liked her, but that was based largely on the instinct for reading people that Rebecca had developed from a lifetime of living in New York and many years working with so many different young women at Colden House. And, of course, she admired O'Connell's determination to open a new shelter. But she'd only known her for a short time, and not all that well. Now she believed it was necessary to learn more about the former madam.

Upon arriving at the ferry house on Atlantic Avenue, Rebecca hurried out to where several hansom cabs for hire were waiting for customers, and hailed one of the vehicles.

A heavily bundled driver with a short clay pipe rooted in his mouth hurried down from his perch at the front of the carriage and opened the door for Rebecca. "You'll need to be careful, ma'am."

She stepped up into the cab with ease. "I'm fine, thank you."

"I mean once we drive, ma'am. You'll want to sit in the middle—away from the windows—and keep your head low."

The man must be drunk, Rebecca thought. "What on earth are you talking about?" She shifted in the seat, edging toward the door, ready to get out again and find another driver.

"It's the militia, ma'am. They put out an order today—every door and window in Brooklyn has to stay closed. Anybody pokes their head out a window is likely to get their face shot off." The driver clamped down harder on his pipe. "The soldiers have been told to shoot on sight."

Rebecca stared at him with disbelief. Could this be true?

"According to what I read in the *Eagle*," he went on, "the order's only for houses and buildings. But no sense takin' chances. Them soldiers have been real trigger-happy, and it wouldn't surprise me if they started shooting at faces in cab windows, too."

Rebecca noticed no sign of intoxication in the driver and decided to stick with him. "Thank you for the warning," she said with a smile of appreciation. The problem wasn't that the driver was drunk; it was that the city was in a state of war.

As the cab reached exclusive Montague Street, without being targeted by gunfire, Rebecca thought back. It hadn't been very long ago that she'd come to this same place in Brooklyn Heights. But then she'd been in the comfort of a brougham and in the company of Vivian O'Connell.

The hansom cab let Rebecca off at the stately brownstone of Mr. Matthew Anderson-Smith. She approached the home and rapped the massive brass knocker on its oak door.

After a couple of minutes—it was Rebecca's experience that the finer the home the longer it took for anyone to answer the door—she was greeted by the same diminutive butler whom she'd encountered before.

"Miss Davies," he said, recognizing her, too. That he was surprised to see her was evidenced by a slight lift of his brow.

"I'd like to see Mr. Anderson-Smith, please," she said.

"I don't believe he is expecting visitors this morning."

"I realize I'm not expected, but it's important that I speak with him." Even though Rebecca's family outranked Anderson-Smith on the social ladder, dropping by unexpectedly was poor form.

The butler hesitated only a moment. "Please come in." He ushered her into the exquisitely furnished foyer that was larger than some Manhattan apartments. "I'll see if Mr. Anderson-Smith is available."

With a stiff bow, he was gone, leaving Rebecca to study a Persian wall hanging.

While she waited, a uniformed maid came to take Rebecca's coat and hat and served her tea and scones from a silver tray. Rebecca used the time to try to think what exactly she would say to Mr. Anderson-Smith should he consent to see her, but failed to come up with any combination of words that seemed suitable.

The butler finally arrived to give her the news that the gentleman of the house would indeed be pleased to meet with her. He led the way back to the study in the rear of the home, where Rebecca found herself in the masculine environment of dark wood, plush leather, somber prints, and thick carpeting.

Anderson-Smith was again seated behind his carved desk, wearing a rather formal suit and an impossibly stiff high collar that was almost hidden by his drooping muttonchop side-whiskers. He rose and bowed slightly as the butler announced Rebecca.

"A pleasure to see you again, Miss Davies," he said. "Even if it is an unexpected one."

"I appreciate you making time for me." She settled into the chair that Anderson-Smith offered. "And I apologize for the suddenness of my visit."

He waved off the apology, dismissed the butler, and sat back down behind his desk.

Rebecca again sought the words to explain her reason for coming, and again failed.

Anderson-Smith spoke up. "I must tell you, however, that if you've come to renew our previous conversation, that matter is closed. My donation to Miss O'Connell was a generous one, and there will be no more coming. You may relay that message to her."

"I am afraid I am not able to give her any messages."

His eyebrows rose.

Her gaze fixed on him, Rebecca explained, "Miss O'Connell was murdered two nights ago."

"Murdered," he repeated, his lips pursing and a slight scowl creasing his forehead. His expression was not of shock or horror; rather, he appeared as if he'd taken a sip of bad wine.

"Yes. That's why I've come."

Anderson-Smith appeared puzzled. "To give me the news?"

"No." Rebecca sought the words to explain.

"I don't understand."

Rebecca decided to simply be direct. "The last time we were here, Miss O'Connell implied that she would speak to your wife about donating to Sayre House—you didn't want her speaking to your wife, and so decided to make a contribution yourself. She basically blackmailed you—I *don't* approve of what she did, by the way, and made that clear to her afterward. And I regret that she used me to gain access to you as she did. She did confirm that you'd been a patron of her house, however, a matter which I'm sure you'd prefer to keep secret."

Anderson-Smith shrugged noncommittally.

"And it occurred to me that your secret is now safe with Miss O'Connell dead. She can't try to blackmail you again."

He stared at her for some moments, and a bemused expression came into his eyes. "You think *I* murdered her?"

"I suspect that a man in your position would not take kindly to a blackmail attempt—especially a successful one."

Anderson-Smith's mouth twitched up in a smile. "I must say, Miss Davies, I'm actually rather flattered at your accusation. I suppose I should be offended, but

I'm not. The thought that someone believes I could be so physically aggressive as to commit murder is flattering to a man of my age."

This wasn't the reaction Rebecca had expected. "I didn't mean to accuse, and certainly not to flatter. I—"

Anderson-Smith held up a manicured hand. "May we speak frankly?"

Rebecca wasn't sure how much franker the discussion could possibly get. "Of course."

Anderson-Smith glanced backward at the gilt-framed portrait of his wife that hung on the wall near his desk. "I am quite fond of my wife, and would prefer not to give her or my family any public embarrassment. However, my occasional visits to houses of the sort that Miss O'Connell used to run are in truth no secret. A man in my position is *entitled* to avail himself of pleasures of the flesh—that is understood by everyone in society. There simply must be some decorum about the matter. I do not tell my wife, for example, so she can pretend otherwise if she prefers. And I am discreet in discussions with my friends." He pushed back from his desk. "In short, the donation I gave Miss O'Connell was worth avoiding some embarrassment. But the matter wasn't worth any more than that—certainly it wouldn't merit killing anyone over."

Rebecca actually hadn't necessarily suspected Anderson-Smith. Vivian O'Connell had told her she'd spoken with several people about donating to Sayre House, and if any of those discussions had gone the way that it had with Anderson-Smith—along the lines of blackmail—there might have been someone with a motive to silence her permanently. "Perhaps *you* wouldn't kill her," said Rebecca. "Maybe she had another customer who would."

He pressed his fingertips together and appeared to

consider the possibility. "I don't see that as likely." He shook his head, causing his side-whiskers to flutter. "As I said before, any man in my position is entitled to his recreations. And a man of lower status . . . well, he wouldn't really have any reputation that he needed to protect anyway, would he?"

Rebecca chose to overlook his arrogance, it was an attitude she'd encountered all too often growing up in the society in which she had. "You can't imagine anyone wanting Miss O'Connell to be permanently kept quiet?"

Anderson-Smith thought briefly. "Perhaps if the gentleman had proclivities of a perverse nature that he didn't want revealed. But Miss O'Connell's establishment didn't cater to that sort of clientele."

Rebecca could think of nothing more, and gathered her skirts, about to stand. "Well, thank you for seeing me."

"Miss Davies," Anderson-Smith said. "It occurs to me that with Miss O'Connell dead, I suppose she won't be needing my money. Can I expect a refund?"

Rebecca stared at him. A woman was dead and his main concern was getting his money back? Or was *that* the reason—

Anderson-Smith appeared to read her thoughts. He chuckled. "No, I wouldn't kill to get my money back, either." With a dismissive wave of his hand. "If you believe that, simply take it yourself as a donation to—" He cocked his head. "What is the name of *your* shelter again?"

"Colden House."

"Take it for Colden House." He rose from his chair. "Now, if there's nothing else . . ."

Rebecca eased back in her own seat. "Actually there is, if I can impose on you for another minute." When he didn't stop her, she went on, "You mentioned the kind of establishment Miss O'Connell ran—can you tell me more about it?" Marshall had mentioned other crimes, like robbery and blackmail, that took place in houses of prostitution; perhaps a man who'd been victimized in her house had decided to get revenge on the retired madam.

Anderson-Smith walked over to the fireplace, warming his back by the glowing embers. "Miss O'Connell ran a fine establishment, as respectable as such a house can be. You could get a meal as good as most restaurants and had a selection of the best wines. As to the young ladies . . . well, they were attractive, courteous, and I know of no one who ever contracted a disease from them."

"Do you know if anyone was ever blackmailed or robbed there?" Rebecca asked. "Or a victim of any other crime?"

"Not that I'm aware of." He shook his head. "A visit to Miss O'Connell's was an expensive indulgence, and my understanding is that her staff was well paid. There was no need for any of them to supplement their income in other ways."

"People sometimes steal for greed, not necessity," Rebecca pointed out.

"True enough. But all I can tell you is that I'm not aware of any such incidents. I was always treated well, and recommended her house to my friends."

One more question occurred to Rebecca. "Did you ever meet a Frenchy Sayre at the house?"

Anderson-Smith smiled. It appeared that the sound of the young woman's name warmed him more than the flickering fire. "Yes, I had the pleasure of making her acquaintance on several occasions."

"Can you tell me anything about her?"

"Not much. She was young—perhaps early twenties. And had a talent which was truly remarkable." He smiled more broadly. "Whenever I was in the mood for that particular service, I called on Miss Sayre."

"She's dead, too."

"Yes, I'm aware of that." He nodded sadly. "I believe her death was part of the reason Miss O'Connell decided to get out of the business."

"Do you know anything about it?"

Anderson-Smith smiled wryly. "Nothing more than I know about Miss O'Connell's unfortunate demise. As I said, I called on Miss Sayre on occasion, but I didn't know her well. She was good at what she did, but at my age I prefer to have companionship and conversation with my, uh, dalliances. And so there were others at the house whom I usually spent my time with."

Rebecca rose. "Thank you again for your time."

"My pleasure." There was a twinkle in his eye, and Rebecca suspected that he had indeed enjoyed discussing such matters so frankly with a lady of her elite background.

"Thank you also for your offer to transfer your donation to Colden House, but it won't be necessary."

"I'll get it back?"

"Sayre House *will* open, just as Miss O'Connell planned."

Anderson-Smith wished her well with the shelter, but the twinkle was gone from his eyes and the smile vanished from his lips.

Marshall Webb found the building on Leonard Street, in a run-down commercial area of Williamsburg. This part of Brooklyn had been hurt badly by the depression and many of its businesses and industries were now closed.

One of them was the brick building he was seeking this evening. Sputtering streetlights were barely bright enough for him to make out the peeling sign above the door: ASTAFAN PAINT COMPANY. It was easy to see the boards nailed across the front door of the abandoned structure.

As he'd been told to do, Webb went around to a side entrance off a darkened alley. Finding the door unlocked, he went right inside, where he was nearly bowled over by the overpowering smells of acrid liniment, rancid sweat, stale beer, and cheap stogies.

What had once housed a paint company now was home to a makeshift boxing gymnasium. A few bare electric bulbs hung from the high ceiling, casting every motion with eerie shadows.

Along one wall, a dozen or so men, most of them young, were working out on punching bags and tossing medicine balls. There were a few older men among them, acting as trainers. Arranged in a rough order were about fifty plain wooden chairs of no consistent style; perhaps twenty were occupied by spectators whose attention was directed toward the ring at the center of the room.

The ring was as makeshift as the rest of the place. It was simply a roped-off square on the plank floor. The ropes were supported by rough boards acting as posts, not one of which was truly vertical. Inside, two barechested, bare-fisted lightweight young men were seated on stools in opposite corners waiting for their bout to commence.

Webb hadn't come to watch a fight, though, so his attention went to the audience, scanning over the faces. He then worked his way through them to an empty chair and sat down.

"You're a difficult man to find, Detective."

Buck Morehouse hadn't noticed that the man who'd just sat next to him was the writer, and surprise showed on his face. Through a mouthful of half-chewed peanuts, he asked, "How'd you find me *here*?" He shifted in his overcoat; there was a chill in the unheated room.

"It wasn't easy." Webb saw no need to explain his trail of bribes, starting with a desk sergeant at Morehouse's station house and ending with a saloonkeeper who gave him the tip about this gym.

Morehouse held out his bag of nuts, offering them to Webb. "Hell, *you* should be the detective."

Webb accepted the compliment and declined the food. "Can we talk for a few minutes?" he asked.

"Sure, but—" Morehouse gestured to the ring, where a referee had just stepped inside. "Fight's about to start. I want to see this boy."

"Which one?"

"The one in red. Name's Robbie Moore. This is just a warm-up fight for him, getting himself ready for a big fight Friday. I want to see how he does."

Webb leaned back in his chair and stretched out his long legs. "I can wait. You have money on him?"

"Not yet." Morehouse smiled slyly.

The first round got under way with both boxers moving cautiously. Moore was a skinny boy who moved his body like an undulating snake; he was a narrow target to begin with, and by moving as he did an opponent would likely miss any punch he threw.

"The kid sure dances around a lot," commented Webb. "But he's got to throw a punch sometime if he wants to win."

"I hear he's got a right hand like—damn!"

From the ring came a sound like a wet towel being snapped. Moore's opponent had managed to land an uppercut to his wiggling midsection, and the skinny young man was doubled over. Moore then took a right hook to the side of his head and fell to his knees. Waving off his opponent, he crawled to his corner where he began to vomit on the floor.

"That was fast," said Webb.

"Damn," Morehouse said again. Then a smile slowly brightened his face. "At least I didn't bet a dime on him, and now I know I never will. That skinny son of a bitch just saved me a bundle."

Two more fighters stepped into the ring as Moore was dragged out of it by a trainer who was cussing his boxer out even more powerfully than the punches that had brought him down.

"You want to see any more?" Webb asked.

"Nah, we can talk." The detective jerked his head toward the wall where a few bottles were set up on a plank like a bar. "How 'bout a shot?"

Webb knew that meant that Morehouse wanted a shot and was hoping for Webb to treat. "Sure," he answered. "It's a cold night."

Morehouse called a name, and a fellow came to serve them their whiskeys and take Webb's thirty cents. The two of them took their drinks to a couple of seats near the rear of the audience, where they could speak in relative privacy.

"I heard they shot a kid today," the detective said.

"Ten-year-old boy. Looked out his bedroom window to see what was happening and a militiaman put a bullet in his head."

"Bastards." Morehouse took a sip of his whiskey.

"And the mayor's asking for five thousand more

troops; he wants the strike smashed," Webb said. "You haven't been on the streets?"

"Nah. Captain Sturup has me on robbery detail—expects me to be staking out Wallabout Market."

"But you're here instead."

Morehouse smiled. "I'm on a lunch break." He downed the rest of his drink and his expression became serious. "What did you want to talk to me about? You learn anything about who could have killed Lonnie Keck?"

"No," Webb admitted. "I'm still looking into it but something else has come up in the meantime."

"What's that?"

"You remember I asked you about Frenchy Sayre, that prostitute who was murdered two years ago?"

Morehouse nodded. "I'm sorry. I haven't had a chance—"

"I understand," Webb cut him off. "The thing is the madam she worked for—Vivian O'Connell—has been murdered, too."

The detective appeared surprised at the news.

"You haven't heard about it at the station house?"

"I've hardly been *at* the station house. Like I said, I been on stakeout. Or in the area of my stakeout anyway."

"O'Connell was killed two nights ago in Washington Park."

"Damn." He wiped his lips. "That's a shame."

Webb was disappointed that Morehouse could give him no details on her murder. "Here's the thing," he said. "I have a friend . . . a young lady . . . and she's the one who wanted me to find out what happened to Frenchy Sayre. Now, with O'Connell dead, too, she thinks somebody is out to kill prostitutes in Brooklyn and if the police don't investigate it, she'll be looking into things on her own—and that worries me. I'd rather you or I did it."

"I wish I could, but . . ." Morehouse shrugged his shoulders helplessly.

"Is there anything you can tell me about Vivian O'Connell? How did she run her house, how did she treat her girls?" Webb was groping now.

Morehouse pondered the questions. "Can't tell you much. Far as I know, her place was respectable—and expensive." He rubbed his bristly chin. "Say, when she went out of business, I believe she arranged for most of her girls to go to Nancy Johnson—she runs a house on De Kalb. You might want to talk to her or some of her girls about O'Connell." He looked up hopefully. "That help any?"

"It's a good idea. Thanks." Webb called for another whiskey, which he gave to Morehouse; the whiskey tasted too suspect for him to want another himself.

After the detective had taken an appreciative sip, Webb went on, "What would really help, though, is if you could investigate her murder."

"I'd like nothing more. You think I want to freeze my ass off watching the markets all night?"

"No, I—"

But Morehouse wasn't listening. He had launched into a monologue about his mistreatment at the hands of Captain Sturup and the lack of appreciation for his years of dedicated service.

After a while, Webb wasn't listening, either. But he was thinking. "Listen," he finally interrupted the detective. "I have an idea for getting you on the murder investigation. Here's what you tell Sturup. . . ."

CHAPTER 19

The station house squadroom always reminded Buck Morehouse of a one-room schoolhouse. Rows of low pine tables were arranged as if they were class desks. At the front of the room, behind the lectern, were an American flag, an unflattering portrait of President Grover Cleveland, and a portable cloth blackboard that could be rolled up when not in use.

What made the room unique to Brooklyn was the flag of the city on prominent display. It was a simple design: a classically robed woman bearing fasces was in the center of the white field, with plain black lettering above her that read CITY OF BROOKLYN and Gothic lettering below that spelled out the city's motto *Een Draght Mackt Maght*—Dutch for "In Unity There Is Strength."

What made it obvious that this was no schoolhouse was the fact that next to the blackboard was an enormous map of the Second Precinct with all streets, railroad tracks, and major buildings laid out and patrolmens' assigned beats clearly marked. The patrolmen were in their seats like well-behaved schoolboys, sitting rigid and straight in their stiff blue uniforms with their helmets on their desks. Some were nearly young enough to be schoolboys, while others were veterans nearer Morehouse's age and appeared attentive only by making an effort. The detective himself was slouched against the back wall, trying to appear inconspicuous since he wasn't even supposed to be at the morning shift's roll call.

The gruff duty sergeant standing behind the lectern finished making his routine announcements and giving the men their assignments, then announced, "Captain Sturup has a few words for you." He quickly scanned the room and barked, "Pay attention!"

The warning was unnecessary. Oscar Sturup had been standing to the side, in full regalia and with a military bearing. His presence was the reason the men had appeared so attentive to the sergeant, Morehouse knew. Normally, they used roll call for a chance to get a few minutes' dozing in or to eat a quick breakfast or to chat among themselves.

Sturup strode briskly to front and center. Unlike the sergeant, he chose to stand in front of the lectern; Morehouse suspected it was so that none of the ribbons and epaulets of his rank would be obscured. He paused for effect, casting a stern gaze about the room of police officers.

Finally, he began speaking in clipped tones. "Men, we are dealing with a situation this city has never faced before: an assault by armed forces of the state militia."

Morehouse noted that Sturup failed to mention that those forces had been invited into the city by Mayor Schieren. He also noted that the photograph of the mayor that used to be displayed next to President Cleveland's had been removed; the events of the strike had caused the mayor to become as unpopular as the militia and the railroad companies.

"The militia," Sturup went on, "has gone far beyond the mission that was assigned to them. Instead of protecting the railroad cars from strikers, the soldiers are taking the lives of innocent civilians." His voice dropped to a theatrically sorrowful tone. "We all mourn for that ten-year-old boy who so tragically lost his life to a soldier's bullet yesterday—as well as for all the other innocent citizens of this great city who have been brutally taken down by bullet and bayonet in recent weeks." He paused and lowered his head slightly as if in prayer. A few of the patrolmen crossed themselves.

Morehouse marveled at the captain's way of speaking. Sturup always managed to sound like both a politician and a commanding officer.

The captain raised his eyes and there was a look of determination in them. "The mission of this department is to protect and serve the people of Brooklyn. I intend that the officers of this precinct carry out that mission—and that includes protecting citizens from murderous soldiers."

A number of the patrolmen exchanged glances as if uncertain of Sturup's meaning.

He promptly made it clear. "Any soldier who fires upon a unarmed civilian is to be placed under arrest and charged with murder." Sturup puffed himself up a bit. "I have already communicated with General McLeer, the commanding officer of the National Guard troops, as well as with Governor Morton. I want the soldier who shot that boy turned over to me for arrest."

It would never happen, Morehouse was sure, but the move was brilliant. Captain Sturup's stand would undoubtedly be wildly popular with the people of

Brooklyn and he could count on their support for whatever future plans he might have. There was no doubt in the detective's mind that Sturup was positioning himself for some kind of political move.

"In the meantime," Sturup said, "I am charging each of you to respond to any additional acts of violence by the militia."

Patrolmen exchanged worried glances with each other.

One veteran, Zach Swann, who had more years on the force than Morehouse and many more pounds around his midsection, gathered his courage and gave voice to what many of his fellow officers were thinking. "How *exactly* are we supposed to respond?" As an afterthought, he added, "Sir."

Sturup's response was terse. "I expect you to respond the same as you would to any other crime: identify and apprehend the perpetrator."

"So if another one of them militia snipers shoots down a civilian, we're supposed to go up to the roof, or wherever he is, and arrest him?" Swann sounded doubtful. "Uh, sir."

"From the looks of you, Officer, I doubt you are capable of getting your fat ass up to a roof. But that *is* what I expect, yes." Sturup clearly did not like explaining himself to subordinates.

Swann was undeterred. "What if they resist? The guardsmen have us outnumbered two-to-one."

"And several thousand more troops are coming in, so soon you'll be outnumbered five-to-one."

Another brave patrolman spoke up. "But what if—"

"That's enough questions." The color of anger was rising in Sturup's face. "You have your orders and I expect you to do your duty." He gave a sharp nod at the duty sergeant, who barked an order of dismissal.

As the officers grabbed up their leather helmets and shuffled glumly out of the squad room, Buck Morehouse walked over to Sturup. "Can I speak with you, Captain?"

Sturup's steely gaze remained fixed on the backs of the departing patrolmen, as if he was trying to impart some of that steel to their flagging backbones. It was some moments before he turned to Morehouse. "What is it, Detective?" He scowled. "What are you doing here, anyway?"

"I came in to speak with you."

"Any progress on the robberies?"

"No . . . Well, yes, in a way . . . there haven't been any more of them since I've been on the case."

"But you haven't caught anyone."

"No."

"Then you've made no progress, have you?"

"No, sir." It was easier simply to concede the point to the captain, Morehouse decided.

"So back to my question: Why are you here?" Sturup looked ready to leave the room.

"It's the strangest thing . . . but something I thought you'd want to know about. So I—"

"Damn it, Detective! Spit it out or shut up."

"Well, sir, it'll sound crazy, but I was contacted by this writer—a fellow named David Byrd. He writes them dime novels you can find on the newstand."

"Why on earth do you think this would be of interest to me?" Sturup then said to the sergeant, "Go ahead. I'll be with you momentarily—if the detective here can get to the point."

Left alone in the squadroom, Morehouse went on. "This Byrd fellow has the craziest notion. He says he's got a theory that Jack the Ripper has come to New York—and he's planning to write a book about it."

Sturup's scowl reconfigured itself from perturbed to perplexed. "That's utterly absurd."

"I think so, too. But there was a prostitute murdered here a few days ago—Vivian O'Connell. You might remember she ran one of the best houses we had in the city."

"Houses of prostitution are illegal," Sturup replied. "If I knew such a place was operating in my precinct, I would have had it shut down."

Morehouse was taken aback by the response. It sounded like Sturup was still speaking politically instead of honestly. "Uh, yes, sir. But anyway, this David Byrd says he's been looking into the murder of prostitutes in New York and he says the numbers have gone up in the last few years—right after the Ripper killings stopped in London."

The captain mulled over the news. "So this writer has a theory. Why should that be of any concern to me?"

"Byrd says most of the prostitute killings have been in Brooklyn—in this precinct, in fact. He mentioned another one who was killed here a couple of years ago—'Frenchy Sayre,' I think her name was."

Sturup appeared to be searching his memory. "I don't recall any such murder. But then one whore more or less is really not a matter of much importance, is it, Detective?"

"You're right, of course, sir. But those Ripper killings sure attracted a lot of public attention. And this writer could make the department look pretty bad in his book—he says we haven't been working to solve the murders and we're leaving the public at risk." Morehouse paused for a breath. "Like I said, sir, just thought you'd want to be aware."

Sturup nodded thoughtfully to himself. He suddenly demanded, "Why did this writer contact *you* of all people?"

"I was in the papers last year after we solved the Joshua Thompson murder. He said that's where he got my name."

The captain growled softly. Morehouse knew that he didn't like to be reminded of the detective's success on the Thompson case; Sturup assumed Morehouse was an idiot and had stumbled on the solution through sheer luck. Even worse, the *Brooklyn Eagle* had failed to give Sturup any credit for the resolution of the case, instead giving it to the detective who'd earned it.

"I did have a thought," Morehouse ventured. "Maybe if I look into the murders—at least the O'Connell killing since that's a fresh one—it will show the department is working on the case. Byrd might still publish his crazy ideas but he wouldn't be able to accuse us of dereliction of duty."

The captain again thought for a few moments. "Who is this writer again?"

"David Byrd. He said he writes for Pritchard's Dime Library."

"I've never heard of him."

"Me either. But I'm not much of a reader."

After more thought, Sturup came to his decision. "Very well, Detective. I'm glad to see that you do think on occasion—because this time you actually came up with a sensible idea."

"You mean—"

"You're off robbery detail. Investigate the murder—or murd*ers.* Don't expect you'll come up with anything, but it might keep that writer from making us look bad. With the strike and citizens being shot in the streets, we have enough bad publicity to worry about."

He dismissed Morehouse with the order "Your job for now is to keep that writer from putting anything derogatory about us in print."

The detective knew that Sturup meant nothing derogatory about *him* should appear in print. And he noticed that Sturup did not tell him to actually solve the murders of the dead prostitutes.

Marshall Webb had finally been able to get an appointment to interview the president of the Atlantic Avenue Railroad Company. Wednesday morning, a clear sunny day with a temperature slightly above the freezing point, he arrived early for his ten o'clock meeting at the imposing Fulton Street building that housed the railroad company's offices.

The railroad executive wasn't as punctual as Webb. It was nearly an hour wait before a wan male secretary in a black suit a size too small for him ushered the writer into the office of Paul Toomey.

The spacious office was made small by all the furnishings, which looked like they had been chosen by a Middle Eastern sultan. Thick Persian rugs covered every inch of the floor, some of them layered over each other. Tapestries of oriental designs and paintings in elaborate gold frames festooned the walls. The furniture was of plush velvet and dark wood with a lot of curves and curlicues. All that was missing was a Turkish hookah.

Seated behind a massive, heavily polished desk decorated with inlays and carved to the point that there was little wood left that could be cut away, was a small round man of about sixty. He was in a thronelike armchair that was much too large for his size, making him appear even smaller. Perhaps to make himself look bigger, the man's snowy hair was curled up around his ears and his muttonchop whiskers were puffed out like a blowfish.

The secretary announced Webb to Toomey and backed out of the office, leaving them alone.

"Thank you for seeing me," said Webb.

Toomey gave a terse nod. "You have fifteen minutes of my time, as agreed." The voice boomed deeply, unexpectedly so for a man of his stature. He pulled a heavy gold watch from the pocket of his silk vest and squinted to check the time through myopic eyes.

Webb glanced at one of the leather armchairs in front of the desk and back at Toomey, but the railroad president did not invite him to sit down. For fifteen minutes he could stand, Webb decided.

A smirk was on Toomey's thin lips. "I take it you're here because you've decided to switch to the winning side, Mr. Webb?"

"I don't have a side."

"Perhaps you *shouldn't* have one, but you do." Toomey idly began toying with the thick watch chain draped over his bulging belly. "I've read your reports in *Harper's*. There's no doubt that you support the strikers. In fact, they were barely 'reports' at all—more like propaganda."

"The Knights of Labor gave me access and information. I was unable to get an appointment with a railroad official until now." In truth, Webb did favor the cause of the strikers, but if he wanted Paul Toomey to provide information he had to convince him that he wasn't in the enemy's camp.

"You should have tried."

"I did. I requested appointments but—"

Toomey slapped the top of the desk. "How can you expect us to make 'appointments' when we were virtually under siege?" The deep voice suddenly went up an octave.

"I understand everything was chaotic when the strike was launched. And I still tried to speak with a Mr. Ryan Akin, one of your directors, at the Fifth Avenue terminal."

"He was busy trying to get the trains out."

"I understand that, and I understand the demands on your time. I hope you'll understand that *Harper's* has a deadline. I had to submit the information that I had available to me at the time, and most of that came from Mr. Coppinger and the Knights of Labor."

Toomey growled softly, something that sounded like a concession. His voice back down to a lower register, he offered, "Have a seat, Mr. Webb."

"Thank you." Webb was soon in the hug of soft thick upholstery.

"You didn't have to make those damn strikers sound *quite* so sympathetic, though," Toomey groused.

"They trotted out the widows and children of men who'd lost their lives in your employ. There is no way *not* to make them appear sympathetic." Webb pulled out his own watch. "So far, I've been explaining myself to you instead of you answering my questions. I assume I still have my fifteen minutes."

Toomey hesitated, then nodded in concession.

"You mentioned having been under siege," Webb began, returning his watch and taking out his notebook. "But the siege appears to be lifting. There is no doubt that the railroad companies will be, as you put it, the 'winning side.'"

"I had no doubt from the beginning," Toomey said. "The strikers were led by a small group of malcontents. *We* are the ones acting in the public interest, and the public is beginning to realize that."

"Actually, the crowds along the streets still seem to support the strikers as do all of the Brooklyn newspapers and—except for the *Times*—most of the New York press." Webb knew that part of the reason Toomey had agreed to see him was in hopes of wooing *Harper's* to the side of the railroad companies.

"The crowds are smaller, though, aren't they?" Toomey was smirking again.

"And do you believe that it's because they are now opposed to the strike, or because there are five thousand armed troops on the streets with orders to shoot down bystanders?"

"I suppose the militia *has* been an effective deterrent." Toomey's smirk turned to a full smile, exposed a neat row of yellow teeth.

"Would you care to comment on the killing of that ten-year-old boy recently? Do you think the shooting was justified?"

Toomey coughed. "Loss of life is tragic, of course. But remember: the militia is not in our employ, so we can not be held responsible for their actions. We had nothing to do with bringing in the Guardsmen. They came at the request of the civil government."

"Specifically at the request of Mayor Schieren," said Webb. "Do you attribute his request to the fact that he is a major shareholder in several of the Brooklyn trolley companies?"

No longer smiling, Toomey again had hold of his watch chain, rubbing his thumb along the gold links. "I attribute the mayor's actions to the fact that he is responsible for preserving order in the city."

"Have the troops brought order?"

"Not yet. Those strikers are acting criminally— cutting the electric lines and sabotaging the system. I don't know if you are aware of it, but only yesterday they completely shut down a De Kalb power station and tore up tracks on the Flatbush and Willoughby lines."

"I didn't know." Webb made a point of writing down the information, and Toomey appeared pleased.

"But the sabotage will be stopped," Toomey vowed. "And the perpetrators will be prosecuted for their crimes."

"It does appear certain that the strike is in its death throes," Webb said. "Even without the additional troops coming in. It's quite a change from the first days, when they had the streetcar lines completely shut down. To what do you attribute the change in fortune?"

"'Death throes,'" Toomey repeated. "I like that." A small smile of satisfaction briefly creased his face. "I attribute the change to several factors. Primarily, the public has realized what an essential service we provide. How can they travel without the railroad companies? We are much less expensive than hiring a hansom cab, and highly efficient in our operations." He spread his hands. "A trolley is cheap, fast, and can take you almost anywhere in the city."

"What about the safety issue?" Webb asked. "There *have* been an inordinate numbers of accidents on the Brooklyn lines in recent years—quite a few people injured or killed."

"I don't know what your definition of 'inordinate' is. People are injured in every form of transportation. Ferry boats sink, horses throw their riders, carriages and wagons collide. A train is a much more complicated piece of machinery than any of those, and there is a correspondingly greater risk." Toomey quickly added, "Of course we are always trying to improve the safety of our operations, though."

Webb again recorded his words. "You said you attribute the declining fortunes of the strikers to 'several factors,'" he reminded Toomey.

"Yes. Another one would be the violent nature that the Knights of Labor and their supporters have demonstrated."

"What acts in particular?"

"Overturning cars, tearing up tracks, blocking the lines. There has been a vicious assault on our property."

"Is that more violent than the shooting and bayoneting that the militia has been doing?"

"The militia came in to *quell* the violence—and they need to use superior force to do so. Remember, not only were there attacks on our property; railroad employees were assaulted, police officers were stoned, and that one patrolman was even shot and killed." He leaned back in his massive chair. "The militia has responded appropriately under the circumstances."

"Do you think that the additional troops are still needed now that the strike is almost over?"

"Oh yes. Order must be established completely and the strikers must be made to realize that their violent actions will not be tolerated in this city." The smirk returned. "In fact, I would venture to say that not only will the strike be over, but the Knights of Labor will cease to exist."

So that was the real goal, Webb realized: to crush the union for good. Realizing that his allotted time was almost up, he quickly went on to his next question. "You mentioned that the militia has done a good job. What do you think of the Brooklyn police?"

Toomey snorted. "They're useless. In the first days of the strike they stood idly by and let the strikers run wild."

"There's one of them whom I should think you'd be indebted to."

Toomey frowned in puzzlement.

Webb explained, "The shooting of Sergeant Lonnie Keck seems to have provided the impetus for bringing in the militia—and it's the militia that has effectively crushed the strike."

"Yes." Toomey adopted a mournful look. "That was a tragic example of how violent the strikers really are."

"Why assume it was a *striker* who killed him?"

"Of course it was. Who else—"

"Killing a police officer was *not* to the strikers' advantage—it would obviously rouse public sentiment against them."

Toomey was again working the watch chain. "Justifiably so."

"Yes, if they had done it. But there has been some speculation that the officer could have been killed by an agent of the railroad owners in order to make the strikers look bad and provide an excuse to bring in the troops."

His voice high again, Toomey squeaked, "That's outrageous. Who could think that we would—" His myopic eyes slowly focused on Webb, and he no doubt realized that the writer thought that it was indeed a possibility. He finally said, "Your time is up, Mr. Webb."

Webb could only hope that the statement referred merely to the time for the interview.

CHAPTER 20

Although he was going into one of the least cheerful places one could imagine, Buck Morehouse was positively buoyant as he walked through the door of the King's County Hospital morgue. He was back on the job, the job he wanted to do: investigating murder.

Stepping inside, Morehouse peeled off his overcoat and removed his derby, giving it a little spin in his hand before hanging it next to the coat. He took a deep breath; the smell of chemicals and death was noxious but the cool air in his lungs was bracing.

Apparently the body count was still high in Brooklyn, for the tables were all occupied and there were now several carts along the wall that also had human forms bulging up from under white linen sheets. Morehouse walked past them to the back of the room where Shannon Elswick was slouched in his desk chair staring absently at the wall through his tiny wire-rim spectacles. The deputy coroner had given Morehouse the briefest glance when he'd first walked in, then turned back to the wall without uttering a word.

Morehouse didn't recall seeing Elswick look so morose before. The detective had been planning to tell him that the tip on boxer Robbie Moore was a bum one, but instead he said, "From the look on your face, Shannon, I'm guessing one of these stiffs must have been a good friend of yours."

Elswick turned to Morehouse; there was no humor in his red, rubbery face. "No, worse. The parents of that ten-year-old boy came to claim his body today—they just left."

"Oh, damn." The detective was sorry he'd attempted a joke. "I sure came at a bad time."

"I tell you, Bucky, no matter how many years I do this, I'll never get used to the kids. The only thing sadder than doing an autopsy on a child is seeing the parents when they come to take their dead child away." He rubbed his hands on the front of his filthy black frock coat as if trying to wipe away the memory. "No child should have to die," he murmured.

"Hell, I'm sorry, Shannon." During his career, Morehouse had had the awful task of dealing with the deaths of children and could understand what his friend was feeling.

Elswick nodded, his thoughts obviously still directed inward. He suddenly sighed. "What I need is a snort."

The coroner's desk was a clutter, as was the table next to it that held a number of pasteboard boxes filled with the possessions of those who were at present laid out around the room. There were stacks of papers, some so high they were in danger of toppling; various medical implements, most as soiled as Elswick's frock coat; and specimen jars, some empty and many filled with fluid and containing body parts that Morehouse didn't even recognize as being human.

Elswick began rummaging. "I got a bottle around here some place." Failing to find it in his crammed desk drawers, he continued working his way through various piles. "Ah! Here it is." He pulled a bottle of Storm King Whiskey from behind a tall jar that contained one of the few things that Morehouse could recognize: a human hand that was missing its thumb.

The coroner next took a couple of dusty but relatively clean Mason Jars, and brought those to his desk along with the bottle. "Care to join me?" He uncorked the bottle.

The atmosphere wasn't one where Morehouse would typically want to ingest anything, but he was starting to get the taste of death in his mouth and was suddenly eager for something to take it away. "Yes, sure."

Elswick poured a healthy shot into each jar and the two of them drank the whiskey down. The bottle was offered again; Morehouse declined a second shot but Elswick immediately had another.

"I'm surprised you still had the kid," said Morehouse. "Thought he'd have been released right away."

"*I* wanted to." Elswick sighed and settled back in his chair. "Did my work immediately so the parents could bury their boy." He looked up at Morehouse sharply. "But your captain held things up."

"Sturup?"

"He wanted to keep the body in case more examinations were needed. And he wanted me to get the bullet out clean—to confirm it's the same kind of ammunition used by the militia." He shook his head. "As if there was any doubt what happened. A hundred people saw the sniper shoot that boy, and the Guard's commanding officer acknowledges it."

"Yeah," said Morehouse. "Sturup wants the soldier prosecuted for murder—as if there's really a chance of that. And if militiamen shoot anyone else he wants them arrested on the spot."

"I read that in the newspapers, but it seems foolish to me."

"Well, people hate the militia for what they've been doing, and Sturup is only going to make himself popular by doing this."

"Is he running for something?"

Morehouse shrugged. "He's always positioning himself to move up somehow. Thing is I have no idea where he's trying to move *to*."

"Save us from politicians," said Elswick, pouring himself another shot.

"And from cops who act like politicians." Morehouse accepted another one for himself. After they drank, he said, "I hate to put you back to work, but I'm investigating two murders."

"Who?" the coroner grunted.

"Vivian O'Connell. Killed in Washington Park a few nights ago. Beaten to death, I think."

"Oh yes. I still have her." Elswick pushed himself up from his desk. His legs were slightly unsteady as he led Morehouse to a table near the door of the morgue, checking name tags as he went. He pulled the sheet down to expose her round lifeless face. "Pretty woman. Damn shame."

"Cause of death?"

"Blow to the back of the head. My guess is a pipe— can't be sure, but it fits what I've seen before."

"Just the one blow?"

"That's all it took. Cracked her head in." Elswick grabbed hold of O'Connell's coppery hair, about to lift her head.

"That's all right. I believe you."

"Probably robbery," Elswick said. "There was no purse or even a coat or hat among her effects."

"Maybe." Morehouse wasn't sure, though. With so

many destitute people making Washington Park their home, she could just as likely have been robbed after death.

"Say, do you know who's going to claim her?" Elswick asked. "Pretty crowded here, as you can see. If nobody takes her body, she might have to be shipped off to potter's field."

"I don't know if she had any relatives. I'll try to find out and let you know." Morehouse was still staring at O'Connell's face; it looked so peaceful, but so unmistakably dead. It wasn't only children who should never have their lives taken so violently, he thought.

"Oh, you said there were *two* bodies you were interested in," Elswick reminded him.

"Yes, but you don't have the other one anymore."

Elswick looked around at the filled tables. "Don't be so sure. Seems like they're just gathering here."

"She was killed two years ago."

"*Two years?*" The coroner blinked rapidly behind his spectacles. "And you're just getting around to investigating the case now?"

"Better late than never."

"But what do you want from me?" Elswick hunched his shoulders. "She's long gone by now."

"I know, but I figured you could check your records."

Elswick sighed; Morehouse knew that he didn't like having to dig through paperwork—no surprise since it was so unorganized. "I suppose I could try." He moved back toward his desk with the detective following. "What's his name—or her name?"

"Her. A prostitute named Frenchy Sayre. Don't have much more information, but she was probably early twenties, and probably beaten to death."

Morehouse took a seat while the coroner rifled through stacks of papers and his desk drawers before

going to a file cabinet as a last resort. There were repeated murmurings of "It's gotta be . . ." but none of
them was followed by the retrieval of any documents.

"Sorry. I just don't have anything." Flushed from
the effort, and from the earlier whiskeys, Elswick sat
back down. "You didn't do the investigation?"

"No," Morehouse answered. "I don't believe there
ever was one."

"Strange." Elswick appeared perplexed. "Two years,
you say?"

"November of 'ninety-three."

"Let me check this." He tried another desk drawer
and pulled out a small ledger book. After turning
pages and running a forefinger along the entries, he
announced, "Here she is!"

"What is that?" Morehouse asked. "That's not an official report."

"No, these are my private notes."

"You keep private notes?"

Elswick shrugged. "Not really *private*. It's just that
things get busy here sometimes. So whenever a customer comes in, I do a quick examination and jot
down some preliminary notes in case I can't get to the
full autopsy for some time."

"There should still be an official report."

"Yes. The official autopsy is what goes into the
report, though; these notes are just for my reference."

"So what do you have on Sayre?"

"Her head was basically crushed."

"Like O'Connell's?" Morehouse wondered if there
was indeed a link between the two murders.

"No." Elswick was squinting to read his own handwriting. "I made a note here that there were multiple
fractures probably made by a brick—I must have noticed some brick dust or pieces in the wounds." He

tilted his head back. "I vaguely remember her, I think." After a struggle to recollect, he shook his head. "Sorry. It isn't coming to me." He smiled sheepishly and gestured at the whiskey bottle.

"That's all you have on her?"

"I'll look again for the report, but I just don't think it's here." He tapped a finger on his desk. "But I might . . ."

Morehouse thought he would be in for another long wait and a fruitless search, but Elswick found the paper he was looking for in only a few minutes.

"Not a report," Elswick said. "But I do keep a record of where the bodies go. And Sayre's . . ." He scanned the paper. "Ah. Hers was claimed by—huh—she was claimed by Miss Vivian O'Connell." He looked up at Morehouse. "Now, there's a coincidence."

"Thanks," Morehouse said. "If you could do another search for the autopsy report, I'd sure appreciate it."

The coroner promised that he would, but Morehouse doubted that it would ever be found.

Marshall Webb enjoyed having Rebecca's touch on his arm, even though their heavy winter garb made it barely perceptible. He also enjoyed being outdoors with her, temporarily free from the serious issues with which they too often had to grapple, and he was glad he was able to convince her to come with him today. The fact that it didn't take much convincing was an indication that she was pleased to get away with him for a while, too.

With Rebecca's hand in the crook of his elbow, the two of them ice-skated together, side by side, as closely as their bulky clothing would permit. The Central Park lake was crowded, and they had to thread their way around male skaters dressed in somber dark overcoats and black derbies, heavily bundled brightly clad children being pulled on sleds or tottering on double-bladed learning skates looking like newborn colts trying to walk, and several clusters of older men sliding heavy stones over the ice in games of curling. They also had to watch for older boys who delighted in swooping among the other skaters as fast as they could.

Those on this part of the lake were almost entirely male, and Webb was aware of looks—some disapproving, some curious, and some appreciative—cast in their direction. Women were supposed to skate at the north end of the lake, in the section reserved for their gender. Rebecca, however, went where she pleased and Webb wanted her with him.

Their progress was held up by the ice itself as much as by the crowds. It was rough, chewed up by a couple months of skating. The red ball that signaled that the ice was solid enough for safe skating had been hoisted in early December, and winter had remained so cold that it never had to be lowered. It was visible atop the bell tower of Belvedere Castle on Vista Rock, the highest point in Central Park. The only structure as prominently in view was Dakota Apartments, an odd, nine-story structure that looked like a cross between a Swiss chalet and a Renaissance French palace. Standing in a largely undeveloped area of Manhattan, at the corner at Seventy-second Street and Central Park West, the massive apartment house loomed over the lake and dominated the western skyline.

Webb and Rebecca skated leisurely, and chatted idly at infrequent intervals. Even at their slow speed, the cold wind in their faces made it difficult to keep their mouths open.

When Webb felt the small chunks of ice that his breath had formed on his mustache, he looked at Rebecca. Her face had gone from healthy pink to a brighter shade of red in the cheeks. "Are you cold?" he asked.

"Mm-hmm. A bit." She spoke through lips that she barely opened and steam came from her mouth.

It was more than just a bit, Webb was sure, and he steered their course toward one of the benches on the shore of the lake. Rebecca stumbled slightly when her skates hit ground, but he caught her easily and guided her onto the bench. Webb knelt at her feet and pulled the kid gloves off his hands so that he could remove the skates from her side-button boots. She tugged up the hem of her ankle-length heavy wool skirt to give him access.

As he fought with the first strap, his numb fingers trying to work the buckle, Webb said, "I suggest as soon as we have our skates off we get something hot to drink. Cider?"

Rebecca laughed. "As long it's laced with brandy."

Webb smiled, cracking the ice that had built up on his mustache. "I'm sure we can find something to warm you up."

After winning his battle with Rebecca's buckles, Webb removed his own skates and the two of them stood.

Rebecca stomped each of her feet a few times. "My toes are numb."

"I'll leave you here to dance for a moment while I get us something to drink," Webb said.

"Once again, I only get to dance by myself," she teased.

Webb made an exaggeratedly gallant bow. "Only because if I tried to dance with you, you would have no toes left to go numb." His refusal to venture onto a dance floor was something she'd been trying to change for a couple of years—with no success.

From a nearby pushcart vendor, Webb purchased some fried oysters and two cups of hot apple cider. The seller offered to "fortify" the cider for an extra fifteen cents a cup, but Webb declined. It was risky enough to eat food from New York street vendors; there was no telling what kind of chemicals they might dispense under the guise of "alcohol."

Carefully juggling the provisions, he returned to Rebecca. "No brandy in this, I'm afraid, but I'm sure we can find a café where we can warm up and get something stronger."

"That sounds good." She took a sip from her cup. "This will tide me over for now. Thank you."

They walked to one of the roadways, where Webb hailed a carriage and gave the driver instructions to take them to Cerdeira's, a café on Madison near the south end of the park. The two of them huddled in the back of the carriage, a lap robe draped over them, and finished off the oysters and cider.

"So, how are things at the house?" Webb asked. They never could go very long without discussing their work.

"Good. One of the girls—Becky Forbes—has left. She's gotten a job in Syracuse working in a ladies' hat shop."

"That *is* good news."

Rebecca nodded. "It should be very nice for her." She looked up at Webb. "But mostly I've been thinking about what to do with Sayre House."

Webb suspected as much. "What *will* you do?"

"It's difficult to say." She tugged the robe a little higher on her lap. "I'm finding it hard to think about it without thinking about Vivian O'Connell. I *need* to find out what happened to her."

"I spoke with the detective again—Buck Morehouse—and he's able to investigate now. In fact, he's working on both Vivian O'Connell's murder *and* Frenchy Sayre's."

There was a flash of hope in Rebecca's eyes and Webb hoped he hadn't given her false hope. "I hope he finds something," she said. "I've been thinking, and I'm sure Miss O'Connell was in that park to meet someone."

"What makes you think so?"

"Well, I was wondering why she would have been in Washington Park by herself late at night. Granted, I didn't know her well, but from what I saw of her it wasn't something she would do."

"Why not?"

"For one thing, she lived and worked in Brooklyn for years so she knew full well that the park is a dangerous place for a woman alone at night. So she had to be *with* somebody."

"Makes sense," Webb conceded.

"And it had to be somebody she didn't want to be seen with."

He didn't see the sense in that conclusion. "Why?"

"She always traveled in style, in her carriage. And she liked hotels and restaurants. If she was entertaining someone, it wouldn't have been in Washington Park unless she wanted the meeting to be secret."

"And whoever she was meeting with killed her?"

Rebecca pursed her lips. "Possibly. Or the person she was with might have at least seen who did do it. Either way, I think it's important to find out why she was there."

"Morehouse did give me the name of someone who might be able to provide some information about Miss O'Connell."

"Who?"

"Nancy Johnson. She's a—she runs a—" Webb was having difficulty. "She's in the same business that Miss O'Connell was in. Runs a house on De Kalb, and according to Morehouse she took on most of the girls who used to work for O'Connell when she retired. I was going to try to see her tomorrow."

Rebecca nodded thoughtfully.

Webb went on, "There's some discouraging news, too, though."

She looked at him expectantly.

"Morehouse was at the coroner's yesterday and they can't find their records on Frenchy Sayre. With no police file and no autopsy report, it might be impossible for him to get anywhere in solving her murder." He thought to himself, but didn't say aloud, that there was probably little to no chance of finding Sayre's killer even with the records.

"No records?"

"No."

"I *hate* that. It's like she never existed."

"Morehouse also had a question."

"What's that?"

"He says that no one has claimed Vivian O'Connell's body. Did she ever mention any family to you? Someone we can contact so they can bury her?"

Rebecca shook her head no. "Come to think of it, she never told me much at all about her personal life."

"Maybe this Miss Johnson will know."

"Yes. She's definitely worth speaking with." Rebecca laid a hand on Webb's forearm. "And, Marshall . . ."

"Yes?"

"I want to be the one to speak with her."

Webb thought it over and decided that it might

make sense for a woman to interview the madam. "Very well," he said. "You can do it."

There was a twinkle in Rebecca's eyes, and he realized that she hadn't been asking for his consent; when she'd said she "wanted" to speak with Nancy Johnson she meant that she was "going" to be the one to speak with her.

CHAPTER 21

The next morning, Rebecca was alone in a hansom cab traveling northeast on De Kalb Avenue. With her contacts, it hadn't been difficult to learn the location of Nancy Johnson's house of prostitution; apparently it was an institution of some renown here in the City of Homes and Churches.

As the cabdriver prodded his horse along through the heavy street traffic, Rebecca stared out the window. The sidewalks were lined with blue-garbed soldiers, their ranks swelled by several thousand in response to the mayor's request for more troops. Other than the soldiers, there were few pedestrians on the street and most windows were shuttered—no one wanted to risk being shot. In along the rails in the middle of the street, the trolleys rolled without incident. They were also virtually devoid of passengers. Although the strike was for all purposes squashed, many Brooklynites were vowing not to ride the trains as long as their city was occupied by state militia.

A mile and a half outside the heart of downtown Brooklyn, near Nostrand Avenue, the cabbie pulled over to the curb. "You sure this is the place you want?" he called to Rebecca.

She checked the address she had written down, and looked at the modest three-story brick dwelling. She'd half expected to see a glowing red light at the doorway, but the house appeared no different from the other residential homes nearby. "This is the place," she answered.

After paying the driver, Rebecca went to the door and rapped with the brass knocker.

After a considerable wait, the door was opened by a sleepy-eyed young colored woman in a disheveled maid's uniform. She greeted Rebecca with "We ain't open yet," and yawned.

"My name is Rebecca Davies and I'd like to see Miss Johnson, if I may. Is she in?"

"She don't see *nobody* this early."

"It's important," Rebecca pressed. "Please tell her I'm a friend of Vivian O'Connell and I need to speak with her."

"Well . . . I'll see. What's your name again?"

Rebecca repeated her own name as well as Vivian O'Connell's a couple more times, hoping the sleepy maid could keep the two of them straight. She was then left to wait outside on the stoop while the maid again promised to give the message to her boss.

It was a good five minutes before the door opened again, and the maid reported, "Miss Johnson says she'll see you. You can come in and wait in the parlor if you want."

Rebecca followed her into a quiet house that was richly furnished. The decor wasn't cheap or tawdry, although the spacious parlor did resemble a crimson cocoon. The carpeting, wallpaper, and plush sofas were all of that color. There was little relief from the red except for a glossy black baby grand piano in one corner, a polished mahogany bar along the back wall, and some rather suggestive oil paintings in gilded frames hanging on the walls.

The maid left Rebecca alone, making no offer to take her coat or provide refreshments. Rebecca took off her own hat and coat and hung them on a rack next to a mirror by the door. She then sat in a fake Louis XIV armchair after first checking that the upholstery was clean.

After another wait, a rather stout woman of about sixty in a bright floral wrapper came into the room. She didn't appear any more awake than the maid. Her pale eyes were haggard, there was no powder or rouge on her droopy face, and her long, unnaturally blond hair hadn't yet been fixed. "Rebecca Davis?" she asked in a hoarse voice.

"Dav-*ies*," Rebecca corrected. "Miss Johnson?" The woman's shape was so similar to Vivian O'Connell's that Rebecca wondered if there were any skinny madams.

"That's me."

"Thank you so much for seeing me. I'm sorry I didn't call ahead, but I couldn't get a telephone listing for you." She hesitated. "I hope I didn't come at too inconvenient a time." She had assumed that the house would have its least business in the morning and that it was therefore the time when the proprietress would most likely be available for a discussion.

Johnson waved off the apology and sat down on a sofa. "We don't open for business until lunchtime. I'm just not usually up this early." She turned her head toward the open doorway and bellowed, "Annie!"

The maid soon appeared. "Yes, ma'am?"

"I need coffee and cigarettes—now." As an afterthought, she asked Rebecca, "Can I offer you anything?"

"Tea if you have it."

Johnson added that to the order, and when the maid left to comply, she called after her again, "Bring some chocolate cake, too! There better be some left in the icebox or somebody's gonna have hell to pay!" To Rebecca, she said, "Hope you don't mind if I have my breakfast."

"Not at all."

A package of Old Judge cigarettes was delivered first, along with the information that the coffee was brewing and the water boiling for tea. Johnson held the cigarette package out, offering one to Rebecca, who declined. The madam then lit one up for herself, inhaled deeply, and blew the smoke out from a corner of her mouth in a decidedly unladylike manner.

Cigarettes were a disgusting habit for anyone, Rebecca thought. Although she was progressive in her thoughts on what women should be able to do, she preferred to see the habit remain a rarity for those of her sex.

After another drag, Johnson asked, "How did you know Vivian O'Connell? Did you work for her?"

"No," Rebecca hastened to reply. "I run a shelter for young women in Manhattan—Colden House. Miss O'Connell came to see me about helping her start a home in Brooklyn for former prostitutes. We worked together on it until she was killed."

"Oh yes. She told me she was opening a place in Flatbush—what was she going to call it?"

"Sayre House. When did she tell you that?"

"Only a few days before she was killed. Tried to talk me into giving her a donation to get the place started."

"Did you?"

Johnson shook her head no.

"You didn't think it was a good idea?"

After a drag on her cigarette, Johnson answered, "My first thought was that it was a *good* idea—a good way to open a house that's out of the way and get girls to work for her cheap."

Rebecca didn't understand.

"With this economy, we're all pressed to save money wherever we can. Vivian could have set up a profitable operation for herself—she's a helluva smart operator and always managed to make money."

Now it was clear. "You really thought she was planning to make Sayre House a brothel?"

Johnson shrugged her shoulders, producing ripples in her flesh. "Why? You think she was on the level?"

The thought that O'Connell hadn't been honest with her hadn't occurred to Rebecca before. Now she considered the possibility, and after brief thought realized that the planned layout for Sayre House wouldn't have served as a brothel; it was indeed intended as a shelter. "She was telling you the truth," Rebecca finally answered.

The maid returned with the coffee, tea, and cake, served them clumsily, and left them alone again.

After allowing her hostess to get her first bites of cake and a few sips of coffee, which she took black, Rebecca asked her, "I only knew Miss O'Connell briefly. What can you tell me about her?"

Johnson paused to dab at some chocolate frosting that had dripped onto her chin and lick it off her fingertip. "Vivian ran a good house—clean, safe, and very profitable. I don't know how she could have sold out like she did when it was doing so well."

"She told me it was because of the death of Frenchy Sayre. She just didn't have the heart to keep the business going after that."

"Yes, I heard that." Johnson put her fork down long

enough to take one more drag on her cigarette before stubbing it out in the ashtray. "She certainly was close with that girl."

"You said she 'sold out.' I thought she just retired."

"A lot of her girls came here afterward. And I had to pay her a pretty penny to get them."

"She *sold* you her girls?" That was slavery, Rebecca thought, horrified at the idea.

"No, not like you're thinking. It was more of a 'finder's fee.' I got some good, experienced girls that she recommended and that's worth something—like I said, she's a good businesswoman. I also bought her customer list."

Rebecca took a sip of tea. "From what you knew of Vivian O'Connell, who would want to kill her?"

Johnson paused from her renewed assault on the cake and reached for another cigarette. "I don't know. She didn't run a crooked joint—nobody got robbed in her place—so there shouldn't have been any unhappy customers." She lit up the cigarette. "And she treated her girls well—*too* well, as far as I'm concerned, because they came here expecting me to treat them the same." A stream of smoke was exhaled in a sigh. "I honestly don't know who would have wanted to kill Vivian. Maybe it was a mugger who didn't even know who she was."

Rebecca conceded that was a possibility and didn't mention that she thought it unlikely. "What about Frenchy Sayre, the girl who was killed two years ago?" she asked. "Did you know her?"

"Only by name and reputation."

"What reputation?"

Johnson smiled slyly. "She was supposed to be a prodigy at her particular specialty."

Rebecca nodded. She'd already heard of Sayre's talents; what she wanted to know was what the person was like. "What about the girls you got from Miss O'Connell? Are there any here who could tell me about her?"

"The girls should be sleeping now—we had a busy night last night, and there should be a full house tonight, too." Johnson suddenly sat a bit straighter. "You know who you should talk to is Sarah Fredrich— she was supposed to be good friends with Frenchy."

"When can I speak with her?"

"You'd have to find her first."

"She's missing?" Rebecca had a sudden fear that Frenchy Sayre and Vivian O'Connell might not be the only murdered prostitutes.

"Sarah quit on me." From the tone of Johnson's voice she considered it an act of betrayal.

"Do you know where she is now?"

"I think she went to Manhattan."

That was little help; New York had more whore-houses than trolley stops. "Do you have *any* idea where in Manhattan?" Rebecca asked.

"No, but it's a safe bet that it's some place expensive. She always thought she was some kind of princess and should command a high price." Johnson picked up her plate again and began scraping up the chocolate remains with her fork.

Rebecca stood. "Well, again, thank you for seeing me." She took a calling card from her purse and handed it to Johnson. "If you think of anything, could you please give me a call?"

Johnson promised that she would and added, "I sure hope they find whoever killed Vivian. Dead whores are bad for business—the girls get skittish and the men stay away."

Prostitution apparently wasn't a business that involved a lot of sentiment, Rebecca thought.

CHAPTER 22

Although it was nearly noon, Marshall Webb hadn't dressed yet. He'd spent the entire morning in his apartment, wearing pajamas and a robe, working at his massive rolltop desk, and pouring black coffee into a stomach that had only had a piece of toast for breakfast.

Webb was trying to make sense of all that had happened during the week for his latest strike article for *Harper's*. As he sorted through his notes scattered about the desk, he had doubts of ever being able to present a logical sequence of events. The fault wasn't really his, he thought, though—it was simply that there *was* no sense to what had transpired.

While agreeing to negotiate with the strikers through the State Board of Arbitration, the Brooklyn railroad companies began importing workers from as far away as Pittsburgh to run their trolleys. Then, during meetings at the St. George Hotel with the union's Executive Committee and the Arbitration Commissioners, agreement was reached that wages would be increased, with some railroad men to receive wages as high as two dollars a day. When the union men agreed to return to work, however, the railroad presidents announced that their jobs were already taken by the newly hired employees from out of state; the rationale was that since the strikers had refused to report for work, the new hires had now established seniority. The meeting ended with the union negotiators feeling betrayed, the Arbitration Commissioners dumbfounded, and the smug railroad owners refusing to engage in any more discussions on the matter.

The strikers subsequently stepped up their efforts at sabotage, cutting lines so frequently that the railroads gave up on running any trolleys at night and could only get a few lines operational during the day. The union also succeeded in convincing many of the scabs to defect to their side, and the railroads were left with little manpower to run their trains.

Just when the strikers appeared to be getting the upper hand, the additional troops came marching in. With seven thousand National Guardsmen patrolling the city, ten of them assigned to each car and fifty to each power station, car barn, and horse stable, the sabotage was effectively stopped. Meanwhile the railroad owners had stepped up their recruiting efforts and were bringing in more replacement workers from all over the Northeast.

Webb was just writing about what might ultimately prove to be the death knell for the strikers—soldiers from the National Guard's Seventh Regiment, under orders from their sword-wielding colonel, fired a volley of bullets into a protesting crowd outside the Halsey Street stables, sending two citizens to the morgue and several more to the hospital—when the telephone rang.

Annoyed at the interruption, Webb tried not to let it show in his voice in case the caller was Rebecca. "Hello?"

"Marshall! So glad I caught you at home!" It was Lawrence Pritchard's reedy voice coming through the receiver.

"Lawrence . . ." Webb wasn't expecting the dime novel editor's call. "I *am* planning to get to work on that book for you."

"That's why I'm calling—to thank you." Pritchard sounded positively cheerful. "And I *love* your idea for the novel."

"You do?" Webb didn't understand; he had no idea what Pritchard was talking about.

"Yes, it's wonderful. I'm so glad you decided to try writing a detective story"—Pritchard cleared his throat, which sounded like a burst of static on the line—"as I suggested."

"Well, I'm *considering* it."

"According to a fellow named Oscar Sturup, you're already working on the book."

"Sturup? You spoke with Oscar Sturup?"

"Yes, he telephoned me yesterday. He's a captain with the Brooklyn Police Department."

Webb chose not to mention that he knew full well who Oscar Sturup was. "Why did he call *you*?"

"He wanted to know if one of my writers—a David Byrd—was working on a book for me."

"He didn't mention my real name?"

"No, and I didn't give it—I know you like your anonymity." Another cough crackled in the receiver. "I merely confirmed that David Byrd was indeed one of my writers and currently working on a novel for Pritchard's Dime Library. Of course, I feared that might only be wishful thinking on my part. . . ."

"I *will* write another book for you." Webb was slightly exasperated with how much reassurance Pritchard needed. "I'm still working on the strike for *Harper's* right now."

"Oh, I understand," Pritchard promptly replied. "And do take your time—from what Captain Sturup told me, it sounds like your story will certainly be worth waiting for."

"What exactly did he tell you?"

"He said you're working on a story about Jack the Ripper being in New York, killing prostitutes in Brooklyn." Pritchard hesitated and Webb could imagine him adjusting his pince-nez on the bridge of his nose. "As a matter of fact, this Sturup fellow sounded concerned about that—said he was worried it might make his police department look bad. And he tried pressing me for details about what was going to be in the book."

"What did you tell him?"

"Since I didn't *have* any details, I played coy. I told him we didn't want to reveal any details ahead of the book's publication because we don't want to diminish the impact when it comes out."

"You think he believed you?"

Pritchard hesitated. "Yes, I believe he did."

It sounded to Webb as if the story he had told Buck Morehouse to give Sturup was working. But maybe too well.

The editor spoke up again. "So . . . when do you think you'll have this book finished?"

Webb briefly debated whether to tell his editor the truth; he decided against it in case Sturup should contact Pritchard again. "As soon as the strike is over— and that looks like it's going to be any day."

After Webb told Pritchard that the sooner he could get back to finishing his current article for *Harper's* the sooner he could write the novel, the editor quickly brought the conversation to a close.

Webb freshened his coffee and went back to his desk, but he didn't immediately resume writing about the strike. Instead, he pondered the reason Oscar Sturup had contacted Pritchard. The police captain had to be worried about something; why else would he be checking up?

Webb was impressed by Buck Morehouse's capacity for ingesting large amounts of food and beer. It was no wonder that he had never seen the detective in clothes that fit him properly; every coat and vest he owned must be strained to the breaking point in the effort to contain his protruding belly.

The two of them had agreed that it would be best if they no longer met in Brooklyn, so this evening Morehouse had come over to Manhattan for dinner at Webb's invitation.

Webb recommended Schmalstig's, an atmospheric German restaurant in Union Square. The sausages, kraut, and spatzel were savory and dark beer flowed like rivers from the taps. They sat at a quiet corner table that was of plain wood with no cloth to hide the names that had been carved in its top over the years. Fresh sawdust covered the floor and around the walls were flags and heraldic designs of various German states and cities.

Buck Morehouse sat against the wall, under the blue and white flag of Bavaria. He was belching from the enormous amount of food he'd already stuffed into his stomach, but eying the remaining sausages on his platter as hungrily as if he hadn't eaten in a week. The detective took a deep breath, a healthy draught of his third stein of Munchener, and poked his fork into one of the sausages.

Webb decided they'd better get to the topic of discussion before Morehouse burst. "Your Captain Sturup is a worried man," he said.

"Worried about what?" Morehouse asked through a mouthful of half-chewed bratwurst.

Webb reported what Pritchard had told him about the police captain's telephone call.

The detective smiled. "I still can't believe Sturup bought that Jack the Ripper story. But I guess maybe he's really concerned that you—or 'David Byrd'— might write something that will make the department or his precinct look bad."

"Perhaps," Webb agreed. "But I don't think so. The Ripper notion is patently absurd—the prostitutes in London were cut to pieces, and both Frenchy Sayre and Vivian O'Connell were beaten to death. A dime novel trying to make a link between the London and Brooklyn killings would obviously be taken as fiction— no reason for him to worry."

Morehouse looked a bit perplexed. Stumped for something to say, he instead put his mouth to use drinking a long swallow of beer.

"He's checking up on something," Webb continued. "At first, I thought perhaps he just wanted to check that you hadn't made up the story about the book to get your duty assignment changed. Then I wondered if his concern was that a writer looking into matters in his precinct might find something that Sturup didn't want to become public knowledge."

"That could be," Morehouse agreed. "You know we can't always do things by the book. So of course there's things we wouldn't want to come out."

"Graft would be one of those things, I'm sure."

The detective cocked his head. "I was never in-volved in none of that—and I got the empty pockets to prove it."

"From what I hear," said Webb, "Oscar Sturup takes payoffs and that dead sergeant, Lonnie Keck, was his bagman."

Morehouse didn't reply.

"I also hear that the boss who runs things in Brooklyn is a fellow named Jason Ward, who works out of a joint in Red Hook. I thought I might go see him about Sturup."

"You don't want to do that."

"Why not?"

"Jason Ward is a powerful man and a ruthless man. He's got his hooks in every racket in the city, and he keeps control of them by killing anyone who might cause him a problem."

"I've dealt with ruthless men before," Webb answered calmly. "Tammany Hall doesn't play by the Marquis of Queensbury rules, either."

"But there's no point," said Morehouse. "Everybody knows about the graft—it's just the way business is done in the city. Hell, it's the way things are done in *every* city. Why would Sturup be worried about something that's an *open* secret anyway?" The detective's brow furrowed. "Unless . . ."

"Unless what?"

"Well, he's up to something. I figured he was planning a run for politics or something when he came out with those orders to arrest Guardsmen—it had to be to get the public on his side." Morehouse shrugged. "But I don't know for sure. Sturup is always planning something to improve his own position."

"And you don't think he'd be worried about the press learning that he's corrupt?"

"Don't think so. It would be like learning that there are gambling joints and whorehouses operating in the city—everybody knows about it."

"All the publicity about what happened to corrupt police officers in New York should have him scared." Webb hated to think that all his work to detail the operations of Tammany Hall and their pawns in the police department wouldn't serve as a deterrent to others.

Morehouse shook his head. "Actually the Tammany

scandal took the heat *off* of Brooklyn. You got the big fish—and the big story. Nobody's much interested in the small fish after that."

Webb was silent. The more he considered the detective's words, the more he realized that there was sense to what he said. And if true it was utterly discouraging. Switching topics, Webb asked, "Have you gotten anywhere with the O'Connell or Sayre murders?"

"Nowhere to speak of. Tell you the truth, I don't think there's any chance with Sayre—the case is too cold."

"What about O'Connell?" Webb remembered Rebecca's idea that O'Connell had been in the park to meet someone. "Did you check to see if she had an appointment book? Maybe she was meeting someone in Washington Park."

Morehouse took another swallow of beer. "I looked through everything in her suite at the Fields—she paid through the end of the month, so all her possessions are still there. No notes, no calendar." He ran the back of his hand over his wet lips. "Could be she got a phone call to meet somebody there, but no way to tell about that now."

"What are you going to do next?"

"Basic footwork. I plan to be at the park every night around the same time she was killed. Talk to everyone who's there and ask if they saw or heard anything when O'Connell was killed."

"That doesn't sound very promising."

"It isn't. Anyone who's in that park at that time of night isn't likely to be forthcoming about what they were doing there." Morehouse looked longingly at the last sausage, then sighed in surrender and looked back up at Webb. "What's next for you?"

Webb thought about it. "I'm not sure." But he still thought that he wanted to know more about Oscar Sturup.

CHAPTER 23

Buck Morehouse didn't consider himself to be a demanding man. He lived a simple life, content to make a one-room walk-up apartment on Myrtle Avenue his home, satisfied with the simple hearty food served in working-class saloons, and resigned to the fact that he would never achieve a higher position than his current rank with the Brooklyn Police Department.

He didn't expect much of life. But was it too much to ask that he could at least park his rear end on a decent chair?

Morehouse looked about his tiny drab office in the Second Precinct station house. He didn't mind that it had been furnished with discards that had to be retrieved from a storage area in the basement. The drawers of his scarred oak desk stuck and the battered pine file cabinet was missing one drawer entirely. He did have an adequate desk chair, though. Until today, that is. Since the last time that he'd been in his office, someone had stolen it and left a slat-back chair with a cracked seat and one short leg as a replacement.

The detective shifted his weight to and fro, making the chair legs clack on the floor as they hit. As he kept slamming down, he grew more and more aggravated with the theft. Then, staring absently at the files and papers on his desktop, he began to rock more easily, without bringing the legs all the way down.

As he rocked idly, Morehouse considered his recent conversation with Marshall Webb. The detective wondered why he had been so defensive when Webb had brought up the possibility of Captain Sturup fearing exposure of precinct operations. There was no reason to defend Sturup; Morehouse had never particularly liked or respected the captain—although he had to admit that he admired Oscar Sturup's innate political talents, which the captain always employed to maneuver himself into positions from which he could better his personal prospects.

Perhaps his reaction to Webb's statements was reflex on Morehouse's part. It had become ingrained in him through decades on the force that those who carried a police badge stuck together. As Morehouse had commented to Webb, "We can't always do things by the book." Probably every officer had had to employ personal judgment and do something that went against regulations. It was only a few weeks ago that Morehouse himself had bribed the deputy coroner into attributing the stabbing death of the vicious mugger Anthony "Tony the Hammer" Aspesi to "exposure." So they all had their secrets, and each officer had to live with his decisions. As for Morehouse, he believed that on the whole he helped protect the welfare of the city, and he had no trouble sleeping at night.

Having mollified himself, the detective looked over at the slim pile of papers on his desk. With no strong leads, Morehouse had undertaken a methodical approach to investigating the murder of Vivian O'Connell. He had spoken with all the beat cops who patrolled the area of Washington Park, and obtained the names or nicknames of all those whom they knew to live in the park or frequent it. Then he pulled arrest records for those who had them—a considerable number since the park was a regular place of business for streetwalkers, muggers, and pickpockets. It was now his task to go through the files and identify those who had the most violent tendencies—the ones who were most likely to kill. He leaned forward and lurched suddenly as his wobbly chair again clattered.

Annoyed, Morehouse tore off the blank bottom half of an arrest sheet and folded it over and over. He got down on his knees and shoved the paper wad under the short chair leg. It was too thick, so he ripped off a few of the folded pieces and tried wedging it again.

"I don't expect you to stand at attention when I come in," came a terse voice from behind him, "but I don't want to be faced with your fat ass, either."

Morehouse scrambled to his feet. "Sorry, Captain. I was just . . . the chair wasn't . . ." He smiled sheepishly. "Sorry, sir."

Sturup hadn't actually come into his office; there wasn't room, so the captain stood in the doorway, tall and straight. "I came for a progress report."

"On . . . ?"

"The cases we discussed, of course."

"Yes. Well, to be honest, sir, I haven't been able to get very far yet. No solid leads on the Vivian O'Connell murder and the Frenchy Sayre case is even colder than she is."

Sturup's stern expression actually softened slightly. "And what about that writer—Mr. Byrd. Have you heard anything more from him?"

Morehouse thought quickly. "Yes, he telephoned me. Wanted some information—"

"You didn't—"

"I didn't tell him anything. Except that the cases are under active investigation by the police department and that we can't reveal any details."

The captain nodded thoughtfully. "Good," he murmured. "Very good."

"He sounded awful frustrated by that," Morehouse added.

Sturup nodded again. "How do you plan to proceed in the investigations from here?"

Morehouse was continuing to think as quickly as he could, and assessing the captain's reactions as thoroughly as possible without appearing to do so. "Well, to be honest, I don't know that I can go much further on the O'Connell and Sayre cases—I just don't have anything to go on. But I'm still a bit worried about this Byrd fellow—he might increase his efforts now that he knows we're investigating. So I've been thinking of trying something that you might not want me to."

Sturup frowned. "What is it?"

"I've checked, and there have been several other prostitutes murdered in Brooklyn over the past few years. Not in our precinct, though. I thought I might look into those a little—just enough to put Mr. Byrd on their scent and maybe keep him away from our precinct for a while. That's if I have your permission to look into crimes that really aren't our cases."

The captain pondered that for a moment; Morehouse thought there was relief more than concern in the man's dark, intelligent eyes. "Yes, that might be worthwhile," Sturup finally conceded. "Just be sure you don't step on anyone's toes—I don't want to get any complaints from other captains about you nosing around their turf uninvited."

"I'll be careful of that."

"Very well." Sturup turned and was already walking away when he added, "Carry on, then, Detective."

Morehouse watched him go, then sat down in his chair, which was now stable. He looked at the files on his desk, and briefly debated getting started on reviewing them. He decided that as a last resort he might go back to the methodical approach, but in all probability Marshall Webb had been correct—it was most likely that Vivian O'Connell had gone to the park to meet someone. Finding that person was the key, not going through files of the petty criminals who roamed the park.

Besides, more intriguing than the prostitute killings was Captain Sturup's behavior. The man had actually been relieved to hear Morehouse's claim of making no headway. And his agreement to divert "David Byrd's" attentions to crimes outside the Second Precinct was peculiar as well.

Morehouse got to thinking about Marshall Webb's contention that Sturup was hiding something. The detective was beginning to believe there might be something to it, and he wondered what it was. Whatever Sturup was up to, it seemed clear that he did not really want the murders of the prostitutes to be the subject of serious investigation either by Morehouse or the dime novel writer.

He forced open the tight top drawer of his desk, reached into a jar of gumdrops, and popped half a dozen into his mouth. As he chewed, he continued to mull things over. One of the things he pondered was that although he had gotten the Anthony Aspesi killing to be deemed "exposure," there was still a file on the man's death. He didn't know how one could get the paperwork to disappear.

Morehouse finally decided on his next step. He

would check with Shannon Elswick and see if the deputy coroner had been able to unearth the Frenchy Sayre file yet.

The four-floor library of the American Museum of Natural History, always a peaceful place, was even quieter than usual. One old man, who looked like a vagrant, was at a table in the corner, hunched over and using a thick leather-bound book for a pillow as he slept. Drool ran from the corner of his mouth onto the binding of the book.

Webb took a random volume from a bookcase and went to another table, where Danny Macklin appeared about to join the other patron in slumber. The short, stocky Tammany sachem had a folio-sized book open on the table in front of him, but his head was tilted back and his eyes were half closed. It was a most unappealing sight; the nostrils of Macklin's red pug nose looked like caverns, with black hair for stalactites, and his mouth was slack, exposing his bad teeth.

"Sorry to interrupt your nap," said Webb.

Macklin started and his breath caught in a swallowed snort. "Wasn't sleeping," he mumbled. He sat upright, shook his ruddy head to clear it, tugged at the upturned collar of his overcoat, and adjusted his cloth cap so that it was tilted down. "Was just restin' my eyes."

"Yes, of course." Webb smiled.

"It's these books," Macklin grumbled, tapping a finger on the open folio. "There's too many words in them and not enough pictures." He looked around the room. "I don't want to meet here no more."

"Where would you prefer?" Webb hoped that the

sachem didn't mean that he didn't want to meet with Webb again at all.

"Downstairs—second floor. I saw they got some dragon bones or somethin' down there. I wanna see the bones."

That would be almost as removed from prying eyes as this spot, Webb was sure, and he agreed to make that their next rendezvous location. "But as long as we're here now, can we talk?"

"Might as well," Macklin agreed. "Why'd you wanna see me?"

"I need some information about a Brooklyn police captain."

"Oscar Sturup?"

Webb was surprised that Macklin could name the subject of his interest. "How did . . . ?"

Macklin shrugged. "Don't got to be no college boy to add two and two. What, you think I don't know things?"

Webb knew Macklin was no college boy. They had both grown up in Five Points, the toughest slums in New York, and got educated in ways that no professor would consider. And it was that kind of education that made Danny Macklin such a useful resource. "I *know* you know things," Webb replied with a smile. "I don't come to see you for the pleasure of your company."

Macklin made a show of pouting. "Now you've hurt my feelings."

Webb chuckled softly. "So, what made you think I was interested in Oscar Sturup?"

"You were asking about Brooklyn police captains last time we met. And Sturup's name has been coming up a lot lately. You still fussin' about whether they take a little graft over there?"

"I'm not sure," Webb admitted. "What do you mean about Sturup's name coming up?"

"He's been in the news—makin' those threats to arrest militiamen." Macklin shook his head with admiration. "The man knows how to curry favor with the public. I'll give him that."

"You hear anything else about Sturup?"

Macklin hesitated; Webb was sure he was calculating how much to reveal. "This *ain't* for publication, right? Just between us."

"It isn't for a story," answered Webb. "I really need to know whatever you can tell me about him."

"All right. Long as we understand each other."

Webb nodded in agreement.

Macklin slid the folio aside and folded his arms on the table. "Here's how it is: everybody's makin' plans for the new city government, and it looks like Sturup is gonna have a place in it."

"He's running for something?" The posturing about arresting militiamen certainly smacked of a political ploy.

"Nah, he'll be appointed."

"To what?"

"The new police department of 'Greater New York.' There's gonna be six inspectors that'll rank just below the police chief and his deputy. The boys in Brooklyn are gonna get one of those inspector slots."

"The 'boys'? You mean the political bosses—like Jason Ward." That was the Brooklyn power broker Macklin had mentioned last time.

Macklin nodded. "Yeah. We're givin' them one position. And you're right: Ward gets to choose the man."

"I'm surprised Tammany Hall is giving anything up to Brooklyn. I thought you'd defend your turf."

"Ah, but if we can *get* more than we *give*, that's good

business, isn't it?" A self-satisfied grin broke over the sachem's red face.

"What are you getting?"

Macklin hesitated. "No offense, but I'd rather not go into particulars as to that point. Let's just say that consolidation means a *lot* of restructuring—police, transportation, public works, you name it. And negotiations are under way to get advantageous deals worked out and divvy up the take. Part of the negotiation is that Brooklyn gets an inspector."

Webb was disheartened. After all his work to expose the crooked dealings of Tammany Hall, all that had happened was some public officials lost their jobs. Now the backroom bosses were back to their old ways, only with an even bigger pie to "divvy." It was hopeless to get New York to function for the benefit of its citizens rather than for the profit of those who used the municipal government to manipulate shady deals and operate payoff schemes. He knew for certain that he would no longer pursue the kind of investigations for *Harper's* that he had before. If this was all that resulted from his efforts, he was better off writing lurid novels for Lawrence Pritchard's Dime Library.

Macklin interrupted his thoughts. "You're quiet."

"Sorry. Just thinking." Webb then asked, "Why Sturup? How did he get chosen?"

"I'm not sure exactly. Like I said, the choice was Jason Ward's. The only thing we required was that he be clean. Gotta keep up appearances, you know, especially after the kind of publicity we been gettin' the last year or so." He glowered at Webb, who was responsible for much of that unfavorable publicity.

Webb knew that Macklin didn't really hold a grudge, though; the sachem had actually provided Webb with some of the information, especially if it reflected badly on his rivals in the Tammany organization. "But you told me last time that all the captains over there take payoffs. If that's true, then Oscar Sturup is *not* clean. And if Jason Ward is getting a cut, he knows Sturup doesn't meet your requirement. So why are you going along with him?"

Macklin smiled. "Sturup's clean enough. The public doesn't mind a little graft here and there—it's what greases the wheels and gets things done. But Ward assures us that Sturup has no major problems that can embarrass us, and with that publicity he got about arresting militiamen he's something of a hero over there now. Makes him a good choice, far as I can tell."

"Do you know anything else about him?" Webb asked.

Macklin appeared to think for a moment. "Nope. Just what I read in the papers and the fact that Jason Ward vouches for him."

Webb knew that Ward must have confidence in Sturup; vouching for the captain meant that Ward was putting his own reputation on the line with Tammany. And sometimes that meant putting one's life on the line. "If you do hear anything more, could you let me know?" he finally asked.

"Sure," said Macklin. "Maybe you'll do me a favor sometime." He looked down at the folio. "But next time we meet by the dragons, right?"

Webb agreed, and chose not to debate with his informant whether or not there really were such things as dragons.

CHAPTER 24

Rebecca Davies couldn't help but stare at the splendid decor and sumptuous furnishings. The walls of the spacious room were mint green with glossy white trim; on them hung tasteful oil paintings in gold frames that were simple enough not to detract from the artwork. Well-cared-for potted ferns and areca palms were placed about the floor, interspersed among colorful Kashan rugs and pedestals that held classical marble statues. There were inviting divans and armchairs upholstered in silk damask, and polished cocktail and end tables of tropical woods. A glowing fire crackled in a magnificent fireplace of Italian marble.

Rebecca couldn't get over the fact that the place seemed far more like a Fifth Avenue drawing room than a brothel. But then, this particular house of prostitution was indeed on Fifth Avenue, just a few blocks from her parents' mansion, and she was in a drawing room that differed little from those of other homes in the exclusive neighborhood. One difference that she did notice was that there were a number of Japanese silk screens positioned about the room like partitions to provide some degree of privacy in the conversations. She could hear a low murmur of a few people speaking in soft tones, but she was sure that there was nothing more going on behind the partitions than talk—this was obviously not the sort of place where the employees and customers cavorted about in the open. Rebecca felt certain that there were exquisitely furnished bedrooms upstairs to which the more amorous activities were relegated.

Rebecca sat on a chair that was as soft as a cloud, sipping tea from a dainty china cup and nibbling sugar cookies that were baked to perfection. She was alone, waiting patiently to meet Sarah Fredrich.

Thinking of how she had come to locate the young woman, Rebecca had to smile to herself. She had first spoken with some of her girls at Colden House, but these poor women knew only of the poorer parts of the city. Nancy Johnson, the Brooklyn madam with whom Rebecca had met, had said that Fredrich was probably practicing her trade at "some place expensive." So after striking out with most of her contacts in the city, Rebecca had finally turned for help to her younger sister, Alice, an expert on those things that were expensive in Manhattan. Sweet, demure Alice had married into the Updegraff family, one of the few in New York that was older and wealthier than their own, and socially prominent enough to consider the Vanderbilts to be Johnny-come-latelys.

Alice had once again come through for Rebecca, instructing her husband, Jacob Updegraff, a Wall Street banker, to make inquiries of his friends. Not only had Updegraff succeeded in finding where the young woman was working—Rebecca didn't know, and didn't want to know, how easy that assignment had been for him to complete—but he'd arranged with the proprietor for Rebecca to come and speak with Sarah Fredrich.

Just as Rebecca recalled Alice's excitement when she gave her the news, a slim young woman dressed in a stylish gown of peach silk and white lace glided gracefully into the room. She had curly strawberry-blond hair tied in a French braid, sparkling green eyes, and a clear complexion that was fashionably pale. From her bearing, movements, and garb, she could easily have fit in with the society women who frequented the Astor ballroom.

"Miss Davies?" she asked in a soft, sweet voice.

"Yes. Miss Fredrich?"

The young woman gave a barely perceptible nod in affirmation.

"Thank you for seeing me. May we talk here?"

"Certainly." Sarah poured Rebecca a spot more of tea, before sitting herself. Rebecca noticed that she settled on the divan next to her with such grace of movement that she appeared to have no weight at all.

Rebecca glanced about; they were far enough from any of the screens that she was comfortable that they could speak without being overheard. "Miss Nancy Johnson suggested that I speak with you," she began.

"I haven't seen her in some time." Sarah Fredrich's soft speech was measured and precise.

"She said you used to work for her."

Sarah nodded.

"She also said that before going to her house you used to work for Vivian O'Connell." Rebecca hesitated. "Did you know that Miss O'Connell was killed recently?"

"Yes. I was very sorry to hear that. Miss O'Connell was a good lady, and treated me well."

"There was another girl who worked with you—Frenchy Sayre. I'm told you were good friends."

At the mention of the name, Sarah started slightly and a flush came to her cheeks. "That was a long time ago."

"Two years, right?"

"Yes. She was murdered." Cracks came into the smooth voice and the diction was no longer as perfect. "Just when she was leaving the business."

Rebecca could tell that Sarah was troubled at the mention of her dead friend. "Do you mind if I ask you about her?"

"I don't want to think about my life back then," was the faint reply. "I have a new life here now."

"But aren't you still . . ." Had Rebecca been wrong? Perhaps the reason this place didn't look like a whorehouse was that it wasn't one. "I was led to believe that you . . ."

Sarah folded her hands primly in her lap. "Yes. I still am. But not the same as before." She pulled herself a little more upright and looked about the room. "See, at Miss O'Connell's and Miss Johnson's most of the other girls learned all that they could do with their bodies and made their money that way. I wanted more—so I worked on my mind and my manners. Now I get to work in a place like this. I see wealthy gentlemen, usually older, and they value conversation and company as much as my body. I light their cigars, pour their brandies, and listen to them talk about anything they want to—sometimes that's all I have to do and I'm paid very well for it." She smiled hopefully. "If I'm lucky, I'll meet a man who'll set me up as his mistress. That's my plan."

"You *have* come a long way from Brooklyn," Rebecca

said. "It's too bad Frenchy Sayre never had the chance to get out."

Sarah's look of hope evaporated.

"I would like to find out what happened to her," Rebecca went on. "I know you don't want to think about your life back then, but if she was your friend don't you want her killer brought to justice?"

Sarah brought her bright eyes directly to bear on Rebecca's. "Do you really think you can do that?" Her accent now was pure Brooklyn.

"I want to try."

Sarah considered it. "I never thought anyone would care about Frenchy anymore."

"Were you ever questioned by the police after she was killed?"

"No. The police didn't do nothin'." The young woman caught herself. "They didn't do *anything*. Miss O'Connell was awfully mad about that, and for a while she tried to find out what happened herself."

"Did she get anywhere?"

"I don't think so. But then . . ." Sarah began to look uncomfortable.

"What?"

"Well, she talked to me, but there was something I didn't tell her."

"What's that?"

"There was a man Frenchy was seeing. I don't think she really liked him, and I know he had a temper— I helped her a few times when he left bruises on her. Anyway, I know he didn't like the idea of her leaving."

"Was she going to leave the area, or just the business?" Rebecca asked.

"Both. It was part of the reason we became friends. Frenchy and I both wanted out. I wanted"—Sarah spread her hands—"I wanted this. Frenchy wanted a home and a normal life."

"Did she have a prospect of that? Is that why she was quitting Vivian O'Connell's house?"

"No. She just thought she had to get out of the business first before she could find a decent man who would want her."

"This man who *was* seeing Frenchy—why didn't you tell Miss O'Connell about him?"

Sarah hesitated. "Miss O'Connell was very *fond* of Frenchy, I think. She wouldn't have liked her seeing a man outside of business. And I know Frenchy never told her about him, so I kept her secret." She sighed. "Although Frenchy was really seeing him by choice— he just demanded that she service him."

"How could he do that?"

"I wondered, too. And then one day, I got a glimpse of him through the door. He was a police officer."

"Do you know his name?"

"No, but I'd seen him at Miss O'Connell's house a couple of other times. He was a sergeant, a young fellow with a blond mustache."

The two of them chatted awhile longer. Rebecca asked more about Frenchy Sayre as well as Vivian O'Connell, but didn't think she learned anything as useful as the fact that Frenchy Sayre had been involved with a Brooklyn police officer.

Buck Morehouse growled at the repetitious noise that was so rudely interrupting his nap. His first reaction was annoyance, and a desire to go back to sleep. When the knocking continued, it finally dawned on him that there was someone at his apartment door.

"Comin', damn it!" he yelled grumpily, hoisting his

body from the overstuffed chair in which he'd dozed off. There was little light coming through his one grimy window, so it must be night already. He shook the sleep from his head, switched on an electric lamp, and, wearing only a union suit that badly needed laundering, walked the few steps across his tiny apartment to open the door.

Bespectacled Shannon Elswick was there. "You look like hell, Bucky. Just wake up?"

"Yeah. What time is it?"

"Six-thirty." Elswick added in answer to Morehouse's blank stare, "At night." He held up a pail of beer. "Brought something that'll wake you up, if you'll move aside and let me in."

"Oh yeah. Sorry." Morehouse waved the deputy coroner in, eying the beer bucket eagerly. Coming through the door along with Elswick was the smell of warm bread from the bakery downstairs. It stirred a hunger in Morehouse, and he wished Elswick had brought supper, too.

Fully awake now, Morehouse found two relatively clean glasses and poured the beer. In the icebox, he found a chunk of salami that was probably still edible and a wedge of cheddar that would be turned down by most rats. He cut both of them up and put them on a plate to share.

The two men sat down, Morehouse in his chair and Elswick on the edge of a decrepit horsehair sofa that was missing much of its stuffing, and each took a long swallow of beer.

"Ah, that's good," said Morehouse. "Where'd you get it?"

"The Horseshoe, over on Duffield. Saloonkeeper had just tapped a fresh keg when I stopped in."

Morehouse took another swallow and smacked his lips appreciatively. "Thanks for bringing it."

"That's not all I brought."

Food? Morehouse suddenly hoped, wondering where Elswick could be carrying it.

"I got the information you wanted about Frenchy Sayre—or about her missing file anyway."

"You did? How?" Morehouse stuck a couple of pieces of cheese and salami together and took a bite of the breadless sandwich.

Elswick waved off the plate that Morehouse held out to him. "I'm only the *deputy* coroner. So I went to the coroner—J. R. Pitcan, retired last year. You remember him."

Morehouse did, although Pitcan wasn't a man to make much of an impression. He had been an aging politician who left the actual work to his deputy coroners and remained inconspicuous in the background content to collect his pay as if it were an annuity. His retirement had only been an official end to a career that had never really begun. "Where is he?" Morehouse asked.

"He's got a little place in Canarsie. I went to see him yesterday."

"What'd he say?"

Elswick chuckled. "Mostly what he said was how good it was to be retired and not have to work anymore—although I don't know how the hell he could be working any *less* than what he used to." In a serious tone, he went on, "But I asked him about the Frenchy Sayre case. And he remembered it." Elswick peered at Morehouse through his spectacles. "Stayed away from almost every bit of work that came our way, but he remembered that one."

Morehouse was fully alert now. "Why would that be?"

"Because he was asked to kill the file—and the case."

"By who?"

"Your Captain Sturup."

Taken aback, Morehouse had to think about that. "He's sure?"

"Yes. Sturup asked him for a favor. He wanted the case squashed—no file, no inquest, no case. It's like it never happened."

"Did Pitcan know why Sturup wanted the favor?"

"No. I asked; he said he had no idea."

"And he just did what Sturup wanted?"

"Pitcan was a politician. Doing favors is a reflex for them."

That made sense to Morehouse, but one thing didn't. "And Pitcan didn't think he needed to keep this a secret."

"He *has* kept it a secret from other people. But he was open about it with me, maybe because I *knew* Frenchy Sayre had come into the morgue. Or maybe because I did his work for him for so many years that he figured we were in it together."

The big question was why Sturup had wanted the murder of a prostitute to be hushed up. When Morehouse had asked Elswick to give the cause of a mugger's death as "exposure" it had been to save himself the work of investigating a hopeless case. But Oscar Sturup wouldn't have been investigating Sayre's death, so he wasn't saving himself work. What *was* he trying to protect?

Morehouse and Elswick finished the pail of beer and never did come up with an answer to that question.

CHAPTER 25

Other than an occasional visitor, Marshall Webb's
bachelor apartment was rarely used for hosting company. So for this evening, he had made an extra effort
to tidy up, which actually didn't take much effort at
all since his combination parlor, library, and dining
room was rather austerely furnished and he routinely
kept it neat. The only place where there was any dis-
array was on his massive rolltop desk, but for a writer
to have a desk cluttered with papers and books was to
be expected; nevertheless, he had arranged these in
neat stacks.

To make conversation easier, Webb had carefully
bled the radiator under the window that overlooked
East Fourteenth Street. Its clanging and hissing was a
definite annoyance and a possible distraction, but
once he'd gotten as much air out of the pipes as he
could the noise was reduced to a tolerable level.

Webb had also made sure to stock up on refreshments, and his guests were enjoying them now. Buck
Morehouse, seated in Webb's roomy leather easy
chair, had a tall glass of lager in his meaty right hand;
he was holding it with what appeared to be a feeling

of affection for the brew. For Rebecca Davies, next to Webb on a comfortable sofa, Webb had brewed a pot of the best Earl Gray tea. On the coffee table, within easy reach of all of them, were plates of fresh sausage and cheese for Morehouse and cake for Rebecca. Webb himself had little appetite, and was content to drink coffee.

After his guests were comfortable and had sampled the food and drink, Webb began, "We've all gotten bits and pieces of information. I thought it was time for the three of us to sit down together, compare notes, and see what sense we can make of matters. Can we all agree to speak openly?" The question was primarily directed at Morehouse, since Webb wasn't sure how the detective would feel about sharing information with Rebecca.

Morehouse and Rebecca both agreed to be forthcoming with whatever they knew. In fact, Webb had noticed that Morehouse appeared to be rather charmed by Rebecca upon meeting her and looked at her almost as admiringly as he looked at his beer.

"There've been three murders," Webb went on, "Frenchy Sayre, Vivian O'Connell, and Lonnie Keck. It seems possible—likely actually—that there are connections between them." He paused, and the others nodded in agreement. "So let's see if we can determine those connections and where else they might lead. I suggest we take them in order of when they were killed. The first was Frenchy Sayre, and we know the least about her."

Rebecca spoke up. "I met with a friend of Sayre's, who worked with her at Vivian O'Connell's. And I did learn something new: Sayre had been seeing a man, although not willingly. He was violent, had beaten her before, and did *not* want her to quit."

Webb put in, "Sounds like that makes him a possible suspect, especially since she was beaten to death. Did Sayre's friend know his name?"

"No, but she saw him. He was young, with a blond mustache—and he was a Brooklyn police sergeant."

Buck Morehouse sat up from his slouched position. "His name is—was—Lonnie Keck."

"The officer who was killed in the riot?" Rebecca asked.

Morehouse said that was the man.

Rebecca frowned slightly. "How do you know? He couldn't be the only blond sergeant in Brooklyn. And this was two years ago—maybe the officer who was seen with Sayre isn't even on the force anymore."

The detective explained, "Two years ago, Lonnie Keck picked up the graft from the whorehouses, illegal saloons, and gambling joints in the precinct. One of his stops was Vivian O'Connell's house. That's probably how he met Frenchy Sayre in the first place." He hesitated. "If you're doing pickups at a saloon, you might take a free beer. If you're picking up at a whorehouse, you might get a little . . ."

Rebecca nodded with understanding. "Sayre's friend said that she had seen the sergeant at the house a few other times. It was probably when he was doing his collections."

Webb spoke up. "If it was a cop who killed Frenchy Sayre, that would explain why there was no investigation of her death."

"A sergeant isn't high enough up to squash an investigation," said Morehouse. "*I'd* be the one to investigate, and I don't answer to sergeants."

"But you were never assigned the case."

"No. It never got to me because the captain had it killed."

"Sturup."

Morehouse nodded. "I've found out that Oscar Sturup was the one who got the coroner's office to cover up the case—no autopsy, no file, no inquest."

"Why would he do that?" asked Rebecca.

After a sip of beer, the detective answered, "Lonnie Keck was carrying the bag for Sturup, so Sturup had to protected his interests, which meant protecting Keck." He shrugged as if the situation was obvious. "The captain had to choose between a dead whore and an officer who could reveal that he was taking payoffs. Sturup chose to protect his boy."

Rebecca said skeptically, "Part of this makes sense: Lonnie Keck is angry that Frenchy Sayre doesn't want to see him anymore, he loses his temper, and beats her to death. But what I don't understand is why he would then go to his captain and admit what he did."

Webb suggested, "Maybe he blackmailed Sturup. Said that if the captain covered up the murder, he would keep quiet about the graft."

"Wouldn't surprise me," said Morehouse. "Fits with what I knew of the little bastard." He caught himself, and added with an apologetic glance at Rebecca, "Sorry, ma'am."

"I didn't have the impression that Sturup was the sort of man to submit to blackmail," said Webb.

Morehouse considered that point. "Maybe Sturup was looking ahead—he has always been a man to look to his own future. He could have been thinking that if he did Keck the favor, the sergeant would be indebted to him and Sturup could count on him to do whatever he wanted in the future."

Rebecca and Webb both agreed that that made sense.

Webb asked, "So what can we *prove* of this?"

The three of them exchanged looks; then Rebecca and Morehouse shook their heads in reply.

Webb had to agree with their assessment. "It fits into a nice theory, but nothing that would hold up in court. Sayre's friend could testify that she saw Keck with Sayre, and maybe we could prove that Oscar Sturup had the coroner's office cover up the case, but there's nothing to prove that Keck was Sayre's killer. Besides, he's dead, too, now." He paused for a sip of coffee. "All right, that leads us to Lonnie Keck's death. Buck, you were there: what do you think?"

Morehouse fortified himself with a piece of cheese and half a sausage, washed them down with half a glass of beer, before answering. "I never believed that the shooting of Lonnie Keck had anything to do with the strike or that it was random. Seems to me, somebody puts a gun to your back and pulls the trigger, *you're* the one they want dead."

"What about the railroad companies?" asked Webb. "I still think they could have hired someone to kill a police officer in order to get the militia brought in. His death certainly was the catalyst for that."

The detective cocked his head, then shook it. "Still don't think they would do it that way. A lot easier to have somebody on a roof or in a window to take shots at a cop. They didn't even need to *kill* a cop; a few shots fired, or an officer wounded, would have been enough to tag the strikers as 'violent.' Nah, Keck was killed, at point-blank range, because somebody wanted to make sure he'd be dead."

What Morehouse said made sense, but Webb was reluctant to give up on his suspicion of the railroad companies yet. "So the railroads simply got *lucky* with Keck being killed?"

Morehouse had another sip of beer. "Basically. I

think there just was no connection. The troops were going to be coming in because Mayor Schieren is in the pocket of the streetcar companies—if the railroads wanted militia brought in, he would call for them. And they could have used any excuse they wanted—it would have been enough to say they were protecting the lines from 'stone-throwing mobs' or the dangers of electric lines being cut. Why risk killing a police officer when it doesn't gain you anything?"

Webb now conceded the point. He got up to refill the detective's beer glass and pour Rebecca more tea. As he did, he wondered to himself, who *would* gain from killing Sergeant Lonnie Keck? He had an idea, but when he sat down next to Rebecca again he asked the detective for his view.

Morehouse held up the glass to admire the perfect head of foam, before taking a swallow that left much of that foam on his upper lip. "I've been giving that a lot of thought," he replied. "I saw Keck in a saloon just before the strike, and we talked a little." He shrugged. "Didn't especially want to talk to the little—" He caught himself and smiled at Rebecca. "I never liked Keck, and didn't really want to talk to him, but he told me something: he said he'd be 'moving up' and 'sitting mighty pretty' as soon as consolidation was final and the new police force organized."

"Why would he confide in you about that?" Webb asked.

"He wasn't confiding. He was *bragging*. Keck loved to run his mouth, always wanting people to think he knew more than they did and that he had a lot of clout in the department." Morehouse, ignoring the linen napkins that Webb had placed on the table, finally wiped his lip with the cuff of his baggy jacket.

"What he told me was 'I put in for a promotion.' At the time, I assumed he was planning to buy himself a higher rank just like he bought his sergeant's stripes in the first place. But now I'm thinking that maybe his way of putting in for a promotion was pushing Oscar Sturup to get him a good position in the new department. Sturup was certainly planning to move up, and Keck would want to ride his coattails."

Webb put in, "And his way of 'pushing' Sturup might have been to try blackmailing him again?"

"Exactly."

"Only this time, Sturup wasn't willing to go along."

"Right," agreed the detective. "But I'm not sure why it would be different this time. They were already in bed together with the graft and in covering up Frenchy Sayre's death."

"'Murder,'" corrected Rebecca.

Morehouse nodded that she was right.

"I think I can explain what's different now," said Webb. Without mentioning his source, he told them what he'd learned from his Tammany Hall contact— that Oscar Sturup was slated to be one of six police inspectors for Greater New York, and that he was presenting himself as a clean candidate for the job. "If it became known that Sturup covered up the murder of a prostitute by one of his officers who had been acting as his bagman—well, that destroys the clean image he's been trying to sell. A little graft might be overlooked, but the murder of Frenchy Sayre would make for the sort of sordid story that newspapers love and politicians fear."

Morehouse said, "And with the way Keck liked to run his mouth, Sturup couldn't trust him."

"Not with stakes this high," agreed Webb. "Sturup was being sponsored for the inspector job by your political boss over there, Jason Ward, as a way to give

Brooklyn a piece of the new department. From what I've heard of Ward, he wouldn't take kindly to learning that Sturup had misled him about his past and cost him a lucrative piece of the new New York."

"From what *I* know of Ward," said Morehouse matter-of-factly, "he'd have Sturup killed within a week."

"I have a question," put in Rebecca, who had been quietly eating a piece of chocolate cake. "How could Captain Sturup kill Sergeant Keck right there on the street without being recognized?"

"Easily," answered Morehouse. "Despite all the people on the streets, the situation was favorable: it was so early that it was still dark; the crowds were facing the street, not looking behind them; and the killer set off a string of firecrackers that masked the gunshots and had everyone ducking for cover. Captain Sturup had it even easier than anyone else: he had made the duty assignments, so he knew where Keck would be, and he claimed to be doing random 'observations' all over the precinct the first days of the strike so no one knew where he would be at any particular time. All he had to do was wear an overcoat to cover up his uniform, go behind Keck, shoot him, then leave in the chaos. After dumping his coat and maybe his gun some place, all he had to do was show up some place else in uniform."

Webb thought that over for a minute. Although he knew the answer, he asked, "Proof?"

Morehouse shrugged. "None."

This was getting frustrating, thought Webb. He got up to pour himself a glass of port from a bottle on the sideboard before returning to the sofa. "Finally," he said, "Vivian O'Connell. What about her?"

Rebecca answered, "Of course she was bringing attention to Frenchy Sayre by starting a shelter named after her."

"If Sturup did cover up her murder," said Morehouse, "he sure wouldn't have liked that. He'd have wanted Frenchy Sayre to be totally forgotten, with nobody asking anything about her."

"There's something else," said Rebecca. "Vivian O'Connell was trying to raise funds to support the home. When I was with her, she basically blackmailed one of her former customers into making a substantial donation. When she was killed, I thought perhaps one of her former customers didn't intend to succumb to blackmail and murdered her to keep his secret. But now—"

Webb finished her thought. "You're thinking it might not have been a *customer* she'd tried to blackmail, but the police captain she'd been paying off."

"Exactly."

Morehouse spoke up. "As Lonnie Keck apparently found out, trying to blackmail Oscar Sturup is a risky move."

The three of them sat in silence for a while, mechanically sampling the food and drink as they mulled things over.

Webb spoke up first. Instead of asking the same question he had posed before, he answered it. "There is no evidence for any of this. Even though our speculation fits the facts, it's still merely speculation."

The detective grumbled, "It's hard to get evidence when the only people who can really give us answers have all been killed and their cases squashed. Frenchy Sayre never existed as far as the department's concerned, and Lonnie Keck died a hero's death protecting the city from violent strikers—no way the department is going to want to change that story."

"What about Vivian O'Connell?" Rebecca asked. "Her case is still open, correct? Is there any chance of finding witnesses in the park?"

"Realistically, no," answered Morehouse sadly. "But I can keep trying—I don't see that there's anything else I *can* do."

There were again some minutes of silence.

Rebecca suddenly burst out, "This is so infuriating! It seems so clear that Captain Sturup was involved in these crimes, but to whom do you go when the police are the criminals?"

Morehouse looked at Webb. "What about the newspapers?"

"I doubt they would take this up," he answered. "Sturup is a local hero now with his promise to arrest militiamen. The papers aren't going to reverse their portrayals of him easily. A local hero against a couple of dead whores? They'd need evidence almost as much as a court of law would to come out on the side of the whores."

"There has to be *some* way," insisted Rebecca.

Webb said sadly, "If we're right about what happened, it looks like a two-time murderer is going to become an inspector of police."

Morehouse appeared thoughtful. Then, still saying nothing, he shook his head no.

CHAPTER 26

Buck Morehouse paced the spacious porch of the Albemarle Hotel, keeping an eye on the traffic along Surf Avenue, Coney Island's main thoroughfare. In summertime, the ocean resort would be packed with people from all walks of life. Now there were fewer pedestrians on the sidewalks and only the occasional carriage rolling over the cobblestones. This was a sunny Saturday afternoon, and even with the beach too cold for swimmers, the resort still had enough other attractions to bring out some crowds.

As he walked back and forth on the porch of the three-story wood-frame hotel, his hands jammed deep in the pockets of his camel hair coat, Morehouse had to force himself to resist the temptation to wait in the hotel bar. He knew it featured the exceptional product of Otto Huber, who operated one of Brooklyn's finest breweries in Bushwick. But the detective wanted to keep his head clear.

At two o'clock, exactly the time he had specified, Morehouse saw Captain Oscar Sturup approaching the hotel from Culver's Railroad Depot, a stone's throw from the hotel, at the corner of West Eighth Street.

Sturup was in civilian attire, highlighted by an impeccable Chesterfield coat, gray with a black velvet collar, and a beaver felt top hat that nearly matched the color of his trim beard. Even without his epaulets, medals, and ribbons, Sturup was a figure of authority; there was strength in his posture and purpose in his stride.

It didn't matter how Sturup looked, however. All that mattered to Buck Morehouse was that his captain was here—that was all it took for him to know for sure that what he'd suspected was true.

Captain Sturup had just traveled eight miles to the southernmost part of Brooklyn, having been summoned by one of his detectives. By all rights, Sturup should have simply told Morehouse to go to hell—and then perhaps fired him for his audacity. But no, here he was, and right on time. Morehouse believed that there was only one possible explanation for that.

Sturup stepped quickly onto the porch of the Albemarle. He greeted Morehouse with "Why the hell did you want to meet here of all places?"

"It's a nice sunny day," Morehouse answered cheerfully. "I thought it would be healthy—especially with all the people around." He meant that it might be good for *his* health; Sturup couldn't try to shut him up the way he did Lonnie Keck out in the open with witnesses.

The captain shot him a suspicious look. "You mentioned the Sayre case," he reminded him.

"Yes, I did." And apparently the name of a whore who'd been dead for two years, and whom the captain had previously claimed not to be aware of, was enough to get him to make the journey today. "Let's walk," said Morehouse, jerking his head toward the street.

The look of caution deepened in Sturup's features and he studied Morehouse with sharp, probing eyes.

Morehouse took an exaggerated breath of the salt

air and exhaled loudly. "Very invigorating. And much safer than walking in a park at night."

Sturup momentarily lost his composure and snapped, "What the hell are you talking about?"

Morehouse stepped past him, out to the sidewalk, and began walking east. He barely looked to see that Sturup was following beside him; he was sure that the captain would stay close to him now. "The problem you have," he said, "is that there are so many people in a park at night—especially Washington Park. Maybe you don't see them, but they're there in the bushes plying their trades, or trying to sleep in a makeshift shelter—this depression has put a lot of people out of their homes, you know."

Sturup snarled, "The sort of insubordination you've been demonstrating is likely to make you one of them."

The detective ignored the threat. "The important thing," he went on, "is that they can see *you*. You don't know who's watching you in that park."

"You're talking nonsense."

"No, I learned about the park while I was looking into the Vivian O'Connell killing."

Sturup made no reply, but from the corner of his eye Morehouse could see he was studying him with a fierce expression.

They walked on, past bathing pavilions, food stands, hotels, and penny arcades, most of them sporting garish signs. Morehouse looked around and said, "This is nothing like Atlantic Avenue when Lonnie Keck was killed. It's so bright here, everyone can see everything." He turned to Sturup. "Nope, can't sneak up on someone and shoot them in the back out here."

"Get to your point." The voice was more nervous than stern now.

Morehouse did come to the point. "I know some

things," he said. "And I figure what I know should be worth something, something more than just the satisfaction of closing a case—or two."

"And what do you know?"

Morehouse looked directly into Sturup's eyes. "We both know what I'm talking about," he said matter-of-factly. "Look, I know you're a clever man, and by now you should realize that I'm not as stupid as you've always assumed."

"I never thought you were stupid. Just lazy."

Morehouse laughed. "Well, then you were right. Unfortunately for you, I'm not lazy enough, though—I can investigate a case thoroughly and solve it when I set my mind to it."

"I'm beginning to get that impression," said the captain, who then demanded again that he get to the point.

Morehouse didn't hesitate. "Lonnie Keck told me about his plans for the future. You were going to make sure he got a plum position in the new department when it got organized. Something a lot better than sergeant."

"And I'm supposed to take your word that Sergeant Keck said such a thing to you?"

"He probably reported to you that he saw me in Grady's Saloon just before the strike."

"Yes, I believe he did. And it was while you were supposed to be on duty, as I recall."

Morehouse suspected as much; Keck couldn't resist squealing on others. "Well, when we were there he told me a few things. You know how he couldn't keep his mouth shut."

There was no reply from Sturup.

"In fact," Morehouse went on easily, "you know that his big mouth was such a risk that it had to be shut permanently."

"If you believe that," answered Sturup, "you're rather foolish to be making the same demands that he did. Don't you feel at risk talking to me like this? We're in the open now, but you can't watch your back forever."

"Sure, there's a risk." Morehouse tried not to let his voice betray the fact that it was a serious one. "But here's the difference: Keck was a talker; I'm not. And Keck was ambitious—he'd have probably kept demanding more and more from you. Have you ever known me to be ambitious?"

"Not until today," Sturup answered wryly.

"All I want is a job when consolidation goes through— just the same job I have now and a chance to make a living. The way it looks now, I'm gonna be left out in the cold with the new department. I'm too old to do something else, and I happen to like eating regularly. I figured the risk is worth it."

"And in exchange?"

Morehouse smiled his best disarming smile. "Like I said, I *am* lazy. Why would I keep nosing into cases that I don't got to? And I never liked Keck anyway; I figure he got what he had coming to him."

"How about Vivian O'Connell?" the captain pressed. "You mentioned witnesses."

"Let's just say the witnesses are in a line of work where they won't want to be comin' forward on their own. Of course, I could get them to talk, but it would take some doing, and what do I care about a dead whore?"

"That leaves the Frenchy Sayre case."

"Hell, she's even deader than the other one. No reason to waste any more of my time on that one."

There was no response for some moments. Then Sturup smiled and said, "You have a sensible view of matters, Detective. I am sure you would be an asset to the new police department. In fact, I believe I can assure you that your services will earn you the appropriate compensation."

Something about his smile sent a chill through Morehouse that had nothing to do with the winter weather.

Marshall Webb was surprised at getting a telephone call from Buck Morehouse so late at night, and utterly astonished at what the detective had told him.

"So you have no doubt?" Webb asked, holding the receiver tight against his ear.

"None at all," Morehouse replied. "Sturup was too cagey to admit anything explicitly, but after we came to our agreement he gave me enough details to fill in some of the blanks—using a lot of 'hypotheticallys' and 'supposings' of course."

"So it's true," Webb murmured, mostly to himself.

"What's that? Couldn't hear you."

"I'm surprised you confronted him," said Webb.

"I didn't see any other way," said Morehouse. "But don't worry. I never mentioned you or Miss Davies." He hesitated. "I'm the only one he might come after."

"I wish you hadn't done that."

"There's still no evidence, but at least we know what happened. And that means we can look in the right direction for the evidence—maybe we can still get something solid on Sturup."

"If he doesn't kill you first."

"Oh, I'm not worried. Is he going to risk killing again right now with attention on him? I doubt it. Besides, I don't have any direct information on him like O'Connell and Keck did. I'm just not really a danger to him." It sounded to Webb like Morehouse was trying to convince himself of that.

CHAPTER 27

Buck Morehouse's action had left Marshall Webb in a quandary. Confronting Sturup as he did was a courageous action on the detective's part, but probably not a wise one.

The more Webb considered the matter, the more he was led to believe that Oscar Sturup was even more dangerous now. Morehouse was in the most danger; the detective might truly believe that he was a low enough risk for Sturup to live with. But Webb had no confidence in a man who had killed at least twice before in a matter of days to silence those who could expose him.

And if Sturup should decide to silence Morehouse, would the ambitious police captain stop there? Not necessarily. Rebecca was going forward with Sayre House—keeping the murdered prostitute's name alive. Sturup might decide that that could be risky for him, too, which meant Rebecca could be his next target. After all, that might have been part of the motive for him killing Vivian O'Connell.

Finally, as Webb considered what to do about the danger, the question Rebecca had raised kept repeating itself in his mind: *To whom do you go when the police are the criminals?*

Eventually the answer came to him: you go to the criminals.

With that as the plan, Webb went to his desk, picked up his pen, and had one of his most productive sessions of writing that he had had in many months.

The Four Deuces Saloon was on Richards Street in Red Hook. Although it was several blocks from the busy Atlantic Docks, the smell of the waterfront was strong in the air, a mixture of fresh pine tar, decomposing fish, and saltwater. Mingled with that odor was the noxious aroma from the nearby Gowanus Canal, which functioned as an open sewer as well as a commercial shipping thoroughfare.

The squat wood-frame dwelling appeared to be of such shoddy construction that it looked more like a saloon that had been put up overnight in some prospecting camp out West. Its windowless exterior consisted of gray weathered board. There was no sign advertising the name of the place, only a crudely painted hand of cards on the door showing the ace of each suit.

Webb pushed his way inside, wondering why so many top political bosses and crime leaders, whose enterprises must have made them rich, made their headquarters in run-down places like this. What was the point in all the risk and effort only to spend their lives in the same shoddy barrooms patronized by any derelict who scraped together five cents for a beer?

There was nothing to distinguish the interior of the Four Deuces from any other seedy saloon in New York. The lighting was dim and the air almost unbreathable. Soot from a small potbellied stove and smoke from cheap cigars mingled with the rank odors of unwashed bodies, overflowing spittoons, stale beer, and inadequate toilet facilities.

Perhaps a dozen men were seated in the small bar-room, some playing cards, others in hushed conversations. Webb was aware that most of their eyes were on him as he walked to the bar; this wasn't the sort of place that welcomed newcomers off the street.

The bartender, whose face and belly indicated that he had a great personal fondness for the wares he sold, stood with his thick arms folded across his chest. His expression was forbidding, and he did not ask Webb what he'd like to drink. Instead, he greeted him with "Believe you're lost, mister."

Webb said, "I'm looking for Jason Ward."

The bartender shook his head. "Never heard of him. Try some other place—in Staten Island maybe."

Webb calmly took out his *Harper's* calling card and placed it on the bar. "Take this to him. I'll wait."

After a brief staring war, the saloonkeeper backed down and picked up the card, straining to read it. Webb wasn't sure if the strain was due to the poor light or the man's literacy. "Brick!" he called.

A muscular young man with hair that no doubt earned him his name got up from a nearby table and answered the summons.

"Got a visitor here." The bartender handed him Webb's card. "Take this into the back, and see what they wanna do."

The young man disappeared through a door next to the bar, and Webb waited patiently. He still wasn't offered a drink and chose not to order one. More than five minutes later, Brick returned and said to Webb, "This way."

Following the young man, Webb had to duck to go

through the low door. He stepped into a room that was no more appealing than the barroom, neither in its decor nor its atmosphere. The only decorations were some woodcuts on the walls of dancing girls and boxers that looked like they had been cut from the pages of the *Police Gazette*. The smoke in this room had a different scent, but not a better one, produced by the short pipe planted in the mouth of the man he'd come to see. At least Webb assumed that the gnome seated behind the plain, battered desk was Jason Ward. The small hunched man had wispy white hair combed forward over his splotched scalp and straggly whiskers of the same color. The one light in the place was a green-shaded desk lamp that gave his face an eerie hue. Behind him stood two beefy young men in cloth caps pulled low on their foreheads and heavy sweaters that accented their bulk, obviously standing guard.

"Mr. Ward?" Webb ventured, offering his hand.

The gnome made no move to take it. "What the hell are you doing here, Mr. Webb?"

"I have a matter of some importance to discuss with you. May we speak privately?"

"This *is* private. My boys know how to keep their ears, mouths, and eyes shut." Webb didn't doubt that; in fact, they looked more like mountains than men. Brick, who remained at Webb's elbow, had assumed a similar posture to the two who stood behind Ward. The old man went on, "But why should I talk to you at all? You wrote some things that caused friends of mine in New York a lot of trouble."

"Very well," said Webb. "How about if *I* talk and you listen? Certainly that can't do you any harm."

Ward thought for moment, then gave a curt nod for Webb to proceed.

Webb reached for an inside pocket of his jacket.

Immediately, Brick had a hand on his wrist, gripping it like a vise. "It's only some paper," Webb said. At another nod from Ward, the young man relaxed his grip but not his vigilance. Webb slowly pulled several sheets of papers from his jacket and unfolded them.

"What's all that?" Ward prodded impatiently.

"It's an article that I'm working on for *Harper's*." Webb added dismissively, "Merely a draft at this point."

"Then maybe I'll just wait for the final story."

"No, I think you'll want to hear it now." Webb motioned to the one spindle-back chair that faced Ward's desk. "May I?"

The gnome grunted something that sounded affirmative.

Webb sat down and began, "I'll tell you the gist of it, and then if you're interested, you're welcome to read what I have so far." Without waiting for Ward to agree, he went on, "It concerns Captain Oscar Sturup. You know him—in fact, it's due to your influence that Sturup is to be made an inspector in the new police department for Greater New York." Ward's face betrayed nothing, but Webb noticed that he took a hard puff on his pipe. "But Sturup has a problem—one that I don't believe you know about."

"What's that?"

Webb felt some satisfaction that he'd succeeded in piquing Ward's interest. "Sturup is supposed to be clean. At least as clean as any cop in a big city can be expected to be. Nobody's going to mind the graft he's been raking in over the years—it was never enough to get the public in an uproar." Webb waved his hand. "Of course, you already know about that—part of his take was going to you. But he has something in his past that could scuttle his appointment—and embarrass you—if it was to come out."

"And what would that be?"

"The sergeant who carried the bag for him, Lonnie Keck, got involved with one of the girls at Vivian O'Connell's house. The girl's name was Frenchy Sayre, and Keck killed her. Sturup got the case hushed up for a while, but lately it's come to light again—and to protect himself, Sturup killed both Keck and O'Connell. Do you think a police captain like that has any chance of making it as an inspector in the new department?"

"You're just telling me a story," growled Ward. "I ain't heard none of this before."

"I expect you'll have no difficulty confirming all this on your own," said Webb. "As for my credibility, as you mentioned yourself I caused some of your Tammany friends a great deal of trouble—what I said about them held up with the Lexow Committee, didn't it? And you'd know better than anyone if what I said about you promoting Sturup for the inspector position is true."

Ward stared at Webb with hooded eyes that were utterly piercing, but made no reply.

Webb went on, "So I'm sure you'll have no difficulty confirming what I told you about Oscar Sturup and those he murdered." Webb was also sure that the Brooklyn boss would do so by subjecting Sturup to an intense interrogation. In case Ward was thinking of helping Sturup in his cover-up of the crimes, Webb continued with the final part of his tale. "Here's something else I'm sure you don't know: Sturup apparently doesn't think he needs you anymore. According to my Tammany contacts, he's making overtures to them. No offense, but your operations here in Brooklyn don't match what Tammany Hall has going on in New York. Sturup is an ambitious man and he's giving his allegiance to the bosses who can do him the most good. In fact, what he's offering Tammany in return for their support is information on you and your operations. If you go down, Tammany picks up a bigger piece of the pie when the city's reorganized." Webb held out the papers. "Read it for yourself."

Jason Ward did just that, scrutinizing the words under the light of his desk lamp, and puffing away at his pipe.

When he'd finished, Ward looked up. "Why show me this?"

"Because so far I don't have any evidence solid enough to put it in print. All I have is what some anonymous sources told me Sturup said. I need something from Sturup directly, or perhaps something from you—anything in there you'd care to correct or comment on?"

"I don't care to have my name in print at *all*, Mr. Webb."

Webb sounded disappointed. "Well, I suppose that leaves Oscar Sturup, then. I doubt he'd want to talk to me, but I could try. Without him, I simply have no story."

Ward tapped a gnarled finger on the paper. "I would not like to see this in print."

"No, I suppose you wouldn't," Webb replied. "Oh, that's not the only copy, by the way. I took the precaution of leaving another one to be published in case I should become, uh, indisposed."

Ward's beady eyes sharpened again. "Can I ask you to hold off on the story at least? Give me time to confirm what you've told me and then perhaps I *will* have a comment or two for you to include."

Webb considered the request. "Certainly. We're a weekly, and I have four days until we go to press. Besides, I could never run it as it is. Like I said, without confirmation from Sturup the story is dead."

CHAPTER 28

Although he had been working on Sayre House for a couple of weeks, Rebecca still couldn't get over the sight of Marshall in his shirtsleeves, hammering and sawing and hauling lumber around. He presented such a different figure laboring here in the wilds of Flatbush than he did dressed in his formal suits in Manhattan.

Not only was his figure different, but Rebecca was happy to see that his spirits were, too. Marshall had seemed happier than he had in some time, and there was an ease to his bearing and a ready smile on his handsome face.

Rebecca looked about the bedroom that Marshall was framing. They had already partitioned several others and begun work on an additional bathroom. "This is really starting to take shape," she said. "I can already picture it finished."

"Oh, does that mean I can stop now?" Webb teased.

"Not until your lunch break," she laughed. She then went back to the mental picture she had of the final construction. "Vivian O'Connell would have been proud of the way it's going to turn out," she said quietly. "Frenchy Sayre, too."

Webb laid his hammer on top of a sawhorse. "Are you sure you're up for running another shelter?" he asked with concern.

"Yes," she answered emphatically. "In fact, I think a change will be good for me. I've been at Colden House a long time. Miss Hummel and Stephanie Quilty are quite capable of running things there while I get this place going."

Webb smiled and picked up his hammer again. "Then I suppose I better get back to work."

Rebecca was still thinking of the dead prostitutes who were the inspiration for the shelter. "The only thing I regret," she said, "is that the men who killed O'Connell and Sayre won't be brought to justice."

Webb drove in a nail with three strokes. "Keck and Sturup are both dead. That's justice enough."

"Yes, I suppose."

Rebecca studied him for a while, remembering that Marshall had said something similar when he'd first told her the news about Oscar Sturup's body being found in the East River. He'd also said to her, "Buck Morehouse was right about Jason Ward. He did have Sturup killed within a week—in fact, it only took him two days."

The odd thing was that the newspapers never said anything about Sturup having been murdered; they attributed the battered state of the police captain's body to being dashed against a pier after drowning. So Rebecca was left to wonder what Marshall had meant, but she chose not to ask. At this point, she was feeling optimistic about the future and had no desire to fret over what was past.